Amy glared at Joss.

'Now you are deliberately teasing me when you know quite well what I mean! I am sure that there are ladies that you admire in a particular way...'

'As a matter of fact, I do.' Joss grinned at her. 'You, Miss Bainbridge, have fallen into the trap of making assumptions. You suppose that my only interest in women is...' He caught her eye and smiled. 'Is of an amorous nature. On the little that you know of me you have decided that I am a gambler and a rake, with no virtues to counteract my vices!'

'Very well!' Amy said with spirit. 'What good qualities can you offer in mitigation of the bad?'

Joss laughed. 'Why, none at all!'

Dear Reader

When I discovered that there had been a lottery in Regency times, just as there is now, I wondered what it would have been like to be a Regency lottery winner. I did some more research and discovered that the state lottery ran from 1569 until 1826, when William Wilberforce achieved its abolition. The lottery raised money for good causes such as hospitals and building programmes in much the same way that the current National Lottery generates funds for charities. Tickets were bought from licensed offices and the draws were public events. Huge sums of money could be won and the lottery was immensely popular with rich and poor alike.

This gave me the idea for *The Earl's Prize*. Miss Amy Bainbridge is the impoverished daughter of a baronet, whose life changes dramatically when she finds a winning lottery ticket and claims a huge prize. Amy is immediately confronted with the dilemmas that face all lottery winners:

Should she tell anyone about her win or keep it a secret? What should she do with her winnings—save them, spend them, or give them to a good cause? What will happen if anyone finds out and how will she deal with begging letters, with the possibility of kidnapping...or blackmail?

I had such fun exploring the Regency lottery—I hope that you enjoy the story!

Best wishes

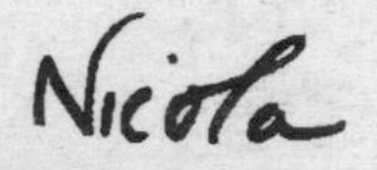

THE EARL'S PRIZE

Nicola Cornick

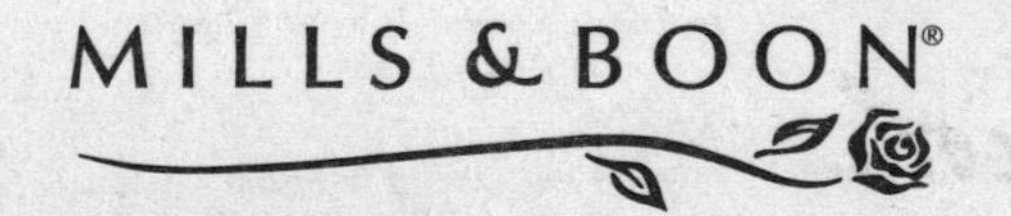

First published in Great Britain 2002
Harlequin Mills & Boon Limited,
Eton House, 18-24 Paradise Road, Richmond, Surrey TW9 1SR

ISBN 0 263 83144 2

Set in Times Roman 10½ on 12.pt.
04-1102-85041

Printed and bound in Spain
by Litografia Rosés S.A., Barcelona

Nicola Cornick became fascinated by history when she was a child, and spent hours poring over historical novels and watching costume drama. She still does! She has worked in a variety of jobs, from serving refreshments on a steam railway to arranging university graduation ceremonies. When she is not writing she enjoys walking in the English countryside and spending time with her husband, dog and two small cats.

Nicola loves to hear from readers and can be contacted via her website at www.nicolacornick.co.uk

Recent titles by the same author:

A COMPANION OF QUALITY*
LADY ALLERTON'S WAGER
THE NOTORIOUS MARRIAGE
AN UNLIKELY SUITOR*
THE RAKE'S BRIDE
(short story in *Regency Brides*. Out now.)

**The Steepwood Scandal* mini-series

Look for Nicola Cornick's next
Historical Romance™ THE CHAPERON BRIDE.
Coming March 2003.

Prologue

Joss—1792

My Lord and Lady Tallant had been quarrelling for the best part of two hours, which was an improvement in their relationship, according to the more cynical members of the servants' hall, for normally they barely exchanged a word. The words that were being exchanged now were less than civil. The Marquis's deep tones vibrated with sufficient anger to shatter the priceless vases on the drawing-room mantelpiece whilst his spouse responded in the shrill accents of one who was determined to break the glass in the fine gilt gesso mirror.

'You've never cared a fig for me, yet now I have the chance of true happiness you have not the generosity of spirit to let me go! Well, I won't stay with you! Never, never, never!'

'Cease this foolish prating, madam, and retire to your room until you can view matters in a more reasonable light. I have tolerated your tiresome infidelities for more years than I care to remember, but give you up to Massingham in this appallingly public manner I will not!'

The sound of breaking china greeted this assertion. The whole structure of the house seemed to shiver. The servants, going about their business via routes that took them close to the drawing-room door, shivered with it.

'I *want* you to divorce me, Bevill!'

'Pray do not be so absurd, madam. Now kindly withdraw.'

'I shall run away!'

'Foolishness! I will never permit it.'

'You are all bluster and no substance. You always were! I know you will not stand in my way.'

The drawing-room door was flung open and the Marchioness of Tallant flounced through in an explosion of silks and neroli perfume. She threw a challenge over her shoulder.

'I am going to pack my portmanteau—'

'Do so.' The Marquis sounded bored. 'It will keep you from making an even greater fool of yourself, at least for an hour or so.'

'Massingham will have a carriage waiting for me…'

'If he brings it closer than Oxford I shall have him horsewhipped from my estate.'

'Oh!'

The Marchioness gathered up the cherry-red silk of her skirts in one hand and ran up the staircase, her slippers pattering on the oaken treads, her petticoats foaming about her ankles. She scattered servants before her like corn in the wind. One of her golden curls had come loose from its elaborate coiffure and curled artlessly in the hollow of her throat. Her blue eyes were wild. She looked beautiful and abandoned.

'Out of my way! Where is Trencher? Send her to me at once!'

On the upper landing, beneath the three-light mullion window, a child was sitting. He was playing with a set of toy soldiers, lining them up, and laying out his battle plan with studied absorption. The light from the window lay across him in coloured bars of red, green and gold. The Marchioness almost tripped over him before she realised that he was there. She swooped down on him in a flurry of silk.

'Joscelyne! What are you doing here? Where is Mr Grayling?'

The boy shrugged. His amber eyes swept over her indifferently for a moment.

'I am sorry, I have no notion, Mama.'

The Marchioness suppressed a shudder. It was not the boy's fault that he looked so like the Marquis, but just at the moment it made her feel quite ill. Joss and his father shared the amber eyes of the Tallants, hair of the richest, darkest auburn, and a tawny complexion to match. They had features that were so pure and classical that the Marchioness had once imagined Bevill Tallant to be some Greek god, come to pluck her from her narrow existence and take her to some other, more exciting plane. But that had been nine years before, when she had not actually known her husband at all. Now she knew better, knew him to be a narrow-minded bigot who denied her even the smallest of pleasures with a self-satisfied smile. But never mind small pleasures now—the greatest pleasure she had found in the past months was waiting for her out there, somewhere beyond the lion gates and the double avenue of elms, waiting in a closed carriage to whisk her away from dreary England and her grey existence, dull as the weather.

Clive Massingham. She shivered again, this time with anticipation.

It would mean losing her children. Her calculating blue gaze fell on Joscelyne once again as, head bent, he brought his cavalry into play. Such a strange child, with his self-absorption and his martial games. But he would barely notice her absence for she seldom saw him as it was, and soon he would be going away to school.

As for his sister upstairs in the nursery, that puling, puking child—she could never be quite sure who had fathered her but she knew that Bevill would do his duty by the girl. She had done hers by giving him an heir of undeniable Tallant blood. Juliana's parentage might be in doubt, but Bevill would never say so openly.

Dropping to her knees on the step below Joss, she looked her son in the eye. The bitter bile rose in her throat.

'I am going away now, Joss darling, but before I do I beg you to remember this piece of advice always. It is the best thing that I can do for you.'

She paused. The boy was looking at her now, unblinkingly, and it was quite uncanny. She put a hand on his arm and felt the tension in his body through the rich copper velvet of his sleeve.

'Never fall in love, my darling boy. Love is for fools and it will only make you unhappy. Do you understand me?'

There was a pause. The boy gave her back look for look.

'Yes, Mama.'

The Marchioness nodded. She got to her feet. 'I am going away for a space but I will see you soon. Be a good boy.'

'Of course, Mama.' There was something faintly

amused in the boy's tone. The Marchioness frowned slightly. It felt odd, saying such things to the child, as though she were giving redundant advice. Joss had always seemed so self-contained.

'Goodbye then, darling.' She patted his cheek. At the top of the stairs she looked back, but Joss's head was already bent over his soldiers again. She sighed. Bevill would never let him join the army, not when he was the heir and there was no spare. Still, that would be none of her concern and already she was late for her rendezvous. She cast one last look at her son, absorbed in his play, and went to pack her cases.

An hour later, the Marchioness had dragged one portmanteau down the oaken stair and her maid, Trencher, had carried the remaining three downstairs, treading heavily on the discarded toy soldiers as she went. All the servants appeared to have vanished and the door of the drawing room remained obstinately closed.

The Marchioness stood in the middle of the white stone floor of the hall and looked around a little uncertainly. Even she could see the ridiculous side of knocking on the drawing-room door to announce to her husband that she was leaving him. After a few minutes, however, that was exactly what she did.

'Bevill, I am about to depart.'

The Marquis was sitting with his back to the door and did not even trouble to rise from his wing chair.

'Then go and be damned to you, madam. Is Massingham here for you? Send a footman to the gates and tell him to drive up to the house!'

'Are you then to let me go so easily after all?'

'Aye, madam.' The Marquis's voice was a low rumble. 'Be damned to you and to all women. Now, get you gone.'

Slightly baffled at her husband's *volte-face*, the Marchioness withdrew and sent Trencher to despatch a footman to the gates of Ashby Tallant. The carriage came, the baggage was loaded, and the Marchioness turned to take a final look at the walls of her prison.

Upstairs at the nursery window, a flash of white caught her eye. Little Lady Juliana Tallant was waving to her. The Marchioness waved back.

Downstairs in the drawing room the Marquis of Tallant replaced the brandy bottle on the small table beside him with a slightly unsteady hand. In the big stone bay window his son knelt on the cushioned seat and pressed his nose to the mullioned glass as he watched the carriage roll away in a cloud of summer dust. The Marquis had kept his son close by in case his errant wife had chosen to snatch the boy away with her. But he should have known better, the Marquis thought heavily. Lady Tallant would never wish to encumber herself and her lover with a seven-year-old boy, not even to spite her husband.

The Marquis stood up and walked over to the window embrasure, where he put a heavy hand on his son's shoulder. The boy seemed to wilt ever so slightly beneath the pressure. He turned his head slightly and his enigmatic amber eyes met those of the older man. Just for a moment, the Marquis thought that he saw an expression there that should never be seen on the face of a seven-year-old child. Just for a moment. But his mind was already cloudy with misery and bitterness and brandy and he dismissed the thought. Really, the Marquis thought, children would do better to avoid any facial expression whatsoever, just as they should be seen and not heard. It was better that way.

The Marquis leaned closer until he could whisper brandy fumes into the boy's ear. 'Listen to me, Joscelyne,' he said to his son and heir. 'Never trust a woman. D'ye hear me? They are perfidious creatures, right enough. Never trust 'em and never fall in love. It will only make you unhappy. Love is for fools, boy, you mark my words.'

In later life Joss Tallant, Earl of Tallant, was to say that he had only ever received one piece of advice that both his mother and his father agreed on and he had lived by it ever since.

Amy—1807

When the carriage came for her, Amy was already half-expecting it. Her mother's most recent letter, determinedly cheerful, had made her suspicious. At fourteen, Amy was adept at reading between the lines.

It had happened before, of course. Several times. There would be the rumble of carriage wheels on the cobbles outside, the muted hum of voices breaking into Amy's sleep, the flare of a light, the urgent hand shaking her awake. Tonight it was just the same. When she opened her eyes she saw her mother's face, pale and resigned in the candlelight, and Miss Melville, the headmistress, her expression tight with disapproval.

'If only you could leave her with me a little longer, Lady Bainbridge! Amy is such a bright and promising pupil, but this constant disruption makes any progress quite hopeless…'

Amy dressed and packed her meagre possessions, and tiptoed away. There was no time for farewells. The other girls slept on, unaware and unconcerned, all but for Amanda Makepeace, who had the bed next to Amy's. Amanda rolled over, groaned as the pale light dazzled her eyes, then sat up.

'Amy, what is happening?'

'It is nothing, Amanda.' There was a lump in Amy's throat. 'I have to go. I do not suppose I will see you again…'

Amanda reached out of bed and hugged her tight. She had always mothered Amy, who was two years younger, and now she felt warm and familiar. Amy choked back a sob.

'Of course we shall meet again!' Amanda whispered. 'You'll see…'

For a long moment they hugged each other in silence, then Amy drew back.

'Goodbye, Amanda.'

She knew that she would not be coming back to Miss Melville's seminary and in a way she was glad. The embarrassment was so difficult to overcome. The last time that her parents had taken her away she had been gone a twelvemonth; when she had returned she had pretended that urgent family business had kept her from school. It was scant protection, but in a sense it was true. All the same, Amy had been aware of the sidelong glances and the giggles of the other girls. Miss Melville herself might be discreet, indeed, Amy suspected that her teacher was sympathetic, but the other pupils had family in the *ton*, family who gossiped and stirred scandal and knew all about her father, 'Guinea George' Bainbridge, a compulsive gambler who was perpetually financially embarrassed. There was no escaping the malicious talk and, even with Amanda to protect her, Amy had felt intensely vulnerable. Whilst outwardly she steeled herself against the sneers, inside she withdrew.

Amy had attended several seminaries for young ladies in her time. There had been two whole years at a school near Oxford, a time of relative stability when her father must have been on an extended winning streak. There had been the snatched months at Miss Melville's, a spell at a school in Bath and almost a year in Hertford. Each time her parents would send her to a different school where her family history could be concealed, at least for a little while. Each time the truth came out and the more spiteful pupils made her life a misery with their sharp teasing. Each time Amy moved on, she lost the few friends she had gained.

This time the journey back to London took just over an hour, for Miss Melville's school was out at Strawberry Hill. Amy, too sleepy and too disheartened to question her mother, curled up in a corner of the carriage and dozed. She awoke as the carriage jerked to a halt.

'Where are we, Mama? Mansfield Street?'

Lady Bainbridge did not reply at once. She made a business of collecting up her reticule and Amy's luggage. In the pale dawn light her face looked deeply lined.

'No, my love. This is Whitechapel. We are…staying here for a little while. A very little, until Papa is ready and we can go to the country.'

'Whitechapel?' Amy flung open the door of the cab and scrambled down. The hansom had come to rest in a narrow street between high buildings that seemed to scrape the streaky dawn sky. It was cool, but the air was heavy with the stench of rotting vegetables, alcohol and something else more unsavoury still. Amy wrinkled up her nose. Splintered barrels and crates littered the street and beside one of them lay a man, deep asleep. An empty bottle lay beside his outstretched hand and a stream of liquid puddled on the cobbles next to his prone body. A woman was sitting in a doorway opposite, her dirty red skirts up about her knees and her filthy bodice barely covering her bosom. She favoured them with a long, slow stare.

'Mama!' Amy had become accustomed to the various indignities that came upon them through her father's improvidence, but this seemed too much to believe. The distance between Miss Melville's genteel classroom and this rookery was too great for her to take it in so suddenly. She looked beseechingly at Lady Bainbridge, but her mother had turned away to pay the surly cab driver. He whipped up his horse and left them standing in the middle of the street, Amy's bags at their feet.

'Mama,' Amy said again, but this time it came out as a whisper. Two gentlemen were turning the corner of the street now, flashy and swaggering, no gentlemen at all, in fact. As they saw Amy one nudged the other and they broke into a run. With an exclamation, Lady Bainbridge picked up the bags and whisked Amy through the door of a house whose wooden signboard boasted the legend: 'Lodgings for Travellers'. She slammed the door behind them and Amy heard the gentlemen run past, their feet thundering on the cobbles, their fists beating on the boarded-up windows. Lady Bainbridge was visibly shaking.

The light was dim in the hallway, but the stench of tallow and rot was all the worse. There were only two doors off the corridor and Lady Bainbridge now opened one of these, drawing Amy inside. The room was barely furnished, containing nothing but a frowsy bed and a couple of broken-down chairs. Lady Bainbridge's hands still shook as they untied Amy's bonnet and helped her with her cloak.

'It is only for a little while, Amy, just a while. Papa will be back soon, you know, and then we may go...'

Amy shivered, though the room was not cold. She took her mother's hands in her own. Lady Bainbridge avoided her gaze.

'Mama, how long have you been staying here?'

Lady Bainbridge shrugged her thin shoulders. Amy could see that her dress was stained and torn. 'A few days only. Soon we shall be gone again.'

'But where is Papa now?' Amy looked around, but the lodging house was silent. 'Why do we have to stay in this dreadful place, Mama?'

'It is only for a little while,' Lady Bainbridge repeated tonelessly. Her face looked grey. She drifted over to one of the chairs and folded herself into it.

'I do hope you are not hungry, my love. There is no food, you see, but it is only for a little while...'

The suggestion of food made Amy feel very hungry. She was a growing girl and her stomach was rumbling loudly, but at the same time she felt almost sick with fear that they should come to this. The house in Mansfield Street had been small and shabbily furnished, but at least it had been at the west end of town. Amy had no very clear idea of where she was now, but she knew that Whitechapel was no place for a lady. She took the chair opposite her mother and hunched herself up, against the hunger, against the fear.

'Is Richard to come with us to the country, Mama?' She asked. Matters might not be so bad if only her brother were with them.

Lady Bainbridge turned her faded blue eyes on her daughter. 'Why, of course not, my love! Richard is at Eton and must remain there. We could not interrupt his education…'

Amy sighed. She knew that Richard would have loved to have his education interrupted, whereas she—

There was a crash as the door of the lodging house was flung open. Loud footsteps echoed on the wooden boards of the hall. Lady Bainbridge jumped up, one hand pressed to her mouth.

'Oh! I wonder—'

The door burst open. A gentleman stood in the aperture, a real gentleman, larger than life, with guinea-gold hair and a gold embroidered waistcoat and high shirt points and a higher colour. Amy leapt to her feet.

'Papa! Oh, Papa!'

His arms closed about her and swung her off the ground. 'There's my pet! Soon we'll be all right and tight, eh?'

He smelled of alcohol and familiar warmth. Amy burrowed close. 'Oh, Papa, I was so afraid! What has happened to the house in Mansfield Street, and why must we go to the country?'

'Guinea George' Bainbridge set her on her feet again. He jingled the coins softly in his pocket. 'No need to fret, sweetheart! What say you we rent a nice house in Curzon Street instead, and a coach and pair? And you will have a governess or go to whichever young ladies' seminary you choose—'

There was a sharp intake of breath from Lady Bainbridge. The pink colour had come into her thin cheeks and a sparkle into her pale blue eyes. She got to her feet and put her hand tentatively on her husband's arm.

'George?' There was a note of entreaty in her voice

and Amy, swamped as she was with excitement and relief, still heard it. She was attuned to such things by now. 'George, you have won again? Oh, you *have* won again!'

Amy saw her father scoop his wife up to him and kiss her hard. 'I have indeed! A new dress for you, my love—twenty dresses if you will have them!'

Lady Bainbridge was laughing, crying and scolding all at the same time. Amy watched her mother as she hung on Sir George Bainbridge's arm, her eyes fixed on his face like a drowning woman. So it would not be today, or even tomorrow, that their ruin would finally catch up with them, but one day, perhaps…one day…Amy turned away. When I marry, she thought fiercely—*if I ever marry*—it will not be to a weak man, a gamester or a wastrel. I shall marry a man that I can love and respect, or I shall not marry at all. And I shall never gamble. They say that it is in the blood, but I will prove them wrong. Why, I should never even be tempted—not for a thousand pounds!

Chapter One

1814

The Marquis of Tallant did not believe in improving his home—what had been good enough for his forebears needed no enhancement from him—and therefore the drawing room at Ashby Tallant was much the same as it had been twenty-five years before. Today sunlight was pouring through the diamond panes of the mullioned windows and its bright light cruelly accentuated the bald patches on the blue velvet curtains and the threadbare rugs where the pattern had almost worn away.

Joscelyne, Earl of Tallant, came into the room with an assured step, pausing only as it seemed empty. Then he smiled a little grimly, for one of the wing chairs had its back turned deliberately to the door.

'Good afternoon, sir.' He came forward to stand in front of the fireplace, looking down at the man huddled in the chair. 'I believe you wished to see me?'

'I cannot say I wished to see you, Joss, but I certainly wanted to speak with you.' The Marquis's voice was harsh, a contrast to his son's light and drawling tones. He made a slight gesture and the sunlight flashed on the diamond ring on his finger, a larger version of the one nestling in the folds of his cravat.

'Sit down. You'll take a glass of something? Pull the bell, then.'

Joss complied, then took the chair opposite his father. The Marquis directed the footman to bring a bottle of canary.

'You are well, sir?' Joss enquired indifferently.

The Marquis shifted uncomfortably in his chair. The diamond flashed again as he grasped his stick a little tighter between gnarled fingers. His chin was sunk on his chest, but his eyes flashed sharply. 'I do well enough. Sorry to hear that, are you, boy? You'd be glad to see the back of me, I dare say!'

'Not at all, sir,' Joss said easily. He rose as the footman entered with the wine, and poured two glasses, handing one to the older man. He raised his own in salutation.

'To your continued good health, sir.'

A grunt was his only reply.

'Juliana sends you her best wishes, sir. She is well.'

'She takes after her mother,' the old man said sourly. 'No discretion. I've heard all the tales about her! I even heard that she is making a set for Clive Massingham, like her mother before her! As well that Myfleet is dead and gone and need not suffer the disgrace of his wife's infidelity.'

Joss shifted a little uncomfortably. 'I beg you not to disparage Juliana, sir. If Myfleet had lived there would have been no infidelity. Juliana was happy with him, and now, of course, she is not—'

'Happy, pah! You speak like a sentimental fool, Joss!

Which of us is happy? Are you?' The Marquis's chin sank down on his chest again, then rose, jutting aggressively. 'I hear all about you, my boy! Gambling dens, prize fights, running with Fleet, the worst rakehell in town! Once I had high hopes for you, before that disgraceful episode when you almost ruined the family with your gambling! Since then you have gone from bad to worse. Why, only last month I was obliged to pay off that blackguard Avery, who swore that you had debauched his daughter—'

'That was unfortunate,' Joss agreed smoothly.

'Aye, unfortunate that I had to part with a considerable sum to keep him quiet!'

'You should not have troubled.' Joss took a sip of his wine. 'I was scarce the first to debauch Angela Avery. Her father must be making a fortune!'

The Marquis flushed puce. 'Maidservants, landlords' daughters, virgins, widows and wives, they are all the same to you!'

'I beg you to be calm, sir.' Joss's drawl was even more pronounced. 'You are getting yourself in a taking over nothing. My exploits are nowhere near as dramatic as you have heard tell. Why, I am even known to attend the occasional tediously respectable ball! I fear your spies have overstated the case.'

The Marquis waved an impatient hand. 'Then it will not be difficult for you to fall in with my plans. I have decided I can tolerate no more of this wild behaviour. Scandal after scandal, dragging the family name into the gutter! You have brought it low—well, now you must redeem it!'

'You must be desperate indeed, sir, if you see me as the saviour of the family honour,' Joss said. 'In what way is this miracle to be achieved?'

'No need for your odious sarcasm, boy.' The Marquis coughed a little and dabbed his handkerchief to his thin lips. He took a draught of the canary wine and sat back with a sigh.

'Needs must that you should marry, Joss. You are nine and twenty, after all, and we need an heir for Ashby Tallant. If you were to wed a charming, accomplished girl, settle here in the country and raise your brood, much of the past might be forgotten. What do you say, eh?'

'A conformable wife and a house in the country...' A mocking smile touched Joss Tallant's firm mouth. 'How deadly dull! No, I thank you, sir. The idea holds little appeal to me.'

'It was not a suggestion,' his father said, an echo of the Tallant arrogance in his tone, 'it was a command! You *will* marry creditably!'

Lines of amusement crinkled briefly at the corner of Joss's eyes. He rose languidly to his feet. 'As a gambling man, I would have to advise you that that is not a safe bet, sir.'

'Be damned to you, boy!' The Marquis grasped his stick and hauled himself to his feet, glaring at his son, his words spitting from his lips. 'You will do as I say! I shall disinherit you else—'

'I do not believe you able to do that, sir,' Joss said mildly.

'Be damned to the entail! I'll leave every last unsecured penny to your cousin Roger! You may have the estate but you'll not be able to keep it! I'll cut your allowance and see how you manage to gamble without that! Then you will need to marry—aye, and an heiress into the bargain!'

'Pray do not make yourself ill on my account, sir,'

Joss murmured, putting a hand out to help his father. 'You know I shall go my own way.'

The Marquis subsided into his chair like a collapsing sack of grain. 'Be damned to you,' he said again, but the venom had gone out of his words. 'You may marry the first female you see for all I care!'

'A whimsical idea, sir,' his son murmured. A gleam came into his amber eyes. 'Perhaps I may do precisely that. Your servant, sir.' He made an elegant bow, which received no acknowledgment, and went out into the hall. A manservant passed him his cloak, hat and gloves. There were no housemaids polishing the banisters, which was perhaps fortunate for Joss's matrimonial plans. He noted the absence and allowed himself a smile.

His curricle was brought around. It was a fresh May morning and before he ascended, Joss stood looking down the double avenue of elms and away across the parkland. The country. What a damnable place. He would return to town at once.

The journey back was uneventful. The first female he saw was the landlady of the hostelry where he stopped to change horses and partake of a pint of ale, but she was already spoken for and the landlord was built like the proverbial brick privy. On the whole, Joss was grateful. It had been an odd, quixotic notion, but he was prone to act on such ideas sometimes. It made life a little less tedious.

'Amy, dear,' Lady Bainbridge said gently, 'do extinguish the second candle. Two candles are quite unnecessary where one will do! Why, I am able to see to read by the light of a single candle so I am sure that you can see to sew just as well.'

Amy put down her knotting and leaned over to extinguish the candle that was on the chest beside her chair. A thick smell of wax and smoke filled the air, making her head ache a little. Her eyes ached also; two candles in the parlour had been barely adequate to light her work and one would certainly not do, particularly as it was on the mantelpiece directly behind Lady Bainbridge's head. Her mother was holding her book up to the light and squinting at the page in a manner that Amy knew could not be good for her eyes, regardless of what she said. She was not entirely sure when Lady Bainbridge had become a miser but the habit was now deeply engrained.

Amy folded her work up neatly and stowed it away in the wooden chest with the shuttle and thread. She had been adding a knotted fringe to an old shawl in the hope that it would make the garment look a little less worn. The thread was a deep ruby colour and her knots were rather pretty, like a string of red beads. Even so, Amy did not delude herself that she had done any more than make a tired old shawl look slightly less frumpish. She had not had any new clothes for several years and had been obliged to titivate her existing ones with lace and ribbon in an attempt to look presentable. The results were not always a success and in more modish company Amy knew she looked a fright. On the other hand, there were very few occasions on which she was required to look presentable, for she seldom went into society.

'I think I shall retire, Mama.' Amy stifled a yawn. The evening had been much like any other. She had taken dinner with Lady Bainbridge, picking over a meal of mutton stew that would have been barely adequate for one and certainly could not stretch to two. After that they had retired to the parlour, the house in Curzon

Street being too small to boast a true drawing room, and Lady Bainbridge had read and Amy had sewed, like any other evening during the past two years since Sir George Bainbridge had died. They had not gone out and no one had called on them. Lady Bainbridge discouraged visitors, as she always felt obliged to offer them refreshment.

'Just as you wish, my love.' Lady Bainbridge frowned. 'There is a candle in the hall, is there not? Pray do not take it upstairs. You should be able to find your way up to your room perfectly well.'

Amy reflected that this was true, but only because she had become accustomed to navigating herself around the house in the dark.

'I shall wait up,' Lady Bainbridge said, with a little self-pitying sigh. 'It may be that your brother will be too tired to remember to lock the door securely when he retires and it would not do for someone to walk in off the street and steal anything.'

Amy thought it more likely that Richard's drinking rather than his tiredness would affect his memory. As for a thief randomly selecting the Bainbridge household, it seemed rather unlikely. She suspected that Lady Bainbridge's parsimony must be a by-word amongst the underworld, who knew they would find no pickings in the house in Curzon Street. Before his death, her father had pawned or sold every item of value that he possessed and it was common knowledge that they had no money. The house, let to them at a minimal rate by an old family friend and furnished in the style of thirty years before, was little more than a roof over their heads. At times during the past ten years they had not even been able to afford to maintain it. These days they had two female servants, a cook housekeeper and maid, and one male servant, Richard's valet, the inestimable Marten. They kept no carriage for they could no longer afford to do so. Lady Bainbridge had argued strenuously against the sale of the carriage the previous year, but Amy had pointed out that the horses were so thin from lack of food that they were likely to fall down in the street and make them a laughing-stock. This line of reasoning had so frightened Lady Bainbridge, who could not bear the censure of others, that she had finally acquiesced.

'I wish you would not stay up until Richard retires, Mama,' Amy said now, in her usual mild tone. 'You know that Marten will take care of him and make sure that all is secure. Besides, the gentlemen are likely to be at their play into the early hours. You will fall asleep in your chair, like as not, and wake up with a crick in your neck and your hair in disarray!'

Lady Bainbridge looked most alarmed. She still possessed the remnant of the beauty that had first captured George Bainbridge and she guarded it zealously. Yet everything about Lady Bainbridge was a little droopy, for she had wilted from the moment that she was widowed, and had never quite recovered. Faded brown ringlets fell about her shoulders from a lace cap that sagged a little. Her gown hung off her sparse figure and her mouth, once a perfect bow, turned down at the corners.

'Oh, I had not thought… If you put in that way, my love… Yet I cannot go up to bed, for I require my other book to help me sleep. This…' she waved the book in her hand '…is Mrs Kitty Cuthbertson's book and I use it to keep me awake. It is Mrs Edgeworth's book that I require for night time.'

Amy had long ago become accustomed to her

mother's personal superstitions. Lady Bainbridge had her own set of beliefs to supplement the more generally accepted maxims of avoiding walking under ladders and refusing to let the maid turn the mattresses on a Friday. One of Lady Bainbridge's most steadfast convictions was that she had to approach her sleep with a particular routine: no looking over her shoulder as she ascended the stair, her slippers to be laid out pointing away from the bed, a certain book to read before bedtime... In these beliefs she was as unshakeable as a mountain.

Amy sighed. 'Where is Mrs Edgeworth's book now, Mama?'

'Oh I do believe...' Lady Bainbridge patted her pockets and the chair cushions ineffectually, 'I do believe I have left it in the dining room. Quite unaccountable, I know, since it should never leave my bedroom. Of all the unfortunate things, that your brother should choose to entertain his cronies at home tonight!'

It was indeed unfortunate and it was also unusual. Sir Richard Bainbridge was seldom at home, preferring to do his gambling at White's or Boodle's. Amy could not remember the last time that her brother had invited his cronies to the house in Curzon Street. It was neither large enough nor grand enough to use for entertaining, but for a small gambling party it was suitably discreet.

'Why not send Patience into the dining room to find your book?' Amy suggested. Patience was their maid of all work, a terrifying puritan of a woman, who was as skilled as a lady's maid as she was diligent with a duster. Patience's stock response to any situation was to disapprove of it. Amy's lip twitched to imagine what she would make of a group of Richard's hard-gambling friends.

Lady Bainbridge brightened, then drooped a little.

'Oh, yes, what a good idea... Oh, I cannot! Patience has sworn that she will not set foot in a room with Richard's friends after one of them tried to pinch her in a...' Lady Bainbridge looked embarrassed '...in an intimate manner. She swore that she was obliged to box his ears and called them all rogues and scoundrels!'

'It was a brave man to try,' Amy murmured, her mind boggling a little at the thought of the hatchet-faced Patience receiving the amorous attentions of one of Richard's cronies. No doubt the man had been in his cups. 'Well, in that case send Marten in. I doubt that he will suffer such a fate!'

'No, indeed, but Marten has gone to visit his sister this evening and I do not believe he has yet returned.'

Amy bit her lip. 'This can scarce be an insuperable problem, Mama! Can you not read another volume instead?'

Lady Bainbridge looked cast down. 'Oh, no, my love, for you know that certain books are daytime reading and others are for the evening. The two cannot mix, I assure you.'

Amy stood up and picked up her shawl, wrapping it about her. 'Very well, I shall go to fetch your book. It will not take above a second.'

Lady Bainbridge gave a little squeak. 'Oh, Amy, my love, you cannot go in *there*! Why, the gentlemen are gambling—'

'I know, Mama.' Amy's expression hardened. 'I anticipate that they will be so engrossed in their play that they will not even notice me. I doubt that I shall suffer Patience's fate!'

'No, indeed,' Lady Bainbridge looked regretful, 'for no gentleman has ever shown *you* any partiality, Amy!

But that is nothing to the purpose. It would be *quite* improper for you to enter a room full of gentlemen.'

'One of them is my brother, Mama,' Amy pointed out. 'Should anything untoward occur, I shall immediately call upon Richard's protection!'

She drew the shawl tight and stepped out into the hall. One candle burned here at the bottom of the stairs and threw long shadows. Amy saw her reflection in the pier glass and thought ruefully that she looked like one of the mummies she had seen at the Egyptology Exhibition the previous year. The shawl was huge, for she liked to have plenty of material to wrap around her and keep the draughts out. The amount of heating available to the Bainbridge household was directly related to the amount of money that Richard gambled away, so she was accustomed to the cold.

She could hear the sound of voices and masculine laughter coming from within the dining room as she approached the door gingerly. As her mother had pointed out, it was utterly inappropriate for an unmarried lady to enter the room, but Amy felt that the sight of her would be unlikely to inflame the passions of any of the drunken gamblers inside. Most were such hardened gamesters that they would like as not fail to notice her at all, and those who did see her would dismiss her—as ever—as Richard's dowd of a sister. *Ton* society worshipped beauty and she possessed little.

She had always been a little brown dab of a girl and her quietness had not helped. During her one and only London Season, Amy had been so silent that some of the more unkind members of society had dubbed her the Simple *ton* and after that there had been no more seasons for Amy and no real suitors either.

She opened the dining-room door and peered in. The

scene inside was much as she had envisaged it. The room was hot and smoky, from a combination of a roaring fire and the twenty or so guttering candles that stood about the table. There was no economy practised here. Presiding over the bunch of drunken gamblers was her brother Richard, an empty brandy bottle at his elbow, and a wooden bowl at his side with a few rouleaus still in it. He was lounging in his chair, his face flushed, the dice box grasped in his hand.

With one swift glance, Amy identified two of her brother's cronies, though the other two men in the room were strangers to her. Lord Humphrey Dainty was so drunk that he looked in danger of sliding out of his seat. He was wearing a frieze coat inside out, and was sweating copiously in the overheated room. Amy thought that he was likely to fall over in a dead faint soon, his malady brought on by a combination of drink and heat. Mr Hallam, looking even more foolish than Lord Humphrey, was wearing a wide-brimmed straw hat adorned with more ribbons and flowers than Amy had decorating any of her bonnets. She shook her head slightly. She was accustomed to her mother's superstitions, but the foolish rituals that gamblers indulged in were another matter again. And Bertie Hallam never seemed to notice that his good-luck charms simply did not work.

Amy's gaze moved on. The other two men were strangers to her. One was fair, large and amiable-looking. He seemed slightly more sober than everyone else. As for the other man…

The draught from the dining-room door set the candle flames dancing and the man looked up just as Amy was studying him. His gaze fixed on her face. She felt a slight shock go through her, not just because his eyes were the most vivid amber colour that she had ever seen, but also because he was looking at her properly. Amy was accustomed to people looking through her or looking over her shoulder at someone prettier or more interesting. This man's gaze narrowed thoughtfully on her face and his brows rose a fraction. Amy pulled her shawl closer about her and tried to efface herself against the dining-room wallpaper.

At the same time, it was difficult not to stare. The man was older than Richard, Amy thought, twenty-nine or thirty, perhaps, to Richard's four and twenty. Long and lean, he appeared relaxed in his chair, his legs crossed at the ankles, his jacket discarded to reveal a pristine white shirt and a somewhat crumpled cravat. He was quite decidedly the most handsome man she had ever seen, with his tawny complexion and perfect, classical features. There was a huge pile of guineas and rouleaus at his side, in comparison to the others, who had barely any at all.

Then he smiled at her, and brushed back the lock of hair that had fallen across his brow, dark auburn hair, thick and straight. Amy frowned repressively. She hardly wanted to encourage gamblers to take the liberty of smiling at her.

Richard was pushing a new bottle of brandy across the green baize cloth. 'Fill up, Joss, fill up, Seb! You're way behind.' The bottle wavered and almost fell, and Richard looked up and saw his sister. He grinned. The candlelight gleamed on his guinea gold hair. His blue eyes danced.

''Pon rep, what are you doing here, sis? Come to check on my losses, have you? Blame Joss—he has the devil's own luck tonight.'

Amy tore her gaze away from the auburn-haired man, smiled politely and edged around the room. Lady Bainbridge had told her that she had left the novel on the window seat, but now the thick red curtains were closed and it was impossible to tell which of the four windows she had meant. Richard's guests were beginning to notice her now, which was most inconvenient. Lord Humphrey Dainty was lying with his head on his arm and was mumbling, 'Y'r servant, Miss Bainbridge, y'r servant, ma'am...' whilst Mr Hallam had jumped up and attempted a bow, almost overbalancing as the drink went straight to his head. Amy put out one hand and pushed him gently back into his chair. She had known Bertie Hallam since they had been children together and he had proposed to her once a year for the last seven years. She saw no need for either of them to stand on ceremony.

'Good evening, Miss Bainbridge. May I be of service in any way?'

The large, fair gentleman had left his seat on Richard's right and was bowing to her. He had a twinkle in his eye and Amy found herself warming to him. She did not wish to do so—her brother's friends, reprobates and wastrels to a man, had nothing to recommend them. Nevertheless, she found herself smiling back, very shyly.

'Thank you, sir. My mother believes that she has left a book down here and swears she cannot sleep without it—'

'There is a novel on the window seat behind you, Seb,' the auburn-haired man said lazily. 'I noticed it when we came in.'

He made no attempt to help in the search, merely sitting back in his chair and watching them with a faintly mocking smile in his eyes. Amy felt her skin prickle with a curious mixture of awareness and irritation. Despite the thickness and utter respectability of her dress and enveloping shawl, she felt very vulnerable. It was a relief when the large gentleman retrieved Lady Bainbridge's book from behind the red curtain, and presented it to her with another slight bow.

'I believe this must be what you seek, Miss Bainbridge. My compliments to Lady Bainbridge and I hope it helps her to sleep well.' He gave Amy another smile. 'Sebastian, Duke of Fleet, entirely at your service.'

The Duke of Fleet! Amy just managed to school her features to impassivity. So much for the gentleman's deceptive air of amiability. Richard was getting in very deep now, for Fleet and his cronies were inveterate gamblers with a reputation for fleecing innocents. Not that Richard could be considered an innocent, precisely. No son of the infamous gamester 'Guinea George' Bainbridge, who had been following his father's example since the age of eighteen, could be considered a complete amateur. Yet Amy knew her brother had not previously tangled with men like these. The Duke of Fleet and the Earl of Tallant ran with gamblers like Golden Ball and Scrope Davies. These men were dangerous. They would gamble thousands of guineas in one sitting and Richard could never sustain such losses.

Despite herself, Amy's gaze turned to the auburn-haired man. He was still watching her and she clutched the novel to her breast, feeling ridiculously self-conscious. If that was Sebastian Fleet, then this…

The man inclined his head. 'Joscelyne Tallant, at your service, Miss Bainbridge,' he said, quite as though he had read her mind. His voice was warm and smooth and it caused a little shiver to ripple along Amy's nerves. She had heard about Joss Tallant, heir to the Marquis of Tallant. Who had not? Gambling was said to be the least of his vices. Gambling and drinking and women, and other excesses that were only hinted at and never explained. As a young man, the Earl of Tallant had been exiled by his father for incurring monstrous gambling debts and almost ruining the family. Whilst abroad he had created another scandal by running off with the wife of his host and in the following five years his name had become a byword for scandal. The Duke of Fleet was still considered to be an excellent catch, redeemable by the love of a good woman, but no one ever suggested redeeming Joss Tallant. The matchmakers would shepherd their charges away with cries of alarm rather than push them forward for his notice.

Amy realised that the Earl was now looking her up and down with an insolent appraisal that made her heart jump uncomfortably. She was utterly unaccustomed to receiving such looks from a gentleman—generally they were reserved for the most attractive of females and Amy had considered them welcome to such calculated attentions. She twitched the material of her gown into place to cover her ankles. Her dress was a little short—she had had it for four years and she had grown an extra inch at the age of eighteen. She saw a smile touch the corner of Joss Tallant's handsome mouth as he noted the modest gesture.

Richard was shaking the dice box impatiently. 'Your call, my lord! Who'll play?'

'Pockets to let,' Lord Humphrey muttered, sliding quietly out of his chair. 'Tallant's taken m'fortune...'

'Not I,' Bertie Hallam said gloomily. 'Not a damned penny left, saving your presence, Miss Bainbridge!'

'Excuse me,' Amy murmured hastily. She smiled at Sebastian Fleet as he held the door open for her, steadfastly refused to spare the Earl of Tallant another glance, and slipped out into the welcome coolness of the hall.

Lady Bainbridge was hovering like a pale ghost at the foot of the stairs. 'Oh, Amy, my love, you were gone so long I wondered what had happened to you. Are you quite safe?'

'Oh, yes, Mama,' Amy said cheerfully, dismissing the memory of Joss Tallant from her mind. 'I have come to no harm at all!'

'Bertie Hallam did not propose to you?'

'No, Mama. Mr Hallam was too...busy.'

'A pity.' Lady Bainbridge sighed. 'It would have been one less mouth to feed.' She clutched Amy's arm. 'How many candles were there?'

'Oh, two or three,' Amy lied brightly. 'Nothing for you to worry about, Mama.'

'And the fire?'

'Yes, there was a small fire.'

'Why does Richard need a fire in May?' Lady Bainbridge mourned. 'It is *so* excessive!'

'Well, it is quite cool in the evenings, Mama.' Amy shivered in the draughty hall. 'Pray do not upset yourself. I am sure that he is making vast sums of money!'

Lady Bainbridge brightened. 'Oh, so you think so, my love? Indeed, he is just like his father! George was a prodigiously talented gambler, you know, and was forever buying me trinkets and treats on the proceeds of his winnings! Well, if that is the case we may all be easy. Now, did you find my book?'

Amy held the volume out to her. 'Here it is, Mama. It was on the window seat, just as you said.'

Lady Bainbridge peered at the book and then recoiled. 'Oh, but this is the book that Lady Ashworth left with me last week! Oh, no, I positively cannot read this now. It will not do at all.'

Amy took a deep breath, cursing the distraction that had led her to accept the book without checking its author. She took her mother's arm. 'Never mind, Mama. I will make you a cup of milk with nutmeg and cloves just as you like it. It will be warming and most efficacious, I promise you, and if that fails there is always the laudanum. I fear that nothing would induce me to set foot in that room again tonight!'

Later, when she could hear Lady Bainbridge snoring happily through the wall, Amy lay awake and listened to the roars of laughter floating up from the dining room. Trinkets and treats, indeed! It was extraordinary that her mother only remembered her husband's generosity and forgot the other, more painful, parts of being a gambler's wife. Amy had not forgotten what it was like to be a gambler's daughter. She would never forget, could never do so since she lived her life now in a genteel poverty that was a direct result of her father's excesses. Least of all could she forget the scandal and misery of two years before, when her father had taken his own life.

She turned her head against the pillow. Richard was like his father in so many ways, generous but feckless. It made her quite cross with him, but she was also very fond of her brother. He was too likeable for it to be otherwise. It was those others, she thought fiercely, the men of fortune such as Fleet and Tallant, whom she hated. They thought nothing of leading her brother out of his depth and robbing him blind. One day soon Richard would find himself in the same desperate straits that George Bainbridge had been in before him. Amy could not bear the thought, yet felt powerless to prevent the worst from happening. She lived constantly with the fear that history would repeat itself. More than anything she detested the likes of Sebastian Fleet and Joss Tallant for their careless confidence and callous disregard for others. Remembering the cool appraisal in Joss Tallant's eyes, Amy shifted uncomfortably in the bed. She hoped devoutly that Richard would not make a habit of inviting his gambling friends to Curzon Street. She had no wish to meet the Earl again.

Chapter Two

It was past five when Sir Richard's guests departed. The house was quiet. Marten, the valet, locked the door and helped his inebriated master up the stairs to bed. Richard was disposed to sing, for he had won two hundred guineas, but Marten successfully managed to dissuade him.

Outside it was a mild May night with the moon shrouded in cloud. The watch called the half-hour. Lord Humphrey Dainty and Bertie Hallam staggered away down the street, their arms about each other for mutual support.

'Youngsters going home to bed,' Joss Tallant drawled with a contemptuous smile, as he watched their shadows merge like a drunken spider. 'What about you, Seb? Can you stand the pace any better?'

The Duke of Fleet squared his shoulders. 'What did you have in mind, dear boy? Abbess Walsh?'

'I thought so.' Joss adjusted the set of his coat. 'I haven't seen the fair Harriet in a month. It seems time to make her re-acquaintance.'

Fleet fell into step beside him. 'It would be something to do, I suppose.'

Joss shot him a look. His friend's sheer indifference amused him, but then they were both cynical about life, albeit for different reasons. 'No more than that, Seb?'

'A pleasant enough interlude.' Fleet shrugged. 'It would lighten the load of these pockets as well. Damned if I ever met a man more talented at losing than Richard Bainbridge! Tonight was the first time I've ever seen him make a profit at the tables! One wonders how he manages to maintain any style at all.'

'Through the money-lending of Howard and Gibbs, so I believe,' Joss said drily. 'Richard apes his father, but he has none of Guinea George's flair and all his bad luck. That trifling sum he won tonight was more than he has scored in the rest of the year so far!'

Fleet laughed. 'His father was scarcely any more fortunate. George Bainbridge lived so far beyond his income that he was forever having to retreat to his house in Warwickshire whilst his creditors cooled off. Eventually he had to sell that too!'

'I remember that,' Joss said slowly. 'Was it not two or three years ago, when Miss Bainbridge had her come-out? Bainbridge lost all his money and shot himself. The family had to sell everything but for that small entailed estate in Oxfordshire and the Curzon Street house. Come to think of it, that doesn't belong to them anyway. Never saw Miss Bainbridge again until this very evening.'

'Funny little sparrow of a girl,' Fleet said. 'Shame she did not catch herself a husband in that first season of hers, but I'm not surprised she didn't take. Too quiet and drab. Confess my taste don't run to spinsterish virgins, though no doubt the Abbess might tout her as a novelty!'

A night coach clattered past.

'She was always very shy,' Joss said. He was surprised to feel a twinge of pity. Normally he never wasted any thought on the plain girls and Amy Bainbridge was decidedly plain. He had ascertained that earlier—and promptly dismissed her from his mind. 'They called her the—'

'Simple *ton*!' Fleet said, laughing. 'I remember! She never spoke and some thought her a lack-wit. Had a pretty little blonde friend, now I recall. Amanda something or other. I wonder what happened to her?'

'Amanda Makepeace. She married Frank Spry,' Joss said succinctly. 'He had property in Ireland, I believe.'

Fleet stared. 'Devil take it, Joss, you sound just like Debrett! Had no idea you had an encyclopaedic memory!'

'Why do you think I win so often?' Joss asked laconically. 'Truth is, I only remember because Juliana and Amanda Spry were in a way to being friends. I hear that Lady Spry is recently widowed and is back in London. Perhaps you should look her up, Seb! Taking little piece, as I recall!'

'So how is the fair Juliana?' Fleet asked with a grin. If ever there was a gamester who could outplay Joss Tallant it was his sister, Lady Juliana Myfleet.

'Oh, Ju is much the same as ever,' Joss drawled. 'High play, low company… Taken up with Clive Massingham, you know.'

Fleet drew his breath in sharply. 'That thought leaves an unpleasant taste in the mouth! Fellow's a wrong 'un, leaving aside the family connection!'

Joss shrugged uncomfortably. 'I agree, but there's damn all I can do about it! Juliana always goes her own way and, although she'll listen to me, I don't flatter myself I've got much influence. Not,' he added with a shade of bitterness, 'that I can play the moralist. To set myself up as such would be absurd. Saw my father yesterday,' he added. 'Thought the old man was about to wash his hands of both of us! It's a toss up as to which of us he disapproves of the most!'

Fleet chuckled. 'Threatened to disinherit you, did he?'

Joss shrugged again. Some residual respect stirred within him. 'Only natural, I suppose, when I fail to meet his expectations in so singular a manner! He wants me to marry and provide an heir. I can't say the idea appeals. Genteel females are all of a piece—insipid pattern-cards! Could marry an actress or some such, I suppose...'

'Or a harlot,' Fleet said slyly. 'The fair Harriet would grace any stately home!'

They had reached Covent Garden. Two ladies of the night, who were emerging from one of the stinking alleyways, regarded them with curiosity and a lascivious gleam.

'Rough,' Fleet said, shaking his head ruefully. 'Very rough indeed.'

In contrast, the entrance hall of Abbess Walsh's establishment was the epitome of tasteful opulence, the perfect fashionable bordello. The Abbess herself glided forward to greet them with a smile. She was a handsome, well-preserved woman of indeterminate age, who had a reputation for providing quality and novelty.

'Gentlemen...it is a pleasure to see you again.' She shepherded them up the marble and gilt staircase. 'Is there anything in particular that I can offer you tonight?'

'Something different, if you please, ma'am,' Fleet said, stifling a yawn. 'I may be fickle but I get so damnably bored...'

'Of course, your Grace…' The Abbess smiled faintly. She turned to Joss. 'My lord? Harriet has missed you…'

Joss's smile did not reach his eyes. He reflected cynically that Miss Harriet Templeton's affections were for sale to the highest bidder and at the moment that privilege was his. Still, that suited him well enough. He had been very fond of his previous mistress, and when Marianne had told him that she had accepted a marriage proposal from another gentleman, Joss had found himself surprisingly chagrined.

He had had a certain regard for Marianne. Indeed, he might even have gone as far as to admit that he cared for her. They had been friends in an easy and undemanding manner, and though he had not been in love since his salad days, he had valued her company and missed her acutely. Fortunately there was no chance of such a situation developing with Harriet. Her affection was only as deep as his wallet and Joss was quite happy for the relationship to remain resolutely unemotional.

He strolled down the familiar corridor and went into the room at the end. Miss Templeton was sitting before her mirror, brushing her hair. At the sight of him, her fair, small-featured face lit with a dazzling smile. She dropped the brush with alacrity and sped forward, enveloping him in a sweetly scented embrace, her body pressed softly against his.

'Joss, darling…' she purred, 'I have been pining away for the sight of you…'

Her fingers were already at work undoing the buttons of his waistcoat. Joss shrugged himself out of his jacket and bent to kiss her.

'I have missed you too, my sweet. Shall we celebrate our reunion?'

He picked her up and tossed her on to the bed. Harriet

giggled delightfully. She lay sprawled beside him as he pulled his boots off, her face alight with laughter and provocation. Her lace peignoir had come undone and there was little of the voluptuous figure beneath that was left to his imagination. Joss felt his body react but his mind stayed cold. Marry a harlot... For a moment he thought of Harriet gracing the corridors of Ashby Tallant as the new Marchioness, but the thought of marriage to anyone was anathema to him. Whenever he tried to imagine it he was left with the picture of two people hurling insults at each other from opposite ends of their great barn of a house. His mind shuddered away from the thought.

He lay back on the pillows as Harriet pulled him down beside her. For a split second he saw Amy Bainbridge's features superimposed on the painted, pretty face that lay beside him. The image gave him a sharp shock. Little Miss Bainbridge, so plain, so disapproving. In the time that he had been observing her he had seen her distaste for him clear in her eyes, had sensed her dislike, even though she had not addressed a single word to him.

No matter. He did not know what had even made him think of her, except that such transparent innocence was wholly at odds with his current surroundings. He had abandoned such innocence many years ago. It was not for him now. He gave himself up to Harriet's skilful hands and allowed his mind to slide away into darkness.

'It's a shambles, Miss Bainbridge! Sheer, wanton untidiness! However could a body be so disorderly? Your brother should confine his gambling to his club.' Patience's angular face quivered with disapproval. She brandished a kitchen knife at Amy. 'I've tried and tried to remove the wax and the stains but Lady Bainbridge doesn't like me to polish too hard. She says that it wears away the furniture!'

Looking around the dining room, Amy could see that Patience had plenty of cause for complaint. Twenty candles had dripped their wax on to every available surface and there were dark rings on the polished wood of the table where the brandy bottle had slopped. There was a stale smell in the air. Amy moved over to the window and pulled the sash up hard, letting the fresh morning air into the room. The bright light made everything look so much more dilapidated. Amy sighed.

'Come, give me that knife, Patience. I will scrape the wax off the furniture if you polish it up afterwards. Why, there is almost enough to make a fresh candle out of the leftovers—'

'You sound just like your mama,' Patience said, but there was a hint of indulgence in her voice now. Her expression softened a little as she looked at Amy. 'Though you tell me, Miss Amy, what use it is you making fresh candles from old when your good-for-nothing brother will only melt them all over my table again!'

Amy winced. Patience took the old retainer's privileges to the very limit sometimes. She knew that Richard was not quite a universal favourite. Though petted by his mother and fawned upon by plenty of ladies for his good looks if not his fortune, he had singularly failed to melt Patience's stern heart. She herself could not approve of his gambling but she could also not help but care for him. It was Richard who had been with her through the dark days after her father's death, giving her the love and support that he needed from her in return.

'I know it is very bad of Richard to gamble as he does,' Amy said, trying to think of any mitigating circumstances that might pacify Patience, 'but he means no harm, and if he wins money at the tables then we may all benefit from it—'

'Humph!' Patience's snort made her feelings quite clear. 'The only benefit of Sir Richard's gambling goes to Sir Richard himself! Easy come and easy go, say I! And it's a crying shame, Miss Amy, when you scrimp and save to keep the household running and have nary a new dress from one year's end to the next.' She plied her duster with force. 'You could be quite a pretty little thing if only you were well turned out—'

Amy went off into a peal of laughter. 'Now there you are fair and far out, Patience! Did you not see me when I had my come-out? The best gowns that money could buy and I still looked a fright. Better to save the housekeeping for less of a lost cause!'

Patience put the duster down and came across to her. 'Those gowns did not suit you because they were too fussy. It was all your mama's doing! Look in the mirror, Miss Amy. What do you see?'

Amy peered obediently into the spotted glass. 'I see brown hair without a curl, a pale face and a figure as flat as a board. No potential there, Patience dear!'

'Strange,' Patience said in acid tones. 'I see beautiful fine hair, pretty blue eyes and a figure as neat and trim as you please. You may not be a diamond of the first water, Miss Amy, but you are a little pearl. You just need the right setting.'

Amy blinked at such an assessment from the unsentimental maid. 'Thank you, dear Patience. You are very kind to me—'

'Aye, and you don't believe a word I say!'

Amy did not reply. It was not that she did not believe Patience; more that she did not want to start to believe. With no money and no prospects it would be the height of folly to start dreaming of fine clothes and high society.

Patience picked up her duster again, dipped it into the pot and spread some polish over the nearest brandy stain. Amy leant over.

'Oh, what is that? It smells very sweet.'

'My own concoction,' Patience said, with grim satisfaction, 'so it costs next to nothing. Wax from the bees and lavender from the garden, with a drop of brandy to lift the stain. Nothing like brandy to lift brandy, I always say! A pity that gambling does not work to cure gambling!'

'I believe it is an obsession,' Amy said cautiously, shaking out the curtains to release the smell of smoke. 'Indeed, it seems that no warning example will persuade Richard to stop. Papa was just the same. They say that it is in the blood.'

'Stuff and nonsense!' Patience bent a stern look on her. 'You are the contradiction of that theory, Miss Amy! You do not gamble!'

'No, indeed, I detest it!' Amy shuddered. 'Yet I hear that there are as many great ladies in thrall to the tables as the men. Why, when I went into society they were for ever trying to tempt me to a game of whist or commerce. It was harmless, they said…' Her voice trailed away. There had been nothing harmless about her father's compulsion to gamble, nor its consequences for the rest of the family.

Patience shook her head. ''Twas a shame you did not take, Miss Amy. You could have had an establishment of your own by now.'

Amy prised a stubborn piece of wax off the table. 'I have the ordering of this house in all but name, and a fine challenge it is with Richard's spending and Mama's economies—'

The door opened and Lady Bainbridge came in. Amy quickly swept all the loose pieces of candle wax off the table and into her apron pocket before her mother could see how much waste there had been.

'Good morning, Mama. I hope that the hot milk procured you a good night's sleep?'

Lady Bainbridge cast a suspicious look around the room, taking in the one candlestick that Amy had left on the mantelpiece. Her gaze rested for a moment on Patience, who was polishing the table very gently.

'I slept quite well, I thank you, my love, and partook of a small breakfast. Now, I do believe Mrs Vestey may be coming to visit this morning. She made mention of it when I was last at the circulating library.' Lady Bainbridge subsided into a chair and waved one white hand languorously. 'Patience, when we have callers, please see to it that only tea and biscuits are served. Anything else will be quite unnecessary, and if we have the misfortune of Mrs Vestey bringing a friend with her, please ensure that there is but one biscuit each. Not cakes. Cakes are too rich and injurious to the digestion.'

'Yes, ma'am.' Patience knelt down and began to sweep out the grate.

'Do not throw those coals away!' Lady Bainbridge said sharply, pointing to some lumps amongst the ash. 'They may be re-used! Amy, dear…' she turned her faded blue eyes on her daughter '…I do believe we should go through the accounts again this afternoon and see where we may retrench. I am sure we will find plenty of opportunity.'

Amy sighed. They went through this particular pantomime at least once a month. 'I do believe, Mama, that it would be better to prevail on Richard to increase the housekeeping rather than try to cut back further. Why, he has an income of at least three thousand a year from Nettlecombe, even if it is the only property left to him!'

'Alas, that three thousand a year is nothing to a man of fashion,' Lady Bainbridge declaimed. 'Poor Richard, I am sure that he could scarce scrape by on twice that amount!'

'We manage to survive on a quarter of that sum,' Amy pointed out. 'There are two of us and we do not repine.' She ignored the snort of disgust that emanated from the hearth, where Patience was still sweeping out the grate.

'Yes, my love, but we have no need of the items that Richard requires,' Lady Bainbridge observed, in kindly fashion. 'Why, he must have a curricle and horses, of course, and money to buy all the odds and ends that a gentleman needs! I do declare, you will be taking the very clothes from his back if you ask for more money! Your brother has a position to uphold in the world, after all—'

'Aye, and his sister has had no new gown for nigh on three years,' came a sepulchral voice from the hearth.

Lady Bainbridge frowned. 'That is enough, Patience! What need has Amy of new clothes? Now, if she were to go out in society it would be a different matter, but Amy has no ambitions for that, have you, my love?' She swept on without waiting for a reply. 'No, indeed, there is plenty of wear in all of Amy's dresses and if there is not she may always add a fringe here and a ruffle there.'

The doorbell pealed. Amy peeked out of the window. 'It is Mrs Vestey, Mama, and I do believe that she has brought Lady Amherst and Mrs Ponting with her.'

'Three of them! How vexing,' murmured her ladyship. 'Patience, I shall receive them in the parlour. Be sure to serve only three biscuits—I shall do without myself.'

Amy, left alone in the relative peace of the dining room, rearranged the good rosewood chairs about the table, moved her mother's armchair to cover a bare patch on the carpet and straightened the curtains. That was better. The room had lost the louche air of gaming that had hung about it and now looked shabby genteel, as indeed it was. As she was. Amy flicked another glance at her reflection. What good was it for Richard to present himself to the world as a gentleman of fortune when the entire *ton* knew that for the hollow sham it was? Once the Bainbridges had had a place in the world and were respected for it, but now Richard lived beyond his means, gambling away what little was left of his inheritance. He would never catch himself an heiress on good looks alone.

Amy closed the dining-room door quietly behind her and went to fetch her coat and bonnet. She had no wish to join Lady Bainbridge and her friends for a pot of tea with no biscuit, but she had plenty of errands to run that morning. There was a parcel of medicines to send to her former nurse, Mrs Benfleet, who lived in Windsor and had recently been ill. Amy wished that she could visit her, but the cost of the medicines meant that a journey was currently out of the question. Then there was the marketing to be done, for Lady Bainbridge entrusted no one but Amy with the purchase of fresh food in a city as ruinously expensive as London. Amy and her mother had had countless discussions about this, with Amy insisting that they could live far more frugally in the country and Lady Bainbridge adamant that Richard needed them to stay in London to look after him. Beneath the pretence, Amy knew that her mother was simply afraid that Richard's gambling would run out of hand without the restraining presence of his family and that they would retire to the country and be forgotten—and starve. It was only their constant presence in Curzon Street that reminded Richard that he had dependents.

Two hours later Amy had managed to stave off starvation for another few days through the judicious purchase of the cheapest fruit and vegetables that she could find. Lady Bainbridge had suggested that they could do without fruit but Amy had said that she had no wish to suffer from scurvy, like some of the navy's more unfortunate sailors. She had managed to find some good bargains in the market—cauliflowers which had outer leaves that were damaged but where the centres were quite fresh; potatoes with only the odd blemish, apples that were only a little fly-blown.

She was on her way back through Covent Garden when she caught sight of a familiar figure—familiar, at least, from the previous night. It was the Earl of Tallant, coming down the steps of a nearby house, adjusting his cuffs and the set of his jacket. The sun gleamed on the rich dark auburn of his hair. Amy froze. With his athletic build and energetic gait he looked like a sportsman rather than a man who had spent the first part of the night at the gaming tables and the second part… Amy felt a crimson blush spread up from her toes to the top of her head. She knew full well that the elegant frontages of these houses concealed the kind of den of iniquity that Richard and his friends were wont to patronise. She turned away hastily, for the last thing she wanted was to catch the Earl's eye. The thought of being obliged to greet him when he had just emerged from taking his pleasure in a bawdy-house almost paralysed her.

She took a blind step forward and the edge of her basket caught the side of a nearby cart, wrenching it from her hands and tipping its contents all over the cobbles. Apples rolled away into the gutter. Amy gave an exclamation and went down on her hands and knees. She could not afford to lose any of her precious food. She even crawled a little way under the cart to try to rescue two potatoes that had disappeared beneath the wheels, bumping her knee painfully in the process. When she emerged, her face was flushed and her hands were dirty and the last thing she wished was to peer out from beneath the wing of the cart to see the Earl of Tallant bending down and extending a hand to her.

'Miss Bainbridge? You appear to be in some difficulty, ma'am. Allow me to assist.'

He had placed one hand under her elbow and helped her to her feet before Amy could refuse. She blushed, stepped back from him and bumped herself on the cart, smoothed her dress down and found that she had managed to spread the soil from the potatoes on to her skirts. She saw Joss Tallant's gaze sweep over her, saw him smile and felt her blush get hotter.

'Thank you, my lord.'

'Have you injured yourself, Miss Bainbridge? I noticed that you winced a little when you stood up.'

Amy took a tentative step and tried not to wince again. 'No, I thank you. I am very well.' She bent to retrieve the basket and slipped the potatoes back inside it, hoping he had not noticed.

'May I escort you somewhere?' Joss Tallant enquired. 'Back to Curzon Street, perhaps?' He was leaning against the side of the cart now and showed no sign of leaving her.

'Oh, no, thank you!' Amy was horrified at the thought. Could the man not simply take himself off? Surely the last thing he would want to do was play the gallant for her. 'I am happy to walk and I am sure that you have other things to do.'

Against her will, her gaze drifted to the bland front door from which he had just emerged. She had no wish to dwell on what his other activities might be, but she found it strangely difficult to drag her mind—and her gaze—away. Despite herself, her inflamed imagination presented her with all sorts of images… And then she met Joss Tallant's gaze and realised that he had read her thoughts most accurately. He raised his eyebrows, a speculative look in his eyes.

Amy discovered that she could not blush any harder. Her whole body was already one burning mass. She looked hastily down at the cobbles, where an apple still lay against the kerb.

'I assure you,' Joss Tallant said, the twinkle still in his eye, 'that I am not engaged until later in the day, Miss Bainbridge. However if you do not wish to accept my escort, perhaps I could procure you a hack?'

'No, thank you,' Amy said again, very quickly. She could not afford to pay for a cab and did not wish to assume that he would do so for her. She grasped her basket tightly. 'I shall walk. Good day, sir.'

'Then you must permit me to walk with you in case you require any assistance,' Joss said, falling into step beside her, 'and please allow me to carry your basket. So many apples and potatoes—I hope they were not damaged?'

'It is quite unnecessary for you to accompany me,' Amy said, holding on to the basket as he took hold of the handle. 'Thank you for your consideration,' she added ungraciously, fearing she might sound too abrupt, 'but I have no need of your help.'

She tugged on the basket; Joss did not let go. She tugged again. He tightened his grip.

'Are we to play tug of war in the street, Miss Bainbridge?'

'This is ridiculous!' Amy let go of the basket and glared at him. 'You cannot possibly walk through the streets of London carrying a marketing basket, my lord—'

'I assure you, my reputation would suffer more were I to permit a lady to carry her own shopping. That would be most ungallant in me.'

'You are absurd!' Amy cast him a furious sideways look. 'You have no need to put yourself to all this trouble! Indeed, I would that you did not!'

Joss merely shrugged, placed the basket over one arm and offered Amy the other, which she pointedly ignored. In this manner they made their way down Shaftesbury Avenue—mainly in silence, since Amy did not offer any remarks of her own and answered Joss's comments on the weather as shortly as possible. After a couple of awkward minutes she turned her head to look at him and saw that he was watching her with quizzical amusement. She turned her face sharply away.

Inside she was seething. The persistence of the man in the face of her obvious reluctance for his company was bad enough; she could not believe that he was really so obtuse not to realise that she wanted rid of him. Then to make her a laughing stock by insisting on carrying the basket as though he were a footman... She could see people staring and pointing and she wished she had accepted the offer of the hackney carriage.

'You are looking as though you wish me in Hades, Miss Bainbridge.'

Joss's words interrupted Amy's furious thoughts and she swallowed hard.

'It is simply that I do not understand your insistence on accompanying me, sir.' Amy forced herself to be civil. 'It is very good of you but quite unnecessary—'

'And quite unappreciated?'

'I do not appreciate having company forced upon me,' Amy agreed coldly.

'I see.' Joss seemed amused. 'Would that be my company in particular, Miss Bainbridge?'

Amy struggled with her annoyance. 'I am flattered by your notice, my lord—'

'I doubt that. You disapprove of me, do you not, Miss Bainbridge?'

Amy looked at him, startled. It was true, but she had not realised that she had made it so obvious. She felt a little ashamed that she had allowed her dislike to show. It was not that she cared whether or not she hurt his feelings, for surely such a hardened rakehell had none, but more that she knew it was bad manners.

'Well, I...' She met his sardonic gaze and raised her chin unconsciously. 'Yes, of course I disapprove of you.'

'It is obligatory for young ladies to do so,' Joss murmured. 'What are your reasons, Miss Bainbridge?'

'As you ask, my lord...' Amy took a deep breath. 'I

do not approve of gaming and I deplore those who lead the young and impressionable astray.'

Joss gave a crack of laughter. 'Good God, surely you do not consider your brother young and impressionable? He could teach most hardened gamblers a thing or two!'

Amy set her jaw. 'Your attitude merely confirms my opinion, my lord. It is all very well for gentlemen such as yourself and the Duke of Fleet, who have the substance to support their obsession, to throw their fortune away as they please! It is another matter for you to encourage those who do not have the means to support their gambling!'

'Nobody forces your brother to gamble,' Joss said pleasantly. 'If he does not have the means to support the habit he should not play for such high stakes.'

Amy felt a rush of dislike for him that almost overwhelmed her. 'I might have known that you would not understand! Or that you would deliberately choose to be obtuse—'

'My dear Miss Bainbridge,' Joss drawled, 'I understand perfectly. You are the one who does not understand. The truth is that if Fleet and I were not taking your brother's money you may be sure that he would be giving it to someone else. The gambling is his problem, not ours.'

Amy's fury was swelling inside her like a vast balloon. Her blue eyes flashed fire. 'You take advantage of his weakness, sir.'

Joss shrugged. 'Maybe.' He shot her a look and she was infuriated to see that he was still smiling. 'Your brother was doubly unlucky, was he not, Miss Bainbridge? For all his charm, it seems that you possess the strength of character that he lacks.'

Amy looked away. She was not about to agree with

his criticisms of her brother, no matter how near the mark they were.

'We shall just have to agree to differ, my lord,' she said tightly, 'and perhaps we should refrain from further conversation until we reach Curzon Street.'

Joss raised his brows. 'Must we, Miss Bainbridge? We are only in Piccadilly and I always find that time passes so much more quickly when one keeps occupied! Perhaps we could talk of something innocuous, however, so that I need not incur your wrath any further.'

Amy was silent. She was not being deliberately stubborn but she was feeling so irritated that she could not think of a single inoffensive topic. After a second, Joss laughed. 'Oh, dear, is it that bad, Miss Bainbridge? And we have already discussed the weather...'

Amy looked at him. He was smiling at her and there was a warmth in his eyes that made her feel uncomfortable in an entirely different way. It was very confusing. She disliked him intensely, particularly for his callous dismissal of her plea about Richard, and yet she was aware of a thaw setting in around the edges of her mind. She deliberately froze it up again.

'We could raise the subject of the weather again,' she said coldly. 'After all, it is very sunny at the moment.'

Joss inclined his head. 'That is true. Though I do believe that if this heat continues we shall have a thunderstorm. Do you dislike thunderstorms, Miss Bainbridge?'

'Yes indeed, I dislike them intensely.' Amy looked around. 'I find the cold preferable to the heat. Too much sun can be very oppressive.'

'Yet too much snow can be most inconvenient.'

'I suppose so.' Amy stopped. 'Oh, look, we are almost at Curzon Street already.'

'How fortuitous. Though I do believe that the weather would have sustained us for several minutes more.' Joss put the basket down by the railings as they reached Number 3.

Amy hesitated. She did not wish to invite him in but civility demanded it. 'Would you care for any refreshment, my lord, following your exertions with that basket?'

Joss smiled. He took her hand. 'No, thank you. I have remembered one of those pressing engagements that you mentioned earlier, so I fear I must go. Thank you for your company, Miss Bainbridge. I hope that you will soon be better—I noticed that you were limping a little.'

'Oh…' Amy blushed self-consciously. 'It is nothing, my lord.' She tried to retrieve her hand. Joss appeared not to notice.

'I did think of carrying you,' he continued, 'but given the fuss that you made over the basket I felt it would be inadvisable.'

'Very wise, my lord,' Amy said crossly, 'though I must thank you for your assistance, I suppose. Good day.'

Joss let her go at last and raised a casual hand in farewell. 'Goodbye, Miss Bainbridge. I am sure we shall meet again soon.'

Amy paused, one hand on the door. 'I doubt it, my lord.'

Joss grinned. 'You may depend upon it, Miss Bainbridge. You might even bet on it—if you were the gambling kind! It is inevitable when you are trying to avoid someone!'

He turned away and Amy watched, a little bemused, as he disappeared around the corner of Clarges Street. She hoped that he was wrong about them meeting again, although there was some truth in the fact that one often bumped into the very person one was trying to avoid, as though some kind of perverse fate was at play. She shrugged a little uncomfortably. There was something about the Earl of Tallant that she found entirely disconcerting and it would be better to forget all about him. They had nothing in common, not the least little thing.

Amy retrieved her basket and went into the cool of the hall. The parlour door was ajar.

'Is that you, Amy?' Lady Bainbridge called. 'Oh, dear, I have just partaken of luncheon and there was not sufficient for two. I was so hoping that you would not be back until later!'

'That is all right, Mama,' Amy said, stifling a sigh. She selected one of the bruised apples from the top of the basket. 'I will have this for my luncheon with some cheese and make the rest of the apples into a stew that will do us for the rest of the week.' She bent to kiss her mother's cheek. 'Is all well with you?'

'Yes, my dear,' Lady Bainbridge said, settling back in her chair. 'I have had a very pleasant morning. Lady Vestey stayed for far longer than she ought, though. I was hard pressed not to serve up another pot of tea.' She bent a look of enquiry on her daughter. 'Were you speaking with someone just now, my love? I thought that I heard a gentleman's voice.'

'No, Mama,' Amy said, avoiding Lady Bainbridge's eye. 'There was no one. No one at all.'

Lady Bainbridge slumped back in her chair. 'A pity. For I have not quite given up hope for you, you know, Amy. I am sure that there is a pleasant gentleman somewhere who wishes for a conformable wife. An older gentleman, perhaps, or a widower looking for a mother for his children…'

'It sounds a delightful prospect, Mama,' Amy said, reflecting how different from these imaginings was the Earl of Tallant. 'However, I fear I know no widowers or older gentlemen looking for a suitable wife. And I have no dowry, nor even my looks to recommend me…'

Lady Bainbridge patted her cheek. 'No, but you are a dear, sweet girl, Amy! We shall not look too high for you, though.'

'Any gentleman will need to look high,' Amy said with a smile, 'to see the shelf that I am on, Mama! Now, if you will excuse me, I shall eat my apple and cheese, and then I have some visits to make.'

'To the poor, I suppose!' Lady Bainbridge waved a languid hand. 'You are so good, Amy! That former landlady of ours, Mrs Wendover… You will persist in keeping in touch with her although you should not feel obliged, you know!'

'No, Mama,' Amy said, selecting the most battered-looking apple from her basket and biting into it, 'but at least I get a good piece of fruitcake when I am visiting in Whitechapel!'

Lady Bainbridge's eyes brightened. 'Then slip a piece into your bag for me, my love! You know I love a good fruitcake!'

Chapter Three

'I'm sure that Patience has beaten these rugs too hard,' Lady Bainbridge said that evening, peering at the carpet in the dining room by the light of one dim candle. 'The pattern is quite faded, you know. One can ruin a carpet with too much beating.'

'I imagine that the rugs are faded because they are old, Mama, not for any other reason,' Amy said. She pushed her apple stew listlessly about the bowl. Dinner had been as lacklustre as ever, but that was not the reason for her blue devils. She had been feeling restless ever since she had returned home from visiting Mrs Wendover and she was at a loss to explain why. The evening stretched ahead of her in the same pattern as every other evening for the previous two years; a book or sewing, a cup of hot milk if there was enough left and it had not curdled, and an early bed. For two years she had been quite satisfied with this routine, but tonight she felt as though she would explode.

A door slammed and Richard's voice echoed down the corridor, then he breezed into the room with his customary flamboyance. Lady Bainbridge, who had been drooping over her bowl, brightened immediately.

'Richard, darling! Do you go to Lady Aston's ball tonight? Oh, you look so elegant!'

A dart of envy, as painful as it was unexpected, pierced Amy. She blinked a little. Ever since the disaster of her come-out she had sworn that she never wished to set foot in a fashionable ballroom again and, until tonight, she had never felt remotely like changing her mind. It seemed extraordinary that she could envy Richard the pleasure, yet now she was jealous. Amy examined her feelings carefully. Yes, she was envious of her brother's good looks, his elegant appearance and, more than anything, his invitation to Lady Aston's ball.

She looked at him. Tall, golden and good-looking in his evening dress, he reminded her so forcibly of their father that for a second her throat ached. Lady Bainbridge was still cooing over him and Amy told herself fairly that it was not surprising. If she saw George Bainbridge in Richard, how much more poignant must it be for their mother.

'Be sure to dance with Miss Loring,' Lady Bainbridge was saying. 'They say that she has fifty thousand pounds—'

'I do not suppose that Richard will see much of the ballroom, Mama,' Amy said. 'Surely it is the card room that will have his attention!'

Both Lady Bainbridge and Richard stopped talking and looked at her and Amy realised that the words had come out in a decidedly waspish tone. Fortunately Richard was so easy going that he never took offence. He gave her a speculative grin.

'You sound as though you're jealous, Amy! I thought you scorned the amusements of the *ton*!'

Amy pressed her napkin to her lips, then threw it down beside the rejected bowl of apples. 'I am sorry,

Richard. I feel blue-devilled tonight! I am sure it will pass.'

'With a bit of judicious sewing, or perhaps a passage or two from an improving book?' Richard had never made a secret of the fact that his own interests and those of his sister were decidedly divergent. 'You would do better to come out with me! Play a hand of whist, dance the waltz!'

Lady Bainbridge started to object. 'Oh, not the waltz, Richard! It is a positively dangerous dance! And Amy cannot go without a chaperon, and certainly not to Lady Aston's. The place is a hotbed of immoral activity!'

'I hope so,' Richard said, grinning.

'Of which the most immoral is whist,' Amy said. 'That is even more dangerous than waltzing for it can be prodigiously expensive!'

Richard leant on the back of a chair and viewed his sister with his very blue eyes. 'I tell you what, Amy, you've been eating too much fruit. It gives one a sour disposition!'

Amy threw her napkin at him. Richard ducked. The chair creaked as he leant his weight against it.

'Children, children!' Lady Bainbridge expostulated. 'Richard, do not break that chair, we cannot afford to replace it!'

'Your pardon, Mama.' Richard retrieved the napkin and sat down. He turned back to Amy. 'Now here's the thing, Amy! I'll escort you to Lady Moon's ball next week—and you cannot say fairer than that, for it is the slowest thing to escort one's own sister—but only if you agree to play a hand of whist! You are for ever complaining about my gambling! Now it is time for you to understand what it is you are complaining about!'

'Lady Moon's ball,' Lady Bainbridge said thoughtfully. 'I am not perfectly sure that we may attend, Richard, for we cannot afford any new clothes—'

'A week is surely long enough to make over something old,' Richard said, brushing a thread off his immaculate evening jacket.

'True,' Lady Bainbridge said. 'It would be pleasant to have some different company and one may eat well enough for a week at a ball. What do you say, Amy?'

'Why not?' Amy said. She viewed her mother's thin figure and tried to imagine her storing enough food for a week, like a camel storing water.

'You might show a little more eagerness, my love,' Lady Bainbridge grumbled. 'It is nigh on twelve months since we attended a proper ball. It will be such a treat for you. Who knows—you may attract the interest of a gentleman...?' Her blue eyes appraised Amy thoughtfully, as did Richard, who had selected an apple from the bowl of fruit on the sideboard and was leaning against the table, chewing heartily. He shook his head.

'I think not, Mama. Amy is almost at her last prayers!'

'I believe you have a ball to attend,' Amy said frostily, watching as Richard straightened up and tossed his apple core carelessly into the fireplace. If only she had an ounce of that golden beauty, she thought suddenly. Then she would show them she was not on the shelf.

Richard bestowed a careless kiss on the top of her head, and a slightly more decorous one on his mother's cheek and strode out, whistling. The front door slammed behind him. Lady Bainbridge stood up and retrieved the fruit bowl.

'Remind Patience not to leave the fruit on display in future, Amy dear. Richard does not need to eat anything at home when he can eat at someone else's expense.'

'Yes, Mama,' Amy said. 'I believe Patience thought it might brighten the room, given that we never have any flowers.'

Lady Bainbridge shuddered. 'Flowers! Wanton extravagance! What use are flowers? One cannot even eat them!'

She disappeared through the door to the servant's hall.

Amy pushed away her bowl of cold fruit stew and got to her feet. Perhaps she might spend the evening helping Patience to polish the silver. That would prevent her from falling into a fit of the dismals. Action, not inaction, was the key. Genteel poverty could be hard, but it was not as desperate as the squalor she had seen in the Whitechapel stews. Even today, when she had visited Mrs Wendover, Amy had been struck afresh by the state of that widow's determined attempts to keep a spotlessly clean house amidst the filth around her. Amy repressed a grin. There were not many young ladies who could boast a stay in Whitechapel, but she had had that privilege twice, the second time when she had been sixteen and her father's finances had reached such a parlous state that there had been no alternative. At least now they could afford to keep a small house in the respectable part of town. Whitechapel had not been respectable but it had certainly been educational. She bent absent-mindedly to bank down the meagre fire, thinking of the time that she had spent there.

A scrap of paper was resting on the carpet beside the fireplace. Amy leant over and picked it up. It was a ticket for the national lottery. She knew that Richard, in common with a huge proportion of the populace, often gambled on the national lottery and on private lotteries as well when they were raising funds for various projects. As far as she knew he had never won a penny. It was just another wager, another way of throwing his money away, another gamble.

Amy smoothed out the crumpled ticket. The draw was dated for the following morning. Richard must have dropped the ticket from his pocket book without realising. She tucked it behind the clock, making a mental note to tell him in the morning. She might not approve of gambling, but some small, superstitious part of her mind prevented her from consigning the ticket to the fire. After all, it might, just might, win a prize. Smiling a little at her own credulity, Amy went off to polish the silver.

After breakfast the following day, Amy retrieved the lottery ticket from its place behind the clock and went out into the hall, intending to give it to Marten, Richard's valet, to hand back to his master. Fortuitously, Marten was just coming down the stairs with one of Richard's coats over his arm. He bowed. Marten never took the liberties that Patience did. He was always deferential.

'Good morning, Marten. Is my brother awake yet?' Amy enquired. Richard was prone to sleep very late on most mornings, especially when he had been playing into the early hours.

Marten sketched another bow. His expression was blander than cream. 'I fear that Sir Richard has not yet returned, ma'am. The ball went on long into the night, I believe.'

'I suppose he has a pressing engagement at the card tables.' Amy gave Marten a sharp look, which he returned with one of even greater impassivity.

'Indeed, ma'am, perhaps so.'

'Or perhaps he retired to another place for the night?' Amy was remembering the discreet house in Covent Garden from which Joss Tallant had emerged the previous day. Marten smiled politely.

'I could not possibly say, ma'am.'

Amy frowned a little. It was most unfortunate that her brother was absent the one time that she needed to see him. Since the lottery draw was taking place that very morning, it was urgent that she should hand the ticket over to him at once. She knew nothing of lotteries, but she did worry that one might have to claim the prize at the draw itself. It would be most galling for Richard if his were the winning numbers and yet he lost the prize because he had left his ticket behind.

Amy sighed. Her father had taught her how to calculate odds when she was a child and the odds against her brother's ticket being the winning one must be huge…oh, forty thousand to one, or some such figure. She knew it was silly even to imagine that he might win. Even so, she felt a certain responsibility to reunite him with his ticket, pointless though it was.

She put the ticket in her pocket, then took it out and looked at it again. It was such a tempting little scrap of paper. Amy felt something stir in her blood. Perhaps, just perhaps, this could be the key to thousands of pounds. No wonder that people prayed so earnestly to win and spent their very last shilling on the gamble. She smiled at the fanciful line her thoughts were taking. It was the first time that she had ever felt even the remotest temptation towards gambling, and the inclination was gone almost as swiftly as it had come.

Marten was still waiting, still deferential, to see how he might serve her. Amy held out the ticket.

'It is very urgent that this lottery ticket is delivered

to Sir Richard, Marten,' she said. 'Do you have *any* notion where he might be this morning?'

The manservant shook his head. 'I regret that I do not, ma'am. Sir Richard made it plain last night that he did not intend to return until late morning, if then. He could be in any number of places, ma'am.'

Amy hesitated. 'Then do you know where the lottery draw takes place? I am sure he must be going there and I could meet with him...' Her voice trailed away and she felt herself blush. It was not that Marten had betrayed any surprise, for indeed his face was as impassive as ever. It was more that Amy felt that he *must* be surprised. She was hardly renowned for frequenting lottery draws any more than she was known for venturing into society.

'The lottery draw takes place at the Guildhall, ma'am,' Marten said calmly, quite as though Amy had only been enquiring after the weather. 'If you would like me to carry a message to Sir Richard—?'

'Yes, perhaps...' Amy wavered. It was simpler by far to send Marten. Except that it was a fine day and she wanted a walk, and, if truth were told, she also wanted a little excitement. Her low spirits of the previous evening had not quite dissipated and a lottery draw would be an interesting spectacle to watch.

'No, it is quite all right!' she said, making a sudden decision and feeling quite reckless. 'I shall go there myself! I have a letter to deliver in Holborn and it is a fine day for a walk.'

'Very well, ma'am,' Marten murmured. 'Pray do not hesitate to call me if I can be of service.'

He strode softly away and closed the door to the servants' quarters behind him. Amy was left in the hall. Before she could change her mind, she sped up the stairs, removed her apron and donned a pelisse and an old chip bonnet. She was still tying the ribbons beneath her chin as she hurried back down the stairs and out of the front door. This was decidedly more exciting than polishing the silver or discussing menus with Cook, and as it was some distance to the Guildhall she had better start at once. It would never do to be late and miss the draw.

Amy had not expected the crowd to be so great. By the time that she reached the Guildhall, the press of people in the building was intense and she could barely move.

She soon realised that the chances of finding her brother in such a throng were very small indeed. She had thoroughly underestimated the appeal of the lottery.

There was a stage at one end of the hall and she could see figures moving upon it, setting up some complicated mechanical contraption that she realised must be the lottery wheel. She could smell gin and sweat and cheap perfume emanating from the bodies that pressed against hers, and she had to swallow hard to prevent herself from retching. The heat was building now and with it an excitement that ebbed and flowed through the crowd like the waves on the seashore. Amy felt it too; it was a tingling in her stomach, a shiver along the nerves. It was intoxicating, like the wine she had occasionally drunk, or the thrill of something unexpected. Very little that was out of the ordinary ever happened in Amy's life, yet now she had a lottery ticket clutched tightly in her fingers and she felt as though anything could happen.

On her left side, Amy was pinned against a pillar by a fat woman with a large marketing basket. Several other people pressed against her back and a huge, red-faced gentleman in a straining, shiny waistcoat was squashed against her right-hand side. Since Amy was so tiny, she could not see over the heads of the people in front of her. After a few ineffectual pleas to be allowed through the crowd, which probably nobody even heard since she was addressing some very broad backs, she realised that she was very likely stuck fast until the lottery draw was over. Richard might be standing a mere twenty feet away, but if he was she had no way of knowing. She began to regret her quest.

She turned her head and caught sight of a familiar figure in the throng. Her heart skipped a beat. The Earl of Tallant was standing over to her left, leaning casually against the wall, engaged in conversation with a large gentleman whom Amy recognised as the Duke of Fleet. She tried to shrink away behind the broad back of the gentleman in the shiny waistcoat. She had no wish for Fleet and Joss Tallant to notice her at a lottery draw of all places. She could not believe that the Earl's point had been proved so quickly. She had wished to avoid him, yet here he was. Some malign fate was definitely in play.

Her involuntary movement caught Joss Tallant's eye and she saw him focus on her, one eyebrow raised in cynical amusement. Amy blushed. It was easy to read that look—she remembered her protestations the last time they had met, her declaration that she did not approve of gaming. Now he had seen her here it was no wonder he had a sceptical view of her claims. Amy felt vexed, her blush turning to one of annoyance.

'Amy! Amy Bainbridge!'

It was not Sir Richard's masculine tones that accosted Amy's ears but the higher-pitched tones of a young lady and an excited one at that. Amy turned with difficulty, peered around the large gentleman, and saw a lady of fashion, with corn-gold hair and blue eyes in a beautiful oval face.

'Excuse me, if you please!' The lady fluttered her eyelashes at the fat man, who moved obligingly, stepping heavily on Amy's foot in the process. Amy and the other girl almost fell into each other's arms as the crowd pushed them together again.

'Amy Bainbridge!'

'Amanda Makepeace!'

'Good gracious, wherever have you been this year past?'

'I wondered what had happened to you!'

'What are you doing here?'

'I am up in London to stay with my aunt for a spell—'

They were both speaking at once, clutching at each other. Amy had last seen Amanda when the two of them had been doing the season three years before, Amanda as a young bride and Amy in her come-out year. Then George Bainbridge had lost all his money, Amy had retired to the country and Amanda's husband had carried her off to Ireland. The friends had kept in touch by letter, although Amanda was an erratic writer, and after she was widowed the letters had stopped altogether.

'I can scarce believe it!' Amanda said, her eyes shining. 'Amy Bainbridge—it is almost too good to be true! I lost your London address a little while ago and thought never to see you again! I should have known I might find you here. The world and his wife come to the lottery!'

'This is my first visit,' Amy said, looking shy. 'I had no notion it would be so busy! Oh, Amanda, it is lovely to see you again! You are looking well...' She eyed Amanda's sky-blue dress and porcelain pale face with envy. She felt hot and frumpish in her ancient sprigged muslin and she was sure that her face was flushed red. 'Where does your aunt live? You must come to tea so that we may talk properly—'

Those nearby turned to shush them, giving them glares and sharp glances.

'The draw is about to take place!' Amanda whispered in Amy's ear. 'We must have a coze later, but for now we must not miss the numbers. Oh, I declare it is *so* exciting!' She fumbled in her reticule to retrieve her ticket. 'I play the lottery every time I am up in Town, which is not that often, of course, but the rest of the time I *dream* about what I would do were I to win! I am quite comfortably circumstanced these days—enough to live in the country anyway—but who would turn away the chance of up to thirty thousand pounds? Thirty thousand, Amy! Lud, it is a fortune!'

Amy felt a little faint. She had had no idea that the lottery prize could be so huge. Yet no doubt Richard could run through thirty thousand pounds in one sitting at White's. Fortunes were relative.

The two wheels were starting to turn now and the crowd was starting to roar. Amy craned to see what was happening. Two boys were up on the stage, drawing numbers from the two wheels.

'Bluecoat boys,' Amanda whispered. 'One picks the number of the winning tickets from the left-hand wheel and the other chooses the amount of the prize from the right.' She was positively dancing with excitement. 'Wait, what number was that? Number two thousand five hundred and eighty-eight wins—what? Twenty thousand pounds?'

'Thirty thousand,' the fat man said, screwing up his own ticket in disgust and looking as though he would spit on the floor were it not for the presence of the ladies. 'One winner takes all today, madam. Thirty thousand pounds.'

'Not I,' Amanda said regretfully, stuffing her ticket back in her reticule. 'Hey day! I must wait another few months, I suppose, for my chance of fortune. Amy... Amy?'

Amy barely heard the excited sound of voices roaring in her ears, for in her hand was a small, crumpled lottery ticket with the numbers two, five, eight and eight on it. She stared until the figures blurred before her eyes.

'I believe that there must be some mistake,' she said faintly.

Amanda squinted at the ticket, then grabbed her arm. 'Amy!' she exclaimed softly. 'You have won thirty thousand pounds!' She threw a sharp look over her shoulder as the crowd jostled them. Everyone was starting to move towards the door now, ripping up their tickets, chattering with good humour or sometimes with bad. Amy saw one man throw his ticket down and jump on it in disgust.

'Put your ticket in your reticule,' Amanda whispered in her ear, 'and do not give any sign that you have won. That would be most dangerous!'

Amy obeyed as though in a dream and obediently allowed Amanda to take her arm and steer her towards the exit. The words *thirty thousand pounds* hammered in her brain. The momentum of the crowd carried her along. All about her was noise and colour, whirling through her head until she thought she might faint. It was with the greatest relief that she felt the fresh air on her face and allowed Amanda to help her on to the steps outside, past ragged groups of people all discussing the draw and the identity of the person who might have won.

'It could have been me,' she heard one woman say regretfully to another, as she ground her ticket beneath her heel. She drew a dirty baby closer to her breast. 'I need food for Emily now that Jack is gone—'

Amy jerked convulsively and Amanda bent closer to her ear. 'Do not listen, Amy! If I know you, you'll be giving your ticket away and the shirt off your back. All the world needs money—why, by the look of you, you could do with a deal of it yourself!'

Amy suddenly remembered just why she could not give the money away even if she wanted. It did not belong to her. It was Richard's ticket and Richard's prize. The thirty thousand pounds belonged to her brother and she would have to hand it over as soon as she saw him. She felt a breathless mixture of relief and rebellion, relief that the decision was out of her hands and rebellion at the thought of wasting a fortune. She knew that Richard would gamble every penny away as surely as the sun rose in the morning. If only the money were hers... There were so many things that she could do with thirty thousand pounds. Amy felt a sudden and entirely natural rush of disappointment. There was no point in thinking what she might do with such a fortune. It was not her money. She would not see a penny of it. For a second her hand clenched on the reticule with its precious cargo and then she relaxed again. It was unfair—*life* was unfair, but there was nothing that she could do about it. She would not be spending the money on herself and she certainly could not use it to do good for others. She had best disabuse herself of any such thoughts at once, before she was tempted.

'Come along, Amy,' Amanda whispered urgently. 'We must get you home safely. It would never do for anyone to realise that you hold the winning ticket! Why, you would be kidnapped before you could go a step!'

Chapter Four

The air outside the Guildhall was fresh and cool and reviving. As her head cleared, Amy realised that she was not sure what happened next and hung back, drawing Amanda into the shelter of the portico.

'I am not perfectly sure what to do,' she murmured. 'Do I not have to go up to claim the prize?'

'No, no.' Amanda cast her an amused look. 'I forgot that you said you had not played the lottery before, Amy. Is this really your first time?'

'Of course it is,' Amy said. She felt confused. No doubt she would wake in her narrow bed in Curzon Street at any moment. 'This is not even my own lottery ticket, you know, Amanda—'

Amanda was not really listening. She was too excited. 'Lud, and you won the prize at the first go! In order to claim the money you need to attend one of the lottery offices. They will pay your winnings. Or, better still, send your man of business. You would likely need a platoon of soldiers to guard you against robbery were you to go yourself! Now, where is your carriage? We need to get you safely home before someone realises who you are and kidnaps you or murders you for your ticket!'

Amy shuddered, clutching her reticule to her. 'Amanda, tell me that you are in jest! I have no carriage and I walked here from Curzon Street.'

Amanda stopped and looked at her, concern replacing the amusement in her eyes. 'Here's a to-do! No carriage! What are we to do now?'

'I was hoping to find Richard here, you see, and thought that he might escort me home.' Amy was prevaricating, thinking that this was scarcely the time to start explaining to her old friend that she did not have the means to run a carriage. She looked around frantically but there was no friendly face in the crowd. People were drifting away now, tearing up their tickets. The pieces fluttered in the breeze.

'We cannot take a hack,' Amanda was saying with a frown. 'Why, you might be down an alleyway and despatched to heaven before one could say lottery!'

Amy gave a little moan. 'I shall give away the ticket before anything ill befalls me—'

'That you shall not!' There was a martial light in Amanda's eyes. 'You need this money, Amy. This simply requires a little thought—'

'Lady Spry, Miss Bainbridge, I thought that I recognised you. May I be of service?'

Amy turned and almost dropped her reticule with the precious ticket in it. The Duke of Fleet had drawn up beside them in his phaeton and now handed the reins to his groom and jumped down beside them. He looked large, genial and, in some respects at least, the answer to their prayers. Amy smiled and curtsied, but though he bowed in reply, she had the strangest feeling that he had not really seen her. The explanation was not far to seek. Fleet's gaze was fixed on Amanda's charming countenance. He looked utterly smitten. Amy suddenly remembered the balls during her come-out season, where Amanda had been like a little golden honey pot around which all the gentlemen buzzed. Amanda had not been spoiled by the attention; she had laughed at her admirers with good humour, treated them all with equal favour but had never done anything to upset Frank Spry, who seemed pleased that his new wife was so sought after. Now, however, Amy was surprised to see that the Duke's chivalry was not warmly received. Indeed Amanda was looking most uncomfortable, her face flushed, her head turned a little away so that the brim of her bonnet shielded her from the gentleman's gaze.

'Thank you, your Grace, but I am sure we shall fare quite well on our own—'

'Miss Bainbridge will vouch for me, I am sure,' Sebastian Fleet said, with another slight bow in Amy's direction. 'I am a friend of her brother and very willing to offer my escort back to Curzon Street if that is what you wish.'

Amy was torn. On the one hand, she barely knew the Duke and what she did know of him scarcely disposed her to be friendly towards him, for was he not a gambler and a wastrel, the very type of man she deplored? On the other hand, they were in a slightly delicate situation and Fleet was a friend of her brother and could surely be relied upon to provide a safe escort…

'I am sure we may safely accept the Duke's offer, Amanda,' Amy said, a little reluctantly. She wondered if her friend was concerned in case the Duke was one of the thieves and kidnappers she had just been mentioning. Surely not. She could not believe that Fleet, for all his faults, would stoop to criminality to fund his gambling. Amanda's reservations must be based on some other concern—the Duke's womanising, perhaps.

She turned to him hopefully. 'I do not suppose, your Grace, that Richard is with you? I have been searching for him this hour past…'

Fleet shook his head. 'I fear not, Miss Bainbridge. Joss Tallant is with me, however, and will be very glad to take you up whilst I escort Lady Spry.'

A strange prickling sensation on the back of her neck prompted Amy to turn her head. The Earl of Tallant was walking towards them. He was immaculately dressed in a black coat, buff pantaloons and black top boots with a high polish. He looked elegantly austere, as though his attire was in direct contradiction to the extravagance of his reputation. As he saw Amy turn towards him, he smiled in quizzical amusement, allowing his gaze to travel over her thoughtfully. His appraisal was as deliberate as it had been the night they had met and Amy found it both curious and disconcerting. She was assailed by a strange breathlessness, which she would have liked to have attributed to the excitement of winning a fortune. Honesty compelled her to admit, however, that it probably had a different cause. There was no doubt that Joss Tallant's company was enough to fluster any young lady, but she did not intend to succumb.

'Joss, my boy,' the Duke drawled as the Earl joined them, 'I was just pledging you to escort Miss Bainbridge back to Curzon Street. I am taking Lady Spry up with me.'

The Earl bowed. 'Thank you, Sebastian. I am, of course, delighted, Miss Bainbridge…'

Amy had always been sensitive to slights—her upbringing and her come-out had made it inevitable. Now she fancied that she heard a note of resigned amusement in Joss's voice and at the same time she thought she recognised the expression in his eyes. It was the one she knew from the faces of all the young men who had approached Amanda for a dance, found she was already engaged, and realised that good manners obliged them to dance with her friend instead when they had no wish to do so. She felt herself blush.

'There is no need to inconvenience yourself, my lord. I am persuaded that we shall soon find my brother—'

Amanda, who had been uncharacteristically silent to this point, added her own protestations. 'Oh, indeed, we may manage very well on our own…'

The Earl flashed Fleet a look of amusement. 'Your fabled charm appears to have failed signally here, Seb! Miss Bainbridge…' he smiled at Amy '…I fear that your brother is not at the Guildhall. He told me last night that he had an appointment at the Cocoa Tree this morning. Lady Spry—' he bowed to Amanda '—I can assure you that Sebastian is the most harmless of fellows and that you are quite safe in his company! I'll have my horses brought around…'

There seemed to be little choice and, indeed, Amy was glad on balance to have the escort. The thought of walking alone through the streets of London with a ticket worth thirty thousand pounds in her reticule was enough to make her blood run cold and, even if it was Richard's money rather than her own, she had a responsibility to get it home safely. Already she was starting to think of ways in which she might influence her brother to part with a little for the benefit of the family, before he gambled the rest away. He was generous—she was sure that he could be persuaded to give her a thousand pounds to make the Curzon Street house more comfortable. They could supplement their diet with some beef, perhaps, and even—Amy felt quite excited—buy a new outfit or two for the autumn.

She stole a look at Joss Tallant as he helped her up into the phaeton. There was something reassuring about a bodyguard even if he did not know that he was performing such a function, although the Earl of Tallant was probably not the man that one would freely choose as a bodyguard—quite the reverse, in fact, if all the rumours were true. Although she was an innocent in the ways of the world, Amy had heard enough of Joss's exploits to know that his company was damaging to a lady's reputation. Further, she had heard that he would damage more than a mere reputation if he so chose. She remembered Lady Bainbridge telling her of a shocking occasion on which the Duke of Fleet and the Earl of Tallant had held up Lord Gibson's coach for a wager and whilst Fleet had relieved the occupants of their money and jewellery, Joss Tallant had relieved Lady Gibson of her virtue. It had been a long time ago but, as far as Amy was concerned, it epitomised the other reason that Joss Tallant was quite beyond the pale—apart from being a wastrel, of course. Really, Amy thought candidly, as she made herself comfortable on the phaeton's seat, the man had nothing to recommend him. His entire life was one big waste of time.

Amy glanced at him again from beneath her lashes. To be fair, Joss Tallant was prodigiously good looking and he was also quite charming, both of which qualities would help in his career of seduction. But she also felt that she was quite safe with him. She had never met any gentleman who had been intent on damaging *her* reputation. She was simply not the sort of girl who attracted amorous overtures from a man.

On that thought Amy relaxed, looked at the view and enjoyed the rare pleasure of being driven. Richard seldom took her up in his curricle these days and she had occasionally taken a drive in the Park with a gentleman during her season, but not very often. This was different. Joss Tallant was a whip of enviable skill and he made the driving seem very easy, which Amy suspected it was not. They had emerged from the Guildhall Yard now and were picking their way through the crowded streets. The noise and crush was enough to make the highly bred team of greys jib, but Joss controlled them with ease. Amy was impressed, although she resolved to keep quiet whilst her companion undertook the difficult task of navigating through the crowds.

'I am surprised to find you at the lottery draw, Miss Bainbridge,' Joss said, when he was able to take his attention from the team for a moment. 'When we spoke yesterday I formed the strong opinion that you disapproved of gambling.'

Amy glanced at him. He was smiling at her in what seemed an entirely genuine manner. She gave him a slight smile of her own in return. She might not like the man, or trust him, more to the point, but he was doing her a service and she could at least be polite.

'Oh, well, I do disapprove of gambling in the general run of things, but I thought to meet Richard at the draw, only it appears that we had a misunderstanding. He had a ticket for the lottery but he left it behind and I was bringing it for him. I would not have attended otherwise.'

'I see.' Joss's amber gaze flicked over her face thoughtfully, making her intensely aware of his scrutiny. 'What did you think of it?'

'The draw?' Amy raised her brows. 'I had not expected it to be so popular. I can understand the appeal of it, I suppose. For most people, winning thirty thousand pounds would change their lives completely. It is a tempting thought.'

'But a dangerous one?'

'Oh, yes.' Amy remembered the excitement that her seized her in the Guildhall as the tension built before the draw. 'It is addictive and costly. If you do not have the money to support your obsession, yet you buy tickets time and time again in the hope of winning—'

'You could end up ruined and in the street,' Joss finished for her.

Amy turned her face away. 'That can happen whatever the form of gambling.' The memory of her father's wilful squandering of the family's fortune was still as fresh in her mind as when it had occurred and she had to swallow hard and push the memory away.

Joss took his hand from the reins and touched hers, so lightly, Amy wondered whether she had imagined it.

'Forgive me, Miss Bainbridge. I see it is a painful subject for you and I should not have raised it.'

Amy met his gaze. They looked at each other for what seemed a long moment, and then she shook her head slowly.

'You are too generous, my lord, letting me off so easily. If I hold strong opinions, then I feel I must defend them and not hide behind convention.'

She saw the smile creep into Joss's eyes like sunlight on water and strangely it made her shiver.

'That is very honest of you, Miss Bainbridge. I admire that.'

Amy shrugged, a little embarrassed. 'I know that I must sound like a reformer at times! In mitigation I can only plead that I have seen the ruinous effects of gambling at first hand and therefore feel at liberty to view it as a most pernicious disease!'

'That is, of course, your privilege, Miss Bainbridge,' Joss said, smiling. 'I can only argue in defence that it gives a lot of us a great deal of pleasure!'

'Including my brother. I believe that we had this conversation yesterday, my lord. I do not think it wise that we should pursue it since we evidently hold such differing views.'

Joss inclined his head. 'We shall not speak of it if that is your wish, Miss Bainbridge, but I confess that one thing puzzles me. I have thought much on this since our discussion yesterday. How comes it that your brother is so ardent a gambler and you are the utter opposite? Such a freak of nature requires explanation!'

Amy was surprised into a laugh. 'Oh! Well, there was my father's example, I suppose. Richard takes after him. They say that gambling breeds gambling.'

'Yet you did not follow your father's example. In your case it bred an utter distaste for the sport!'

'It is not a sport, my lord,' Amy said severely. 'I consider sport to be something requiring more physical effort than the throwing of a dice!'

Despite herself, she could not help running her eye over him and could not deny that he was in infinitely better shape than a man deserved to be who spent all his time at the gaming tables or in bawdy houses. Then she saw the amusement in his eyes and felt herself blush scarlet.

'What is it, Miss Bainbridge? Do I not look suitably dissipated to fit your image of a wastrel?'

'Oh!' Amy was mortified. Not only had he caught her staring, but he was uncannily good at reading her thoughts. 'I beg your pardon—'

'Do not. I would rather have your brand of honesty than the artifice of most conversation!' Joss smiled. 'Tell me, Miss Bainbridge, have you ever dared to play yourself?' He flicked her a mocking glance. 'A hand of whist? A game of vingt-et-un, perhaps? You might find that you actually enjoyed yourself!'

'You make it sound quite tempting and the height of decadence, sir,' Amy said, a dimple appearing in her cheek as she smiled back. She was struggling against feeling in charity with him and was finding it surprisingly difficult. The man's charm was almost tangible and she was not so naïve that she did not realise he was turning it deliberately on her. The only thing left to wonder at was why he was bothering to do so. It could hardly mean anything.

'I have played cards, of course, but never for money. How could I when I have no fortune—' She broke off, remembering the fortune that she carried with her now. Thirty thousand pounds. It was a huge sum of money and the thought of it made her feel quite faint.

'A lack of fortune seems to be no hindrance to most gamblers,' Joss drawled. 'They play upon nothing but a promise.'

'Your words describe Richard to the life,' Amy said, a little sadly. 'Which is why, my lord, I have no wish to fall into the same trap myself. Two gamblers in the Bainbridge family would be two too many.'

They turned into the Aldwych. The horses' hooves rang on the cobbles. The light breeze stung Amy's cheeks to a pretty pink.

'Do you really believe that gambling runs in families?' Joss asked, watching her with interest. 'Is that why you are not inclined to try it? Are you afraid to step onto the slippery slope yourself, Miss Bainbridge, for fear of very ruin? It is a piquant thought!'

Amy blushed. 'I have no fear of being led astray, my lord,' she said, with a very direct look. 'If you are speaking of gambling, I think that it is an excuse to see it as an inherited tendency. One does not fall heir to it, like so much gold or a parcel of land! It is no more than a weakness indulged in by people with too much time on their hands and not enough direction!' She shot him a look that was slightly ashamed, saw that he was smiling quizzically and let her breath out on a long sigh. 'I beg your pardon, my lord. I had no wish to sound so opinionated, but in my defence I should add that you did provoke me.'

'I did indeed,' Joss murmured. For a second Amy could have sworn that she saw a flash of admiration in his eyes. It seemed unlikely, however, and after a moment his gaze was fixed on the road once again. 'I had no idea, Miss Bainbridge, that the result of my provocation would be so stimulating. You have stronger mettle than you show.'

Amy looked away, staring with determination at the familiar sights of Pall Mall. It was curious but true that conversing with Joss Tallant did have a strange attraction that she had never experienced before. Never in her life would she have imagined that she could have so interesting a discussion with a man with whom she had nothing in common. And therein lay the rub. Joss Tallant inhabited a society that might be parallel to her own but was in all particulars utterly different. She did not belong to the world of society balls, dashing rakes and inveterate gamblers. She had neither the means nor the inclination. She did not even like Joss's pursuits; she despised them. The whole thing was ridiculous.

Amy sighed. Soon they would be in Piccadilly and then home, and she knew she would not see Joss Tallant again. She would give Richard his lottery ticket and the good news of his win and then she would watch him gamble it all away to line the pockets of men such as Joss and the Duke of Fleet.

The Duke's phaeton was ahead of them as they drove down Piccadilly and Amy could see that the Duke was speaking to Amanda, and that her friend's animated face was turned up to his as she smiled and replied. Evidently Amanda's reserve had melted under the onslaught of Fleet's charm. Amy had thought on that first night that these men were dangerous but now she was beginning to see just how perilous they could be, with their careless charm and polished address. Her head was screwed on with practicality and commonsense, but she could feel it turning even so.

Amy cast a sideways look at Joss's face. He was concentrating on the driving, for they had reached a place where the road narrowed and a brewery dray was drawn up ahead whilst the carter rolled barrels of ale across the street. Joss's dark brows were drawn together slightly in concentration and the amber eyes were narrowed, but there was still a hint of a smile about that firm mouth. The sight of it did strange things to Amy's equilibrium.

Joss turned his head and smiled at her and her heart performed a sudden and erratic leap. Amy was immediately cross with herself. She did not even like the man and had previously been thinking of him in terms of direst disapproval, yet now—just because he had smiled at her—she was in a fair way to forgiving him for being a scoundrel. It was not good enough.

'It is an unusual female who can forbear to talk all

the time, Miss Bainbridge,' Joss said easily as the phaeton regained the clear road, 'but then I am beginning to think that you are…quite unusual.'

Amy's heart fluttered again and she quelled it ruthlessly. 'Oh, I was only concerned that I should not distract you from your driving,' she said airily. 'For though I have heard tell that you are a prodigious whip, my lord, it seems that these carriages are somewhat dangerous and I had no wish to be overturned in the gutter.'

Joss burst out laughing. 'Upon my word, Miss Bainbridge, you have a way of depressing a fellow's pretensions! I'll have you know that I have never overturned a phaeton in my life!'

Amy smiled sweetly. 'There could always be a first time, my lord!'

'For everything, so they say.' Suddenly there was a disturbing light in Joss's eyes and Amy felt herself go hot all over, without knowing quite why. She looked away.

'Logically that must be so,' she said crisply. 'I cannot let your observation pass, however, my lord! It seems to me that you must have a low opinion of females. I assure you that some of us are quiet by nature, though we are all different, of course.'

Joss grimaced. 'I feel suitably reproved, Miss Bainbridge.'

'So I should hope!' Amy frowned. 'I have the strangest feeling, my lord, that you do not view the female sex in any very positive light—'

'Ah, now you are quite mistaken, Miss Bainbridge.' Joss's drawl was pronounced. 'I have a very high opinion of females and their *attributes*!'

Amy blushed but persisted. 'I did not mean like that—'

'Like what, precisely?'

Amy glared at him. 'Now you are deliberately teasing me when you know quite well what I mean! I am sure that there are ladies that you admire in a particular way…' She caught the amusement in his eye and subsided. 'Very well. We shall end the conversation there!'

'Pray do not! I am vastly enjoying myself.'

Amy sighed. 'You know perfectly well what I meant!'

'As a matter of fact, I do.' Joss grinned at her. 'You, Miss Bainbridge, have fallen into the trap of making assumptions. You suppose that my only interest in women is…' He caught her eye and smiled. 'Is of an amorous nature. On the little that you know of me, you have decided that I am a gambler and a rake, with no virtues to counteract my vices! You are as guilty of making generalisations as I am!'

Amy blinked. Put like that, she could see the justice of his remark. 'Very well!' she said with spirit. 'What good qualities can you offer in mitigation for the bad?'

Joss laughed. 'Why, none at all! In my case it is quite true. But you see, Miss Bainbridge—' the twinkle in his eye became more pronounced '—I do not see anything wrong in my behaviour. I make no judgements about right and wrong. I do not have your certainty!'

Amy felt confused. 'But gambling is wrong, just as theft is wrong—' She broke off, remembering the ragged children in Whitechapel who had been punished for stealing a loaf of bread to survive. 'That is, theft is wrong but sometimes there may be reasons to excuse it. But gambling is always wrong and there are no excuses!'

Joss's lips twitched. 'Very well, Miss Bainbridge. I concede. You would make a fine judge!'

Amy felt hot and frustrated. She had never previously thought that her ideas were inflexible and now that she examined her views she was still convinced of their rightness. The only thing that worried her slightly was that no one had challenged her before. It was an entirely new experience.

The press of traffic had brought them to a temporary standstill, which was not what Amy wanted. She wanted to be home very quickly and to put an end to this disturbing conversation. It was not to be, however, so she searched around for a lighter tone.

'Speaking of gambling, my lord—'

'Yes, Miss Bainbridge?'

'I confess that there is one thing about it that has always puzzled me. Perhaps you could explain to me, my lord, what pleasure there is in losing? It seems to me that some people take almost as much joy in the one as the other. As such an ardent gamester yourself, perhaps you could enlighten me?'

Joss laughed. 'That is a very interesting question but not one that I can answer! Did no one ever tell you that I never lose, Miss Bainbridge?'

Amy stared at him. 'Truly? You are funning me! The odds against winning all the time must be immense.'

Joss laughed again. 'I see that you know plenty about betting, Miss Bainbridge! What would you say are the odds against winning the lottery?'

Amy's gaze narrowed thoughtfully. Lady Bainbridge had once told her that most men did not like females of a mathematical bent but she had thought it was one of the most foolish things she had ever heard.

'I would calculate…about forty thousand to one?'

'Very good. Apparently it is about thirty-five thousand to one. You must have a keen mind for arithmetic—or an inbred talent for weighing the odds. Perhaps your family would make more money if your brother gave up gambling and you took it up in his place? I am sorry to have to say it, but his talent appears to be for losing!'

Amy pursed her lips. 'I have observed it myself. Perhaps I should address my question to Richard, then, rather than yourself?'

Joss inclined his head. 'As to that, I think I can explain. It is the game that is the thing, Miss Bainbridge. The excitement is in the challenge of play. It matters not one whit whether one wins or loses—to play is all!'

Amy shook her head. 'I am sorry—that makes no sense at all.'

Joss grinned. 'Perhaps not, to one of your practical disposition. Can you imagine, Miss Bainbridge, the excitement of waiting on the roll of the dice? The pure chance of it? In hazard, for example, you know that all rests on the one throw. You might lose or you might win all. Just as in the lottery your ticket may come up and you might be…oh, thirty thousand pounds the richer! You see—' his gaze had sharpened on her and Amy felt a shiver go through her '—you do feel it! No one is immune from that excitement.'

Amy shivered again, sharply. Whatever she said, she did understand the lure. For a moment she too had been swept up in the excitement of playing and winning, until she had remembered that she was winning the lottery on someone else's behalf. That had brought her swiftly down to earth.

'Did you have a lottery ticket for today's draw, Miss Bainbridge?'

The question took Amy off guard and she jumped, blushing. For some reason she did not wish to admit to

Joss that she was in possession of the winning ticket. It seemed too much like hypocrisy after her words earlier. She paused, frowning. Surely his opinion of her should not matter in the slightest...

'I...yes...no...certainly not! I would never buy a ticket! I only went to the Guildhall to meet Richard—' She broke off, flustered. Joss was watching her with interest, which only served to fluster her all the more.

'I see. Yes, I remember you saying you were taking Richard's ticket for him. Yet suppose that you had... found...a ticket of your own, Miss Bainbridge. What would you have done then?'

Amy flushed scarlet. 'I have no notion, sir. The matter does not arise.'

She stopped, a little shocked that she had been less than truthful with him. It seemed absurd to be so guarded because once she had given the ticket to Richard and told him the good news of his win he would surely share his good fortune with his friends. No doubt he would share it literally, in fact, by gambling all the money away to them. There was no real reason why she could not tell Joss that Richard's ticket had won the thirty thousand pounds, except... Except that she felt a curious protectiveness about the money and the win. God help her, she was already starting to think of it as *her* money.

Amy grimaced. She had to cure herself of that delusion before it led her further astray. Any moment now she would be asking herself whether she really had to tell Richard at all. She could arrange for the family's man of business, Churchward, to collect the prize. He was very discreet and would tell no one if she asked him. Then she could use the money for various good causes—in small portions, of course, so as not to arouse suspicion. There were hundreds of people more worthy than her brother, people who deserved her help. Mrs Wendover, for example, bringing up four small children in that slum in Whitechapel, and Mrs Benfleet, the nurse, suffering her ill health uncomplainingly out at Windsor... Amy's heart did a huge lurch. It was so tempting, but, of course, it was theft; had she not just said that theft was wrong—although there were sometimes mitigating circumstances.

'Stop!' Amy had not realised that she had spoken aloud, desperate to halt her wayward train of thought before it tempted her any further. Joss was looking startled.

'I beg your pardon, Miss Bainbridge. Is there some problem?'

'No,' Amy said, screwing her eyes up tightly in mortification. 'I was merely thinking of the lottery and did not realise that I had spoken aloud.'

'I see. Was it the thought of all that dreadful gambling that distressed you, or the heady temptation of it all?' Joss's voice dropped to a soft murmur. 'It is so terribly tempting, is it not? So seductive...'

Amy opened her eyes and stared at him. The Earl of Tallant was a very perceptive man, which somehow seemed quite wrong, given his reputation. He was also a very dangerous man. Once again she felt that stirring of excitement that had rippled through her body when he had spoken of the lure of gambling. It was not simply a question of enticing innocents to part with their money. The temptation was inside everyone. It was subtle, wicked. She looked at Joss accusingly.

'I do believe that you are a very wicked person, my lord, to speak so persuasively of something that is so bad...'

Joss laughed. 'You are correct, Miss Bainbridge. There is no end to my wickedness!'

They were back in Curzon Street at last. Amy gave a little, unconscious sigh, suddenly uncertain whether she was glad or sorry to be back home. Whilst she felt a certain relief to be back on familiar ground, she also felt disappointed.

'Thank you very much, my lord. It was very kind of you to escort me back.'

'Not at all, Miss Bainbridge.' Joss Tallant inclined his head. 'I have enjoyed your company.'

They drew to a halt outside Number 3. Fleet was already helping Amanda down from his phaeton. Amy thought that her friend looked flushed and slightly ruffled, as though she was torn between enjoyment and disapproval. Amy knew just how she felt.

Before she was quite prepared, Joss took her hand and swung her down from the phaeton to the ground, his arm hard about her waist. For a second her palm rested against his chest and she could have sworn, fancifully, that she felt the beat of his heart. It was all over swiftly, yet Amy was left with an impression of strength and power and felt a curious, quivering awareness through her whole body. She did not feel quite steady as Joss set her on her feet and let go of her, very gently.

'Good day, Miss Bainbridge. Lady Spry…'

Fleet was directing the grooms to take the phaetons away. Both he and Joss gave the ladies a punctilious bow, before striding off in the direction of St James.

'So that is that, then,' Amy said, feeling curiously flat and finding it difficult to tear her gaze away from Joss's retreating figure. 'What a very odd day this is! Would you care to come in for a cup of tea, Amanda, and we may have that chat we promised ourselves?'

Amy was amused to see that Amanda's gaze was riveted on the Duke of Fleet and that she had to repeat her question before she was heard.

'Amanda? Amanda, are you feeling quite the thing?'

'Oh, yes!' Amanda said, her blue eyes shining. She turned away and focussed on Amy's face. 'I beg your pardon, I was woolgathering. A cup of tea would be most delightful, Amy!' She cast a look over her shoulder. Joss and Sebastian Fleet had just turned the corner into Clarges Street.

'I wonder... They say that he is the most dreadful rake and I know I should avoid him, but—' She broke off and gave a tiny shrug. 'Ah, well. The Duke has invited me to accompany him to a ball next week and I am not at all sure I should accept!'

'But do you think you will go?' Amy enquired, opening the door and ushering her friend inside. 'You may be more accustomed to such society than I am, Amanda, but I find the company of rakes and gamblers a little too exciting for my tastes!'

'Oh, I live quite retired now and a Duke is far above my touch,' Amanda said, her blue eyes twinkling. 'When we were first introduced I was determined to be cool to him, for Fleet is most unsuitable! All the same, he was vastly agreeable to me, Amy, and I think I may accept his invitation.'

'Did he flirt with you just now?'

'Oh yes, of course!' Amanda giggled. 'That was part of the fun of the journey!'

'I cannot flirt,' Amy said, a little regretfully, as she took her cloak off and helped Amanda with hers. 'I do not know how to do it. I am too shy, I suppose.'

Amanda looked at her thoughtfully. 'I'll allow that you have always seemed reserved on the surface,

Amy—with gentlemen, at least, but I would not say that you are shy, precisely. You have a sharp wit when you choose to exercise it! Besides, think how your family have relied upon you to keep matters together since your father's death. You should be proud of that, I think!'

Amy looked self-conscious. 'You are kind to me, Amanda! You always were when we were at school together. But there is no denying it—I did not take at my come-out and I have no means to attract the gentlemen.' A frown wrinkled her forehead. 'Not that I am entirely sure I would wish to do so...'

Amanda smiled. 'If you wish to learn to flirt, it is surely a skill I could teach you!'

'No, thank you.' Amy viewed her reflection, sparrow brown, in the hall mirror for a moment. 'I think not. I do not look the part.'

'It is but a matter of dress and presentation.' Amanda had moved to stand at her shoulder. 'You have good taste, Amy, and with a few new clothes you will look the very thing. Now that you have the money, there is no difficulty.'

Amy clutched convulsively at her reticule. This was the moment to put her friend to rights about the lottery win, before there were any more misunderstandings. Before she was tempted once again to keep the money for herself.

'Amanda,' she began, 'the money is not—'

The parlour door opened.

'Lady Bainbridge!' Amanda turned with a rustle of silks and perfume. 'How charming to see you again, ma'am.' Before Amy could gesture her to silence, she had burst out, 'You will not believe the most wonderful news—Amy has won the lottery!'

Chapter Five

Joss Tallant cast aside the *Morning Chronicle* and reached for his glass of claret. On the sofa opposite him slumbered the Duke of Fleet, sleeping off the previous night's excesses, his large bulk shaken every so often by a sonorous snore. Fleet had declared that the lottery draw had taken the last of his strength. The Club was quiet and almost empty. Only the occasional rattle of the dice box and rustle of a newspaper disturbed the early afternoon peace.

Joss had given up temporarily on the affairs of the nation, for he had been amused and surprised to find his thoughts veering towards something rather more close to home. Miss Amy Bainbridge, to be precise. Miss Bainbridge, who had proved to be no pattern-card female, who had roundly condemned gambling and who had, he suspected, stolen his winning lottery ticket.

Perhaps stolen was putting it a little strongly, Joss reflected, with a grimace. He took another sip of the wine and sat back, considering. Certainly he could not blame Miss Bainbridge for his own carelessness in losing his ticket in the first place. Until the draw had taken place he had not even been aware that it was lost, but as soon as he realised that it was gone, he had traced his actions back to the dining room at 3 Curzon Street and the gambling session two nights before. How simple to drop a small piece of paper and not to notice! How easy for Miss Bainbridge to come along in the morning, pick it up, go to the lottery draw and find herself the winner—of thirty thousand pounds!

He could be wrong, of course, but he had a gambler's instinct that he was on the right track and there were various clues to help him. First, there had been Miss Bainbridge's excessive attachment to her reticule. Every so often she would glance down at it to make sure that it was still there. She had been clutching the bag as though it were a lifeline—or as though it contained something very precious.

Then there was the fact that she had looked very dazed and confused when he had first come up to her outside the Guildhall. Joss had had that effect on any number of females, but on this occasion he was not vain enough to ascribe Miss Bainbridge's condition to his charm. No, indeed, she had looked like someone who had won a huge sum of money but could not quite believe it. Or someone who knew they had won a huge sum of money by means that were not quite proper...

Later on, he had deliberately asked her if she had obtained a ticket for the draw and she had stammered and blushed with a look of absolute guilt. He had asked her what she would do if she had found a ticket and she had turned scarlet. She was no natural conspirator, but she was certainly hiding something.

Joss swallowed another mouthful of claret and gazed thoughtfully into space. He had a good memory for figures and he could recall the exact number on his lottery ticket. Two thousand, five hundred and eighty-eight, winning thirty thousand pounds. He did not need the thirty thousand pounds from a financial point of view, although it would still have been welcome, but his sense of fair play told him that money was rightfully his.

So what should he do? Joss smiled faintly. He could ask Miss Bainbridge directly, of course, or he could mention to Richard that he had dropped a lottery ticket in his dining room and see what kind of response that elicited. Those were by far the most sensible, the most prosaic courses of action. He could even dismiss the whole matter from his mind, given that thirty thousand pounds was a mere drop in the ocean of the restored Tallant fortune. However, such a sensible course was also a trifle dull and he detested the ordinary. So, instead, he could watch Miss Amy Bainbridge for signs of sudden prosperity—see when a modish gown from Bond Street's finest couturier replaced the dress of faded lavender.

His lips twisted cynically. Miss Bainbridge was undoubtedly an unusual woman. He had actually enjoyed her company, which in itself was rather startling. It had been a novelty for him to hold a conversation with a woman who employed no arts to attract him and in whom he had not the slightest romantic interest. She was not conventional; he had suspected it when he had first met her in Covent Garden. Their recent conversation in the phaeton, which had started predictably enough, had soon veered off in an unexpected direction. Joss had been intrigued. Instead of the ordinary conversational gambits that he had intended to employ to pass the journey, he had allowed himself to enter into a genuine debate, a debate that had been decidedly stimulating. Nor was little Miss Bainbridge as reserved as he had at first imagined. No, indeed, there was a core of strength beneath that quiet exterior.

Was it a core of strength that had permitted her to deliberately appropriate someone else's property and use it for her own financial gain? Joss could not be sure. On the one hand, she had struck him as thoroughly honest, but the requisitioning of his lottery ticket for her own ends did suggest an adaptable attitude towards morality. Joss raised his glass in a mocking tribute to the absent lady. There was no doubt that Miss Bainbridge was a decidedly unusual woman. It would be no hardship to study her a little. No, indeed, no hardship at all.

'I am not sure that a lottery win is respectable,' Lady Bainbridge said thoughtfully. 'We must make sure that no one knows the truth of it. Cits and nabobs are disreputable enough, but a win on the lottery is quite beyond the pale!'

It was early afternoon and Amy, Amanda and Lady Bainbridge were ensconced in the parlour with a pot of tea and chocolate biscuits in celebration of the occasion. Lady Bainbridge had insisted on celebrating, even when Amy had finally managed to make both her friend and her mother stop talking for long enough for her to explain that the lottery ticket belonged to Richard. They had both looked disappointed for a moment and then Lady Bainbridge had ventured the opinion that it need not matter and had immediately gone back to the fascinating topic of what to do with the money.

'No, it is not at all respectable,' Amanda was agreeing with a laugh, 'but you must own, Lady Bainbridge, that it is vastly exciting to be in possession of thirty thousand pounds.'

Lady Bainbridge nodded with more animation than

Amanda had seen in her in years. 'Well, of course. It is not *tonnish* to win money, of course, especially not for a woman. In fact, it is quite scandalous! And no amount of cash makes one truly acceptable to society. That need not matter in Amy's case, however! We shall simply put about a story that she has inherited a fortune! No one need know where it has really come from!'

Amy frowned slightly. She was a little puzzled at the direction the conversation was taking, for it seemed that Lady Bainbridge was wilfully misunderstanding the situation. She sat forward on her chair.

'But, Mama, I thought that you understood? We cannot spend any of the money. The ticket must belong to Richard. I did not buy it and I found it in the dining room!'

Lady Bainbridge looked slightly shifty. 'I do not recall that your brother mentioned buying a lottery ticket, my love. Ten to one you will find it was not his! Maybe it blew in from the street—'

'Or a bird dropped it down the chimney!' Amanda finished eagerly.

Amy looked at them suspiciously, and then the penny dropped. 'Oh, I see! You do not wish it to be Richard's ticket! Mama, how could you?'

Lady Bainbridge drooped. 'I know it is dreadfully dishonest, my love, but your brother has an income of his own whilst you have nothing, and besides, he would only gamble it away…'

Since this was exactly what Amy had thought from the first moment, she could not really dispute it. She pulled a face. 'I know that is so, Mama, but we cannot pretend that it is mine—'

'Oh, why not?' Lady Bainbridge looked anguished. 'You could say that you found it in the street, or that it was stuck to the doorstep! Any number of excuses could do!'

Amy put her teacup down and moved across to the window seat. 'Mama, I am as concerned as you yourself that Richard will gamble the whole fortune away—'

'Then why give it to him?' Lady Bainbridge twisted her hands together. 'Oh, Amy, we would be able to live so much more comfortably—refurnish the house and buy a few more candles...' She wavered to a halt at the look on Amy's face. 'Must you be so tiresomely virtuous about this? Why not give Richard half, if your conscience troubles you? Even fifteen thousand pounds would be something.'

'Make it twenty thousand,' Amanda advised. 'That way Amy might have the chance of an advantageous marriage.'

'Wait! Wait!' Amy besought. 'I have no wish to marry, certainly not to a man who is only interested in me for my fortune! Amanda, you must remember all those dreadful men we met during our come-out! Why, half of them had no conversation, and the other half had conversation that consisted of talking about nothing except themselves. It was dreadfully boring.'

Amanda was nodding sagely. 'I know, Amy, but you may find that matters will be very different now.'

'A man can make himself extremely agreeable for the sake of thirty thousand pounds,' Lady Bainbridge added.

Amy frowned. 'I do not wish a man to make himself agreeable for my money, I wish him to do so because he likes me for myself! Oh, this is ridiculous! I do not wish to go into society and I do not wish to marry and the whole thing is speculative anyway since I have not won the money—'

'My dear Amy!' her mother said, in the tones of one addressing a simpleton. 'Surely you do not expect us to continue living retired now that we have come into money?'

'Why, yes!' Amy said. 'Even were the money mine, I have no wish to go out into society!'

Amanda and Lady Bainbridge exchanged a look. 'My love,' Lady Bainbridge said carefully, putting down her teacup with solid emphasis, 'I believe you must have misunderstood our situation. We do not live retired because we wish to do so. We live retired because it is cheaper!'

'Yes, Mama.' Amy fidgeted a little uncomfortably. 'I understand that, but I prefer to live quietly. The balls and entertainments of the *ton* do not appeal to me.'

Lady Bainbridge blinked. 'How can you know that, my love, when you had only one season and that was so tragically foreshortened by your father's death? You will find that society is an entirely different matter when you are courted as an heiress.'

Amanda was nodding enthusiastically. 'Oh, yes, Amy! Lady Bainbridge is in the right of it, you know!'

Amy felt as though she was struggling in a quicksand. Both her mother and Amanda had glossed over the issue of the rightful ownership of the lottery fortune and had moved on to Amy's prospects with breathtaking speed. She drew breath to argue, but before she could say anything else, the door opened and Richard Bainbridge strolled in, home at last. He bent to give Lady Bainbridge a dutiful kiss, then straightened up, grinned at Amy and gave Amanda an elegant bow and an admiring glance.

'Lady Spry, is it not? Your servant, ma'am. Mama, is there a cup for me?'

'Of course, dearest!' Lady Bainbridge rang the bell. 'Richard, you will not believe! The most extraordinary good luck—'

'Please, Mama!' Amy said quickly, leaping in before her mother entangled them all in a web of untruths. 'Richard, did you have a lottery ticket for the draw to-day?'

Richard looked confused. 'Why do you ask, Amy? No, I did not. I was going to buy one but I never got around to it.' He took a chocolate biscuit and bit into it. 'How delicious. Are we celebrating?'

'Yes!' Lady Bainbridge seized the moment. 'Richard, your sister has won thirty thousand pounds on the lottery! Is it not fine? We have just been making a few plans...'

'A moment, Mama!' Amy said desperately. She swung round on her brother. 'Richard, are you certain that you did not have a ticket?'

'Of course I'm certain!' Richard looked quizzical. 'As for you, buying tickets on the sly...I can only congratulate you!'

Amy blushed. 'Oh, but I did not—'

Lady Bainbridge cleared her throat meaningfully. 'Amy means that she did not expect to win, Richard.'

'Mama!' Amy glared.

'I should go,' Amanda said, getting reluctantly to her feet. 'I am sure that you must have a million and one things to discuss *en famille!* Dear Amy—' she swooped on her friend with a scented kiss '—you have no idea how much I envy you your good fortune! I trust we shall be able to meet up again soon.'

Amy grasped her sleeve. 'Oh, but we have not had chance to exchange our news! Please come to see me tomorrow.'

'Of course,' Amanda said, with an enchanting smile. She dropped a curtsy to Lady Bainbridge. 'Good day, ma'am.'

'Richard, go to procure Lady Spry a hack,' Lady Bainbridge said authoritatively as her son, nothing loath, escorted Amanda from the room. 'Such a pretty child,' she added, as the door closed behind them. 'It is a shame that her fortune is no more than ordinary, for Richard really needs to marry an heiress.'

'Mama,' Amy said, 'I had no notion that your thoughts ran along so mercenary a route! You have quite shocked me today.'

Lady Bainbridge opened her eyes wide. 'My dear Amy, I am only trying to do the best for my children and if I have not seemed to put myself out before it is because we did not have the fortune to do the thing in style!' She smiled contentedly. 'But now all that is changed, of course. It is high time that Richard was wed and an heiress will be just the thing for him. As for you, now you have a fortune of your own it will be monstrous easy to see you settled! I think we shall invent an elderly spinster aunt from whom you have inherited. Yes, indeed, old Aunt Bessie from Kent, lived quite retired for many years, but devoted to you, my love, and surprisingly rich…'

'Mama!' Amy said again, horrified at her mother's duplicity.

'Well?' Lady Bainbridge looked defiant. 'You heard your brother, my love. The ticket is not his!'

The door opened again as Richard came back into the room. 'What a charming girl your friend is, Amy. 'Tis a pity she has no fortune, for then she would be more engaging still!' He sat down and swung a careless leg over the arm of his chair. 'Is there any cake, Mama?

Surely we can run to that now that Amy is so rich?' He grinned at his sister. 'Can you lend me a couple of thousand guineas, just to tide me over? There's a game on at the Cocoa Tree tonight...'

Amy made a despairing gesture. 'Richard, it is not as simple as that—'

'Too soon?' Her brother looked disappointed. 'I dare say you have not had chance to claim the money yet? I'll go for you if you give me the ticket, or better still, send Churchward! Time the poor chap had some pleasant business to undertake for this family!'

'Exactly what I thought,' Lady Bainbridge nodded and smiled. 'Churchward will see to it, Amy. He can make a few sound investments for you, my love, and then we will have the rest to spend. You need a couple of new dresses, but not too many,' she added hastily. 'We must still be careful to make sure the money is not wasted!'

Amy blinked hard. Matters were moving very quickly and she felt as though she could not quite catch up. The lottery ticket in the dining room had not been Richard's after all... Whilst her mother rattled on, she tried to think. If Richard had not been the owner of the ticket she had found in the dining room then it must have belonged to one of his cronies who had been playing hazard two nights ago, to Bertie Hallam or Humphrey Dainty, or the Duke of Fleet...or Joss Tallant. She suddenly went cold all over. She had appropriated a lottery ticket that belonged to someone else...

Richard got up to hold the door as Patience came in with a laden tray. 'Excellent! More tea and fresh biscuits! Do we have any cake, Patience?'

Patience looked outraged. 'Cake? I should think not, Sir Richard. Pure extravagance!'

'We are celebrating, Patience,' Lady Bainbridge said hastily. 'Amy has inherited a sum of money—'

'I'm sure I wish you very happy, miss,' Patience said, her stern face almost cracking into a smile. 'Perhaps there will be some money to spend on you now!'

She swished out with a righteous rustle of black crepe.

Richard winked at her and Amy felt herself blush hard. The tales were already being spun; the story was already running out of control. Soon it would be half-way around London. She had to put a stop to this once and for all.

'Mama! Richard!' she said, so sharply that Lady Bainbridge jumped and spilt her tea. 'You do not understand. I have been trying to explain to you this age that the lottery ticket does not belong to me! I found it!'

There was a short silence. Richard and Lady Bainbridge looked at each other and then back at Amy.

'So?' Lady Bainbridge said, as though expecting more. 'That merely makes you twice as lucky, my love!'

'No!' Amy frowned fiercely. 'It makes it imperative that I find the rightful owner.' She swung round on her brother. 'I found it in the dining room. I thought that it must be yours, Richard, for it was lying beside your chair.'

Richard's face was a picture. 'In our dining room! Well, perhaps I did buy one after all—'

'No, you did not!' Amy got to her feet and paced restlessly across the room. 'You said earlier that you had not got around to buying one. Do not try to gammon me! It must belong to one of your cronies—to Bertie, or Humphrey Dainty, or the Duke of Fleet, or...or the Earl of Tallant.' Her voice wavered a little on the last name.

Lady Bainbridge was looking bewildered. She started to pull her delicate lace handkerchief through her fingers. 'I do not understand! Surely you are not suggesting that the *money* belongs to someone else, Amy?'

'It must do, Mama!' Amy swung round on her. 'I have been trying to get that point across to you this half-hour past! The ticket is not mine and it is not Richard's! The servants do not gamble and I do not suppose that you had a lottery ticket in your possession?'

'No, indeed.' Lady Bainbridge sagged a little. 'Though if I had known that I should win thirty thousand pounds I would most certainly have procured one!'

Amy frowned a little. 'We digress, Mama! The ticket *must* belong to one of Richard's friends and we should give it back!'

'Oh, no!' Lady Bainbridge moaned softly. 'All that money. I cannot bear it!'

Richard had his head in his hands. He looked up, his eyes bright with hope. 'It cannot belong to either Bertie or Humphrey, for they were both with me at the Cocoa Tree this morning and neither of them made mention of the lottery draw. Seb and Joss, I do not know. I could ask them, I suppose...' He looked most unhappy at the thought.

'The Earl of Tallant drove Amy back from the Guildhall and the Duke of Fleet escorted Amanda Spry,' Lady Bainbridge said eagerly. 'Surely they would have said something if either of them had dropped a ticket here that night?'

'I am sure they would.' Richard stood up and stretched. 'So really we need not regard it.'

Amy looked at her relatives wrathfully. 'Really and

truly I cannot believe what I am hearing! You both think that we should just forget that the money belongs to someone else?'

Richard flushed and Lady Bainbridge looked defiant in a genteel manner.

'If it was Joss or Seb who had found the ticket and won the money, they would keep it for themselves,' Richard argued hotly. 'They need not know that it was you who found it! Besides, they are both rich and do not need the money as we do. Winner takes all!'

'Oh, yes,' Lady Bainbridge said quickly, 'I am sure that must be true, Amy dearest! We are far more deserving.'

Amy shook her head. 'It is immoral, Mama—'

'So is gambling,' Richard said, with a quick grin, 'yet you are the one holding the winning lottery ticket, sis.'

'I went to the draw to try to find you!' Amy snapped, her patience at an end. 'I thought the money was yours—'

'Then give it to me if it salves your conscience!' Richard reached for her reticule.

'Oh, no, you don't!' Amy grabbed at it. 'I shall hand this over to no one but Mr Churchward and I shall ask him to hold the money safely until I have discovered the real winner. Now, I am going to lie down. My head aches and I need to decide what to do.'

'All this excitement is so fatiguing,' Lady Bainbridge agreed. She exchanged a significant look with her son. 'I feel sure that when you are rested, Amy dear, you will see that it is well nigh impossible to find the rightful owner of that ticket now. Why, if you asked a gentleman if he had dropped a lottery ticket in our dining room, I dare say he would be bound to say yes out of sheer curiosity! You could end up handing the money over to a complete fraud, and one who is a gambler and a wastrel into the bargain!'

'In which case,' Richard said mockingly as he held the door for her, 'you might as well have done and give it to me now, sis! I fulfil all those criteria!'

Amy was burning with indignation as she made her way up the narrow stairs to her tiny bedroom. She clenched her reticule so hard that the beaded workings scored her fingers. To find that her relatives had such a dubious view of morality and one that did not in the least accord with her own was quite a shock. She thought them too worldly and no doubt they thought her a principled fool, but she knew she had to discover the true owner of the thirty thousand pounds. Since Richard seemed unlikely to help her, she would just have to do it herself. She would have to speak to Bertie Hallam and Humphrey Dainty and she would have to seek out the Duke of Fleet and Joss Tallant. She felt quite shaky at the thought, but she knew it had to be done.

Sitting down on her bed, Amy pressed her fingers to her aching temples and tried to think straight. She could hardly go to visit any of the gentlemen privately if she had a care for her own reputation. What she needed was a social event at which she might casually approach them all and sort the matter out with the minimum of fuss. She frowned. The difficulty was that they so seldom received invitations these days. *Ton* society had practically forgotten that they existed, for although Richard had the entree to any number of events, his mother and sister lived quite retired.

Amy lay down on the bed and closed her eyes. After a moment she sat up, placed the reticule beneath her pillow and lay down again. It was not that she did not trust her mother and brother precisely, but until she could speak to Mr Churchward she simply would not feel safe.

She remembered the single invitation card on the mantelpiece in the dining room. Lady Moon's ball was in four days and Richard had already agreed to escort them. Assuming that the other gentlemen were present, she could speak with them and ascertain the identity of the mystery winner. Amy started to relax. Her headache receded a little. Yes, she could see a strategy now. Soon all would be well.

It was not the sound of someone creeping into her room to steal the reticule that roused Amy later that night, but a rather loud crash outside the house, followed by the sound of the front door opening, hushed voices and something being dragged across the floor. Amy climbed out of bed, lit her candle and trod silently to the top of the stair. Down in the hall, Richard was sitting on the floor, his head lolling against the wainscot, his face a pale, waxy green in the candlelight. Marten was kneeling beside him on the carpet and Joss Tallant was just closing the door.

'You will never get him upstairs on your own,' Amy heard him say. 'It was all I could do to get him into the carriage. Let me give you a hand, man—'

'Oh!' Amy's candle wavered and some hot wax fell on her hand, and the men in the hall looked up and saw her standing there. A look of dismay passed quickly over Marten's normally impassive face, but Amy was focussing on Joss Tallant and saw that he looked thoroughly exasperated to see her.

'Miss Bainbridge.' He gave her a punctilious bow.

'Might I suggest that you return to your bed, ma'am? There is nothing you need do here—'

Ignoring him completely, Amy ran down the stairs and knelt at Marten's side. Richard groaned and rolled his head against the panelling but he did not open his eyes.

'Marten, is my brother ill?' Amy touched Richard's forehead gently but recoiled at the cold sweat beneath her fingers. 'Ugh! I believe he must be suffering an ague—'

'Sir Richard is jug-bitten, miss,' the valet said unhappily. 'Nothing for you to worry about, as Lord Tallant says. If you would like to go back upstairs, I will take care of Sir Richard.'

Amy frowned. She got slowly to her feet, vaguely aware that Joss Tallant had helped her up with a somewhat weary chivalry. 'Jug-bitten, Marten? You mean that he is drunk? But he must have taken far too much...he looks so ill! Does this happen often?'

She saw a hint of a smile touch Joss Tallant's mouth and turned on him swiftly. 'You need not look so superior, my lord! I am perfectly aware that *gentlemen*—' she invested the word with a heavy sarcasm '—drink far too much sometimes, but this...' she gestured to Richard's prone form '...this is beyond anything! I had no notion...'

'I will take Sir Richard upstairs,' Marten murmured, suiting actions to words by slinging Richard over his shoulder as though he were a lightweight. 'Thank you, my lord...'

Amy, belatedly realising that Joss Tallant must have brought Richard home, looked at him a little uncertainly. 'I suppose that I should also thank you, my lord...'

Joss favoured her with a slight smile. 'Pray do not if you find it sticks in your throat, Miss Bainbridge! Now, may I urge you to retire? It is past three.'

Glancing at the long-case clock, Amy realised that this was true. 'I suppose that you were all drinking and gambling heavily tonight? You and Fleet and Humphrey Dainty—'

'Do I seem foxed to you?' Joss sounded irritated. 'Miss Bainbridge, it is bad enough you blaming me for your brother's gambling, but I will not take responsibility for his drinking as well! Why, I could have left him to the mercies of the Club servants, but instead I thought to bring him home. I almost wish that I had not bothered!'

Amy sighed. 'Did Richard lose very heavily tonight, my lord? Generally he only drinks himself insensible when his losses are great…'

'He did not lose to me,' Joss said drily. 'Any questions about tonight should be addressed to your brother, and not to me.' He pulled on his gloves and moved towards the door. 'Good night, Miss Bainbridge—'

'Oh, but—' Amy started forward, determined that he should not escape without telling her more of what had happened. 'I want to talk to you—'

Joss turned and looked at her. His amber gaze, mocking now and not in the least deferential, drifted over her with thoughtful appraisal. His gaze lingered on her unbound hair like a caress, slid down the length of her whole body, pausing briefly on the curve of her breast beneath her nightgown, and came to rest on her bare feet.

'Do you really?' he said slowly.

Amy abruptly forgot what she had been about to ask him. She felt as though she was rooted to the spot, vulnerable and shockingly aware. Then there was a thud from above as Marten deposited Richard on his bed, and Amy jumped, blushed scarlet and glared at Joss.

'You have very pretty feet,' he said, with a grin. 'Goodnight, Miss Bainbridge.'

Chapter Six

'Oh, Amy, I am so glad we were able to come tonight!' Amanda clasped her friend's arm with all the excitement of a child. 'It is years since I have been to Vauxhall. How prodigiously exciting it all is!'

They were strolling down one of Vauxhall's gravel walks towards the central square, where they were to take supper in one of the boxes and to hear a concert of Mr Handel's music. Amanda had professed herself disappointed that they had missed the jugglers and acrobats who had been performing the previous night, but Amy thought that the gardens, with their lamplit grottoes and groves, were exciting enough.

She smiled. 'It all looks very pretty, does it not? I do not think that I have been here since the year Papa died…'

Her voice faded away and Amanda gave her arm a sympathetic squeeze. 'Your mother seems to be enjoying herself,' she whispered. 'She is looking most animated.'

Amy watched with amusement as her mother nodded regally to one of her acquaintances in passing.

'There is something of the stately dowager about her

this evening,' she agreed. 'I do believe that now we are to go out into society, she feels she has regained her place in the world.'

'And all because of your winnings,' Amanda said, with a sly, teasing look. 'I knew that you would come round to the idea of re-entering the *ton*—and of spending the money on yourself! You look very fine tonight. You see what I mean about clothes making the woman!'

Amy smiled and thanked her. She had no intention of telling Amanda that she still intended to find the rightful owner of the thirty thousand pounds. After all, there were aspects of what Amanda had said that she could not deny. She had spent some of the money on herself—and she had enjoyed it. She liked her new clothes and liked even more the sensation of looking elegant. She cast a glance at Amanda, who was wearing a raspberry pink silk dress cut daringly low. Amanda was truly beautiful, Amy thought, with a little repressed sigh of envy. Her hair gleamed corn-gold and her blue eyes were bright with excitement, and all the gentlemen were staring. Amy knew that she would never stop the carriages in Hyde Park, but still, she was looking better than she had done for years and that gave her a confidence she had previously lacked.

Amy stroked the cream sarsnet gown, with its bodice of emerald green and matching cream scarf. The sleeves of the dress were slashed for the color to show though and she had a green velvet ribbon holding her curls in place. Amy had ruthlessly refused to have any of the blonde lace that her mother had insisted should adorn the dress. Now that she could finally choose exactly what she wanted, she had no intention of being dressed up like the Christmas capon.

The lace had not been the only area of disagreement

when the sarsnet dress had been purchased. At first Amy had been loath to spend any of the lottery money, until Lady Bainbridge had stated, not unreasonably, that she could not go to *ton* events in one of her four-year-old gowns. In the end, Amy had reluctantly accompanied her mother and Amanda to Bond Street, where she had agreed to buy two evening gowns. She had utterly refused all the other underclothes, day dresses, evening dresses, slippers, hats and shawls that her mother had accumulated hopefully whilst she had been trying on the sarsnet dress. They had left Madame Louise's shop somewhat out of sorts, with Lady Bainbridge muttering under her breath about Amy's lack of family loyalty and misplaced principles. Amy had been obliged to treat her mother to an ice cream at Gunter's in order to restore her spirits. So now the lottery money was already a little diminished but Amy was certain that Mr Churchward would be able to help her find enough to make good the loss when she came to hand the winnings over.

A gentleman passed them, ogling the girls through his quizzing-glass. Amy blushed and looked away. Amanda giggled.

'It is Mr Quarles, Stanton's heir. Do you remember him from your come-out, Amy? He seemed to admire you, as I recall!'

Amy shuddered. 'I remember. He was very full of his own importance.'

The gentleman had turned for a second look.

'And he still admires you,' Amanda commented. 'He is still watching you! No, don't look!'

Amy tried not to turn and stare. For some reason, being told not to look made her itch to do so, even though she was indifferent to Mr Quarles's admiration. In an effort to look the other way, she scanned the supper boxes in the nearest colonnade. And forgot about Mr Quarles entirely.

The Earl of Tallant was leaning against the balustrade of the nearest box. Behind him, a number of ladies and gentlemen were partaking of a chicken-and-ham supper and there was much laughter and banter coming from the group. Joss Tallant's gaze met Amy's and he bowed slightly, and Amy looked away, annoyed at having been caught staring. Then, utterly unable to resist this time, she glanced back. To her horror, the Earl had left the box and was walking towards them across the floor. Amy shrank back.

She had not seen the Earl since their most improper exchange in the hallway at Curzon Street at three in the morning, yet when she had been buying the cream sarsnet dress, Amy had found herself wondering whether Joss would admire her in it. The thought had made her very cross with herself, for the answer was almost certainly no. It was only her feet that had excited his admiration, after all, and he should never have seen them in the first place.

'Lord Tallant is coming over!' Amanda said excitedly and superfluously. 'Oh, I wonder if the Duke of Fleet will join us? I am not sure who the others are in his party, except that I think the lady in green is his sister and I do believe that the lady in the frumpish purple gown is Lady Parrish.' She leaned closer to Amy's ear. 'It is the most monstrous scandal, you know. Lord Parrish is the most terrible rake,' Amanda whispered happily, 'just like Fleet and Joss Tallant. I pity his poor bride! They have only been married two months!'

Amy's gaze moved on to Lord Parrish. He was very dark and wicked-looking in a thoroughly piratical manner. No doubt the ladies were swooning for him.

She grimaced. 'Thoroughly bad company!'

'And good evening to you too, Miss Bainbridge!'

Exactly on cue, Joss Tallant came to a halt before them. Amy, realising that he had heard Amanda's last remark and her own rejoinder, sought to efface herself behind a group of statuary. Joss bowed to Lady Bainbridge and Amanda, then took Amy's hand in his, drawing her a little to one side. Hard as she tried, Amy could not avoid a glance down at her feet, clad tonight in delicate slippers to match her dress. Joss saw the glance and smiled.

The Duke of Fleet had come over now to speak with Amanda and his sister was exchanging polite commonplaces with Lady Bainbridge, who looked delighted to be noticed.

'How pleasant to see you again, Miss Bainbridge,' Joss Tallant said, in his lazy drawl. He relinquished her hand with studied slowness. 'I appreciate that it must be a trial for you to acknowledge such dangerous acquaintances as myself and Fleet, and I admire your fortitude!'

'I do not believe that there is any likelihood of my being overset by the experience, my lord,' Amy said coolly. 'We will not be keeping you from your party for long, I am sure.'

Joss smiled faintly. 'If you wished to keep me from my companions I should be delighted, Miss Bainbridge! They are at daggers' drawn and it is most tiring! May I tempt you to a stroll down the *Dark Walk* instead?'

Amy gave him a very straight look. 'No, my lord, you may not.'

'A pity.' Joss's speculative expression made her face burn. He considered the cream-coloured gown and ribbons, and put out one gloved hand to touch the matching scarf lightly.

'You look very pretty tonight, Miss Bainbridge. And I believe I must congratulate you—I have heard rumours that you have come into a fortune.'

Amy flicked the scarf out of his fingers. Despite the lightness of his words there was a very different expression in his eyes. It looked oddly like anger—or disappointment—and the set of his mouth was grim for a moment. Then he saw her watching him and relaxed.

'It is only a temporary fortune,' she said swiftly, wondering as she spoke why on earth she felt the need to justify herself to him. It was strange, but with Joss she always seemed to say more than she intended. Perhaps it was because he made her self-conscious and so she chattered to cover her discomfort. Whatever the cause, there was an uncomfortable awareness fizzing through her blood.

'A temporary fortune?' Joss raised his brows. 'How original! Does it turn to dust and ashes at midnight?'

'Pray do not be ridiculous, sir,' Amy said, trying not to laugh. 'The fortune itself is not temporary, merely my tenure of it! I am looking after it for someone…'

She stopped, wishing that she had said nothing. This was awkward, for although she knew she might have to speak to Joss about the ownership of the lottery money at some point, this was hardly the time or place to eliminate him from her enquiries.

'And you have been spending some of it for them, by the looks of things,' Joss said drily, his gaze skimming her gown again. 'Indeed, how could you resist?'

Amy frowned a little. Given her previous misgivings about spending the money, this touched a nerve. 'I do not know what business it is of yours,' she said, a little sharply.

Joss took her hand again and held on when she tried to pull it from his grip. 'I beg your pardon. It is none of my business indeed. Indulge my curiosity, Miss Bainbridge… Why did you purchase a beautiful new outfit and yet wear it with darned gloves?'

His thumb was smoothing the top of her glove as he spoke, the soft, repeated caress sending a tingle through her blood. Amy's eyes jerked up to meet his, then she broke the contact equally swiftly. She felt very hot and bothered for such a cool evening.

'They are only tiny darns. I could not discard a pair of gloves for so trivial a reason—'

'But you could have bought new ones—'

'Extravagance!' Amy said. 'As I told you, the money is not mine.' She would have sounded like Lady Bainbridge deploring wastefulness were it not for the fact that Joss's touch was undermining her composure and her voice came out with a husky edge. She knew he had heard it too; she saw his gaze sharpen on her with all the predatory intent of a man who knew exactly the effect he could have on a woman. Their eyes locked, his bright and hard with an emotion that took her breath. Amy gave a little gasp as a shiver went through her. He felt it; she saw a slight smile touch his mouth as he held her gaze very deliberately with his.

'Amy!' Lady Bainbridge's fluting tones brought her straight out of the dream. 'Here is Mr Quarles asking to escort you to supper. Excuse me, my lord…' She looked at Joss meaningfully, evidently hoping he would take himself off and leave the field clear for a genuine suitor.

Joss released Amy's hand gently. 'Then I shall relinquish you, Miss Bainbridge, but I shall hope to see you again soon.'

He gave her a bow, acknowledged the hovering Mr Quarles with the very slightest inclination of the head, and fell into step beside Fleet as they strolled back to their box. Amy let her breath out on a long sigh as she felt her body relax slightly. The blood was still singing through her veins and she felt shaken.

'What a shame that the gentlemen are already engaged for supper,' Lady Bainbridge said, clearly torn between enjoying the exalted company and disapproving of the gentlemen's reputations. Quarles offered Amy his arm as they moved off to find their own box.

'I do not believe that you should cultivate the company of such gentlemen, madam,' he said, in the querulous, reedy voice that Amy remembered. 'Tallant has an unsavoury reputation and Fleet is little better. Sadly unsteady, ma'am, sadly unsteady!'

Lady Bainbridge looked crushed and Amy thought that she heard Richard smother a guffaw. No doubt Mr Quarles was correct and she should prefer his steady presence to the more mercurial charm of the Earl of Tallant. Unfortunately, some perverse part of her, the part that could still feel the echo of Joss's touch, persisted in thinking that the Earl was more exciting company. Not that that meant she would seek him out. Indeed, that would be a very foolish course. Joss was experienced and she was not, and Amy's common sense told her that his attentions to her could have no real substance. It was a sophisticated game of flirtation that she had no intention of playing.

The following afternoon, a footman delivered a pair of beautifully embroidered gloves that fitted her without a wrinkle. There was no card, but Amy knew perfectly well where they had come from and she spent plenty of time thinking about it whilst she helped Patience to polish the windows. Common sense was all very well, she thought with a sigh, but the attentions of a rake were more exhilarating, even when she should know better.

'Dear Sir Humphrey, please try to remember!' Amy said. 'It was only a week ago!'

It was the night of Lady Moon's ball and Amy's campaign to find the owner of the lottery ticket had begun in earnest. She had quizzed Bertie Hallam when he had called in Curzon Street that afternoon, and had been downcast to find that the ticket was not his. She had wanted it to belong to Bertie for it would have been so much more comfortable not to have had to speak to the others, particularly to Fleet and Joss Tallant. Unfortunately, this was precisely what she had to do.

Seeing a chance shortly after supper, she had lured Sir Humphrey Dainty out on to the terrace and had put the same question to him, only to discover that the absent-minded baronet simply could not remember.

'Last week... Let me see...' Sir Humphrey's gaze darted away from Amy's face and fixed rather desperately on the door of the card room. His body was tense as though he was going to dart off in the same direction. 'Now, I might have had a lottery ticket... Or was that the private lottery to fund the Foundling Hospital? Yes, I do believe it was!' He brightened. 'I won two hundred and thirty pounds and doubled it at play the same night! What luck, eh?'

Amy tried not to drum her fingers impatiently on the stone balcony. She knew that Sir Humphrey had always had the most appalling memory. A neighbour of the

Bainbridge family in Warwickshire, he had been perfectly suited to the life of country squire until a substantial inheritance had transformed him into an ardent gamester and transported him to the depths of London's gambling clubs. The inheritance was long gone, but Sir Humphrey found himself unable to break away and return to the country.

'Yes, Sir Humphrey,' she said, struggling to erase the impatience from her tone, 'but what about the most recent draw? Last week—'

'Oh, no,' Sir Humphrey said decisively, 'I did not have a ticket for that. I was playing hazard with your brother at the Cocoa Tree, Miss Bainbridge.'

Amy began to realise that as long as they could measure time and place by Sir Humphrey's gambling, they would stay on approximately the right track.

'You are sure, Sir Humphrey, for this is very important. You might not have dropped a ticket when you came to play in Curzon Street a sennight ago?'

'No, indeed,' Sir Humphrey said again, fidgeting as though an invisible string was drawing him towards the card room, 'for my pockets were to let that night. If I had had a lottery ticket I could have used it as a stake! So it follows I cannot have had one. There! I knew I should remember in the end.'

There was a certain logic to this explanation, Amy felt. It did not help her to find the missing lottery winner, but at least it eliminated the second of the four possibilities. As she watched Sir Humphrey make his impatient way back to the whist table she was tolerably certain that he was not the one. Two down and two to go. She had left the two most difficult until last, hoping that the mystery would be solved by then.

Amy sighed and walked slowly back through the long

windows and into the ballroom. The long drapes stirred in the evening breeze. Inside the room the lights blazed and it was considerably hotter. A cotillion was in progress; Amy watched Amanda twirling in the arms of the Duke of Fleet. Her heart missed a beat at the thought of quizzing him about the lottery ticket, but she felt even more nervous at the thought of approaching the Earl of Tallant.

Amy accepted a glass of lemonade from a passing footman and stood in the shadow of the doorway, watching the ball. It was much the same as any ball she had attended during her come-out and she was certainly not overwhelmed with partners. She was wearing her other new purchase, a dress in jonquil silk. It had scarcely made the gentlemen sit up and notice her, but one or two had been kind enough to favour her with a dance and a little conversation. She had also had a chat with Anne Parrish, whom she had first seen on the night of the visit to Vauxhall. Amy felt a certain affinity with Lady Parrish; they were both outsiders in the *ton*, although surely Lady Parrish's situation was far worse than hers, with the *on dit* going the rounds that Adam Parrish had never wanted to marry her and was dancing attendance on every lightskirt in town.

Across the ballroom, Lady Bainbridge was seated in a knot of chaperons, chatting nineteen to the dozen. The ostrich feathers in her turban waved gently. After a moment she turned and gave Amy a significant look. Mrs Vestey, Lady Amherst and Mrs Ponting all followed her gaze. Their mouths formed perfectly round, excited 'ooohs.' Amy rather suspected that she could guess the conversation, in which a certain fictitious Aunt Bessie was likely to figure. Her mother seemed utterly incapable of accepting that Amy was giving the money away, which made the discovery of the rightful owner of the thirty thousand pounds even more urgent. Amy placed her empty lemonade glass on the windowsill and turned to find the Duke of Fleet at her elbow.

'Would you care to dance, Miss Bainbridge?' Fleet was smiling down at her. Amy's heart skipped a beat, but not because the Duke was so handsome and so charming and so utterly above her touch. She knew she was obliged to cross-question him about the lottery ticket. She had been dreading the moment and now there was no escape.

They exchanged a few of the usual commonplaces about the ball as they took their place in the set of country dances, then Amy plunged straight in.

'We were most grateful for your escort home from the Guildhall last week, your Grace,' she murmured.

'I was glad to be of service,' Fleet replied, with a smile and an eloquent glance in the direction of Amanda, who was further down the set. 'I understand that you are an old school friend of Lady Spry, Miss Bainbridge? It must be pleasant for you both to have met up again.'

Amy reflected that it did not take a great deal of intellect to see which way the conversation would tend if the Duke had his way. It reminded her of her come-out season, when she had spent a vast amount of time chatting to Amanda's hopeful admirers about her friend's many charms. Without exception the men who had sought her out had done so to get closer to Amanda, just as the Duke was doing now. Unfortunately, she could not afford to indulge the Duke of Fleet on this occasion. She had a far more pressing matter to investigate.

'Yes, of course, it is delightful to see Amanda again!'

she said brightly. 'We are the greatest of friends. So tell me—were you attending the lottery draw at the Guildhall because you had a ticket of your own, your Grace?'

Fleet smiled down at her, his expression a little puzzled. 'Yes, I was. I buy a ticket quite often. Miss Bainbridge, do you know if Lady Spry is to stay in Town for long? She would not vouchsafe her plans to me!'

Amy covered her irritation with a patient smile. If he could be persistent, so could she. 'I am not certain what Amanda plans to do, your Grace. Perhaps you should apply directly to her for the information. Did your lottery ticket win anything?'

'Unfortunately not.' Amy could tell now that Fleet was definitely puzzled at her determination to pursue the subject. She knew she could not persist much further, for he was not a stupid man and might guess the reason that she was asking. It was difficult because she had to be absolutely certain—without giving away the fact that she was looking for the rightful owner of thirty thousand pounds.

'But you are quite sure you did not win?' she persevered. 'You had your ticket with you?'

'I had it with me and unfortunately it did not win,' Fleet repeated. 'What is this sudden interest in my gambling habits, Miss Bainbridge? One might imagine—'

Fortunately the dance obliged them to step apart at that moment and did not bring them together again for quite a while. When they finally met up again the dance was coming to an end. There was a quizzical twinkle in the Duke's eye as he bowed to her and he showed no signs of wanting to relinquish her company.

'Thank you for the dance, Miss Bainbridge. Now, as for your interest in my lottery ticket—'

'Oh, that was just idle curiosity on my part,' Amy

said, looking around for the chance of escape. She was not engaged for the next and could not immediately perceive a means to extricate herself.

'I see.' Fleet's smile was rueful. 'I confess that the subject interests me—'

'Oh, I fear it does not interest me!' Amy said with blatant untruth, hiding a yawn behind her fan. 'You must know that I detest gambling, your Grace—'

'I had heard as much,' Fleet murmured, 'which only makes your persistence on the topic all the more remarkable, Miss Bainbridge. However, if the subject bores you suddenly, I suppose I must let the matter go, for it would never do to vex a lady.'

Amy felt the relief wash over her. Thank goodness for the Duke's good manners! Now all she had to do was to find a means of escape. Fleet had escorted her back to her rout chair but showed no signs of departing. Indeed, he was watching her with a mixture of curiosity and amusement. Amy felt flustered. She did not think that the Duke was interested in her for herself—after all, he had made his admiration for Amanda more than plain—but she knew she had piqued his curiosity with her unsubtle tactics on the dance floor. She was sure he would raise the topic of the lottery again in a moment so she fanned herself and commented that it was very hot and prayed for deliverance. It arrived, but not quite in the form that she had hoped.

'I see Joss Tallant is coming over, no doubt with the intention of asking you to dance,' Fleet murmured. 'You are honoured, Miss Bainbridge! Joss never singles out any young ladies for his attention!'

Amy's heart, which had just settled down to a steady beat, leapt into her throat again at his words. She turned her head and watched the Earl of Tallant as he came towards her across the room. She felt hot and shivery at the same time and found herself unable to pull her gaze away from him. It felt strange—she had not seen Joss for a couple of days, but he had seldom been far from her thoughts.

Nor was she the only one disturbed at Joss's approach. The débutantes were scattering from before his path with a kind of enjoyable alarm. They need not have worried; Amy saw that he paid them not the slightest attention as he cut his way through the throng to her side.

'Good evening, Joss.' Fleet was looking amused as he looked from one to the other. 'I assume you have come to wrest Miss Bainbridge from me?'

Joss bowed. 'Good evening, Sebastian. Your servant, Miss Bainbridge. Would you care to dance?'

Fleet, obviously anticipating her acquiescence, smiled and wandered off. Amy would dearly have liked to cry off, but she knew that she had to speak to Joss. All the other candidates had fallen by the wayside and he alone must be the owner of the lottery ticket and the thirty-thousand-pound fortune. She had to tell him so. Besides, she had not yet thanked him for the gift of the gloves, improper as it was.

Beyond Joss's shoulder she could see that her mother had broken off her conversation with the other chaperons, who were all watching with their mouths forming the same round, excited 'ooohs' as previously, though this time no doubt for a vastly different reason. She put her hand on Joss's proffered arm.

'Thank you, Lord Tallant. I shall be delighted.'

They moved towards the dance floor.

'Thank you for the gift of the gloves,' Amy said, a little shyly. 'They are very pretty.'

'I did not like to think of you wearing darned gloves,' Joss said abruptly. He glanced down at her hand, where it rested on his sleeve. 'I see that you do not wear them tonight. Did you not like them?'

'Oh, yes.' Amy darted a look at him. 'It was just that I did not think that it would be quite proper.'

Joss smiled. For a second his hand covered hers. 'It would not be, although there are many things more improper. If you like them, Miss Bainbridge, be damned to convention and wear them!'

It was only as they took their places on the floor that Amy realised that the orchestra was striking up for a waltz. She moved gingerly into Joss's arms, not daring to look up into his face. The waltz was new since her come-out and, although she knew the steps, she had seldom danced it in public. The last time, she recalled, had been with an elderly General who had stepped on her feet several times and had utterly failed to make her feel as though she was lighter than air. Dancing with Joss was easy in one sense and difficult in another. Until that moment Amy had never experienced such an acute physical awareness in her whole life, and the feeling was overwhelming. She did not know whether to pull away from Joss in maidenly withdrawal, or relax into what promised to be a sinfully sensual experience.

Joss solved the problem for her by drawing her closer to him. Her cheek brushed his shoulder and for a second she was certain that his lips had touched her hair, and she had to close her eyes to compose herself whilst her feet moved with the mechanical perfection the waltz demanded. Inside she felt hot and vulnerable and somehow astounded at what was happening to her.

'We seem to have managed to scandalise the entire ballroom simply by dancing together, Miss Bainbridge.'

Joss's voice was low and edged with amusement. 'I am sorry to have made you the focus of all eyes—unless you wished to be, of course.'

Amy glanced round and realised the truth of his words. Everyone was staring, the fans were fluttering, the débutantes whispering. Lady Bainbridge was so red in the face that Amy feared she might have a fit, and somehow the united horror of the crowd served to steady her for their outrage seemed so ridiculous. She looked up into Joss's face.

'I cannot see why there is such a fuss,' she said. 'We are but dancing, my lord.'

'True.' A whimsical smile touch Joss's mouth. 'Perhaps I should enlighten you, Miss Bainbridge. Firstly there is the fact that I seldom dance with débutantes, and when I do most people assume I am intending to seduce them.'

Amy raised her brows. 'Then we need have no fear, for I am not a débutante.'

She heard him laugh. 'Perhaps I should have phrased myself a little differently for the sake of clarity, if not propriety. How can I put this? Miss Bainbridge…' he slanted a look down at her '…if I dance with *any* lady, the world assumes I am intending seduction.'

Amy smiled. 'How extraordinary. That would be so exhausting for you, my lord. Can it possibly be true?'

'No,' Joss said ruefully, 'but gossip seldom takes account of the truth, Miss Bainbridge.'

'All the same, the gossip must have started somewhere, my lord.'

'Ah, now there you have me.' Joss smiled. 'There is always some truth in rumour, I suppose. Are you sure you feel quite safe with me, Miss Bainbridge?'

'Because the waltz is licentious and dangerous?' Amy enquired.

'Or because I am myself.'

Amy opened her eyes wide. 'I do not fear for my safety in a crowded ballroom, sir.'

'Very sensible. But you disappoint me, Miss Bainbridge. How is my rakish reputation to be maintained if you steadfastly refuse to believe in it?'

'No doubt you will think of a way, my lord,' Amy responded. 'Besides, though you may fail to frighten *me*, there are a dozen young ladies in our vicinity who are only too willing to be terrified of you!'

'You reassure me. However, when I wish to lose my dishonourable repute I shall come to see you. I am persuaded that it will melt away beneath such blistering common sense!'

They had completed one circuit of the floor and Amy was presented, once again, with her mother's disapproving frown. It was extraordinary, quite as though she expected the Earl of Tallant to seduce her daughter there and then on the dance floor. Amy, reflecting on the foolishness of this, repressed a little regretful sigh.

'So what was the second reason, my lord? You said *firstly* we were scandalising everyone because of your reputation as a rake. So, secondly?'

'Secondly, it will not have escaped the notice of anyone in the ballroom that I am enjoying your company, Miss Bainbridge.' There was a strange expression on Joss's face for a fleeting moment. 'I doubt that anyone here will remember a like occasion.'

Amy felt a warmth steal through her. It was impossible not to feel flattered even if she was not sure of his sincerity. 'Then I am honoured, my lord.'

A smile quirked Joss's lips. 'Cut line, Miss Bainbridge! I doubt you are! What is your opinion of me—a gambler and a wastrel…?'

'And a rake, of course.'

'I am obliged to you for reminding me. So you cannot be honoured by my attentions, given that you have a low opinion of all of those activities.'

Amy smiled back. 'I was only trying to be kind.'

'That is certainly a novelty for me.' Joss inclined his head. 'Let us change the subject before my esteem suffers any further blows. It is pleasant to see you out in society again, Miss Bainbridge. I thought that you lived quite retired these days?'

'Generally I do, my lord,' Amy returned, 'but Lady Spry is up in London for a short while and persuaded me that I would enjoy the ball. I confess it is quite entertaining.'

'Did you then expect that it would not be?'

'Oh, no, not precisely.' Amy hesitated. 'I do not have happy memories of my début, my lord, for I was very shy and did not take.'

'I remember.' Joss gave her a searching look. 'You barely spoke a word. So what has happened to you in between, Miss Bainbridge?'

Amy looked up at him, startled. 'Why, nothing. Whatever do you mean, my lord?'

'Well, you are not shy now. What happened to change that?'

Amy was taken aback. It was true that she had engaged in conversation with Joss very easily once the initial shock of being in his arms had faded. Their repartee had been light and amusing, and as such was far different from the laboured conversations she was accustomed to holding with her partners. But that was just… She struggled a little, because the truth was that it was only with Joss that she felt at such ease. She felt able to express her views and opinions openly and found him interesting to converse with. And that particular fact was not one she wished to examine too closely.

'I am still a reserved character, my lord—'

'I say fustian to that, ma'am! How can you possibly say so? You have had no difficulty in expressing your views to me from the moment we met.'

'But that was because—' Amy stopped dead. She had almost said, 'That was because I had no wish to attract you,' but managed to prevent herself just in time. One of the things that had hampered her during her season was her mother's fervent insistence that she find a suitable man to marry. Amy had tried because she too was desperate to find a way out of the violent swings of fortune that composed life in the Bainbridge household. She wanted to live in calmer waters. So she had viewed each young man she met as a potential suitor but had found them all lacking one way or another. There was no common ground; they did not appear interested in talking to her and seemed disappointed that she was so plain. Her mother harried her and nagged her to become suitably established but it was all in vain—Amy could not attract any offers.

Yet when she had met the Earl of Tallant she had disapproved of him so thoroughly that it had seemed irrelevant to view him in the light of a potential suitor. She had not even tried and thus had managed to speak to him perfectly normally. Now, thinking about it, she could not repress a gurgle of laughter at so outrageous an idea as Joss courting her.

Joss was watching her, his eyebrows lifted questioningly.

'Really, Miss Bainbridge, are you not to explain yourself? That was because...what?'

'Oh, I beg your pardon.' Amy smiled at him. 'You are quite right, my lord. I have been most outspoken in expressing my views to you.'

'I thought that we had agreed that already. I was interested in the reason why.'

'Oh...' Amy cudgelled her brain to come up with a suitable explanation. Could she say that speaking to him was like talking to an elder brother? No, that would not wash. It was far more interesting than conversing with Richard. What about telling him that she felt comfortable with him? That was not precisely true either. His company was too stimulating for that.

The thought brought her up sharply. Stimulating—Joss Tallant. The gamester and womaniser. The man she disapproved of so thoroughly, who was leading Richard astray with his excessive gambling. Her smile faded. How was it possible that she could distrust Joss and yet enjoy his company so much? It was as mysterious as it was disturbing.

'I believe that I may have acquired more town bronze since then, my lord, that is all,' she said.

'Enough indeed to be able to produce a convincing excuse when you need one,' Joss observed drily. 'You are to be congratulated, Miss Bainbridge.'

He bowed to her and escorted her round the floor, but they did not speak again and it was as though some constraint had fallen between them. Amy had totally forgotten that she was intending to quiz Joss about his lottery ticket and it was only when Lord Anston approached her for the next dance, neatly cutting out Mr Cavendish, who had been advancing from the left, that she remembered that there was business unfinished between them. It was too late, however; Lord Anston was triumphantly claiming her hand and Joss walked off with negligent elegance in the direction of the card room.

After that there seemed to be a queue of gentlemen suddenly eager to make her acquaintance. Amy could not believe that dancing with Joss Tallant had brought her into fashion and darkly suspected that it must be her mother's hints of a fortune that had made her so sought after. Whatever the case, it was after supper that Bertie Hallam finally caught up with her to demand a dance. After they had finished he took her arm in a surprisingly masterful grip and steered her towards the candlelit conservatory. Amy, suspecting that Bertie was about to make one of his regular proposals, tried to deflect him.

'Oh, is not Lady Alice Broughton over there? I am sure you said that you admired her, Bertie. Why do you not ask her to dance?'

Bertie was not to be deflected.

'Now see here, Amy,' he said, when they were seated on a bench beneath the sparkling fairy lanterns, 'I've decided that really you must marry me. It's not right that you should spend your days fetching and carrying for Lady Bainbridge, reading and sewing and…' Bertie wrinkled up his face, evidently trying to imagine what else Amy might do with her time '…and other things,' he finished, a little lamely. 'You are not as young as you were and it's time you had your own establishment.' He took her hands in his. 'I know you're accustomed to refusing me and I know you disapprove of my gambling, but dash it, Amy, you ought to accept my proposal!'

Amy sighed. Over the years she had grown accustomed to receiving an offer of marriage from Bertie Hallam. The habit had started when he was six and she was five, and he had shown a dogged devotion ever since. It was quite dark in the conservatory, but by the faint light of the coloured lanterns she could see that he was looking at her with a hopeful expression on his lugubrious face.

'Dearest Bertie,' she said gently, 'it is very kind of you to ask me but I fear that the answer is still no.'

She had just finished speaking when she became aware that they were not alone in the shadowy conservatory. The shadows moved and shifted and then a tall figure was standing beside the bench and a cool voice said,

'I do apologise for my intrusion, Miss Bainbridge. I had merely come to ask you to spare me another dance. I had no notion that I was interrupting at such a delicate moment. Pray excuse me. Your servant, Hallam.'

The Earl of Tallant. Amy recognised the voice, with its undercurrent of amusement, and felt the colour burn her face that he had found her in such a situation. Bertie got to his feet with what Amy recognised was an attempt to match the Earl's own sangfroid. He failed miserably, for his demeanour was stiff and his good-humoured tone a little forced. Amy recognised his discomfort and felt a rush of sympathy for him—and a burning annoyance with Joss Tallant for being cool and amused and so nonchalant; everything that Bertie was not. Then she felt irritated with herself, for she was the one who had rejected Bertie's proposal of marriage and it was hardly fair to take out her guilt and bad temper on someone else.

'Servant, Tallant,' Bertie said heartily. 'Amy, do you wish to go back into the ballroom?'

Amy knew that that was the proper course of action, but she had suddenly remembered that she had to ask Joss about the lottery ticket and that this would probably be her only opportunity. The field had narrowed—to one. There was only Joss left, and for some reason she felt very nervous about asking him. She would just have to get the matter over with quickly.

'You go on without me, Bertie,' she said quickly. 'There is something that I wish to ask Lord Tallant.'

Bertie hesitated, clearly struck by the impropriety of this. 'Amy, I really do not think that I should leave you here—'

'I shall only be a moment,' Amy said. Clearly her erstwhile suitor had now reverted to acting as an elder brother. Whilst she felt more comfortable with Bertie in that role, she did not wish him to exercise a fraternal interest just now. She turned towards Joss, leaving Bertie standing open-mouthed and startled. 'Lord Tallant, would you walk with me a little, if you please?'

'With great pleasure, Miss Bainbridge.' Joss Tallant fell into step beside her and gave her a searching look. 'What a surprising young lady you are turning out to me, Miss Bainbridge! Seeking out my company in such a way is most singular!'

His sleeve brushed against hers. Amy repressed a shiver.

'I know it,' she said a little uncertainly. 'It may seem a little odd…'

'It does,' Joss agreed pleasantly, 'not to mention bold and surprisingly out of character, Miss Bainbridge! You are surely aware that to ask a gentleman to walk with you through a dark and deserted conservatory could be interpreted in rather a dubious light?'

'That would depend on the gentleman, I dare say,' Amy said.

'Very probably.' Joss slanted a look down at her and Amy could tell that he was smiling. 'Some would take it as an invitation, Miss Bainbridge.'

'But you would not make that mistake, would you, my lord?'

'We have already discussed that, have we not, Miss Bainbridge? You are quite aware of my reputation.'

'I am,' Amy said crisply, 'and I am certain that I am in no danger.'

It was true. Despite his rake's reputation and the fact that they were alone together, Amy had the strangest feeling that they understood one another. How they had reached such a rapport was curious and she might even have imagined it, yet she felt entirely safe with him.

'You are intrepid indeed, Miss Bainbridge.' Joss laughed 'So, having dismissed that issue, we may talk. What is it that you wished to ask me?'

Amy cleared her throat. 'I have asked the same question of several different gentlemen including Mr Hallam—'

'How intriguing.' Joss turned suddenly, taking Amy's hands in his. His touch was warm. 'So, will it necessitate the same actions as your conversation with Mr Hallam?'

Amy snatched her hands away. She wished she was seated so that she might make assurance doubly sure by sitting on them.

'Of course not! How absurd you are! Mr Hallam was holding my hands because—' She stopped, cross with herself. It was none of Joss Tallant's business what she had been talking about with Bertie. 'Well, that is nothing to the purpose anyway—'

'He was holding your hands because he was making you an offer,' Joss said. The undertone of mockery in his drawling voice made Amy's annoyance worse. 'I am sorry for interrupting you at such a deucedly awkward moment. I hope it did not ruin matters for you.'

'Of course not! Mr Hallam proposes to me every year and I fear it has become something of a habit with him,' Amy said. 'Not that it is any business of yours, sir.'

'It is not, but satisfy my curiosity further. Did you refuse him?'

Amy was glad of the darkness that covered her blushes. 'You are impertinent, sir—'

'I am. Did you refuse him?'

'Yes, I did.' Amy spoke in a rush. 'I do not love him.'

There was a short silence. 'I suppose you require the grand passion to persuade you into matrimony, or at least the appearance of it?' The mockery was still in Joss's voice and Amy prickled with annoyance. 'You disappoint me, Miss Bainbridge. Most young ladies are tiresomely sentimental, but I had thought that you might be different.'

'I certainly require to have more than mere liking for the gentleman I marry,' Amy said sharply, 'if you consider that sentimentality! However, I do believe that you do my sex little justice, sir. At least half of us are prepared to marry for money and position alone!'

Joss laughed again, this time with genuine humour. 'This kitten has very sharp claws! I am relieved that I need not repine, Miss Bainbridge. Somewhere there will be a lady prepared to overlook my faults and marry me for my money alone.'

'I was not aware that your lordship wished to marry,' Amy said. The thought gave her a strange feeling inside.

'Your behaviour does not suggest it. You are a self-confessed rake, after all.'

'So?' Joss laughed. 'I have yet to learn that that is a bar to marriage.'

'And you are evidently a cynic too! It seems a shame to embark on matrimony with such an attitude.'

'Ah, so we are to talk morality now, as we spoke of gambling before? How stimulating!'

'No, I do not wish to debate morality with you, my lord,' Amy said. 'There are plenty of reform societies for you to visit if that is your wish.'

She sighed. Debating with him was like wrestling a slippery fish, only much more enjoyable than fishing. Seldom were her wits tested to this extent in her daily conversations with Richard or Lady Bainbridge. It felt exciting, as though she was straying into deep waters. Part of her wanted to go with the tide and the other part, the sensible part, held back.

'Thank you.' Joss inclined his head. 'I am obliged to you for pointing that out although I feel that a conversation with you might have been more enjoyable, Miss Bainbridge. Crossing wits with you is peculiarly interesting.'

'Thank you,' Amy said briskly. 'We seem to have drifted quite a distance from the topic in hand, my lord. I had a question for you, if you recall. It was simply this. Did you have a lottery ticket for the draw last week?'

There was a pause, and then Joss bowed slightly. 'No, Miss Bainbridge. I did not have a ticket. Why do you ask?'

'Oh, no reason,' Amy said airily. She felt both relieved and disappointed at the same time. 'I was merely curious—'

'About my gambling habits? They are extreme, I am afraid. But of course you know that—and deplore it. But I should call time on you for that Banbury tale, Miss Bainbridge. There must be a better reason for your question than simple curiosity.'

Amy pressed her hands together. The Duke of Fleet had not persisted in questioning her, but she had had a feeling from the first that Joss Tallant would not be quite so amenable. And now she had a greater problem. Since the ticket did not belong to any of Richard's gambling cronies, nor was it clear who else might claim it, what was she to do? She frowned slightly, thinking aloud.

'I found a lottery ticket in the dining room at Curzon Street, my lord, and it won the prize last week. I have been trying to reunite the money with its rightful owner, but I cannot seem to find him.'

Joss raised his brows. His tone was incredulous. 'You found a winning lottery ticket and you wish to give the money away? Miss Bainbridge, you astound me!'

Amy threw him a look that was part ashamed, part challenging. 'Why so?'

'Come, you must know the reason! Firstly, I am amazed that you would tell me such a thing and, secondly, I cannot believe that you would give the money away! It beggars belief!'

Amy gave an angry sigh. 'Why must everyone make me feel as though I am doing wrong rather than doing right? All I am trying to do is to see that the rightful owner is given the money!'

Joss laughed. 'Who is everyone?'

'Oh, you and Lady Spry, my mother and Richard! It is the most shocking thing, my lord! All the world would keep the winnings for themselves and cannot understand why I believe I must give them back!'

'Your honesty will be making people uncomfortable, I believe,' Joss said slowly. 'Not one man in ten—and I include women as well—would do as you are doing, Miss Bainbridge, and they will not like you for it.'

Amy frowned. 'Surely there would be plenty of people who would not keep what is not rightfully theirs? I cannot believe the world so venal as you describe it, my lord!'

'Believe it, my dear Miss Bainbridge. I fear you are naïve!'

'Well, there is no need to patronise me!' Amy said crossly. 'Just because you would do differently yourself.'

'Ah, yes, of course—so I would.' There was an odd note in Joss's voice. 'Yet still I may be helpful, perhaps. Have you interrogated all the servants to check on their gaming habits? Perhaps one of them would admit to it—for thirty thousand pounds?'

'None of the servants play the lottery and the ticket belongs to none of Richard's guests, nor to me or to Mama or Richard himself. Amanda—Lady Spry—wondered if it had been blown in off the street, perhaps, or been dropped down the chimney by a bird.'

'How imaginative of Lady Spry—and how convenient.' Joss smiled. 'It would undoubtedly be simpler to accept her views.'

Amanda frowned again. 'Well, I cannot see what else I can do now!'

'Forget the matter and spend the money on yourself would be my advice. Or give it to Richard so that I may win it all from him!'

'Certainly not!' Amy gave him a repressive look. 'If I must keep it, my lord, I shall use it to do good.'

Joss sighed. 'Must you? How tiresome. Can you not allow yourself to be corrupted by the possession of it?'

'No, indeed. How absurd you are!' Amy sobered. 'There is just one small matter...'

'Yes?'

'I wonder—would you not tell anyone about my winnings? I have no intention of going about in society very much and will give the money to good causes, but I could not bear if it was rumoured that I was the lottery heiress, or some such ridiculous soubriquet.'

'Of course.' Joss's hand covered her own for a brief second on his sleeve. 'There is just one thing, Miss Bainbridge...'

'Yes?' Amy found her voice a little unsteady. That brief touch had lit something inside her and she moved back a step. 'What is it?'

'Did you tell anyone else the reason for your enquiries? I mean, did you tell Hallam, or Dainty—or Fleet?'

'No.' Amy hesitated. 'I was trying to be discreet and did not wish anyone else to know.'

'Then why tell me?'

There was a silence. Amy felt tense. She did not wish to answer the question, did not even know the answer. She had known Bertie Hallam for years and trusted him as a brother, yet it was not to Bertie that she had confided the truth but to Joss Tallant.

'I am not entirely sure,' she said uncertainly.

The silence stretched, taut as a drum.

'Yet you trust me with this information?'

'I...yes.' Amy had a sinking feeling in her stomach. She remembered what Lady Bainbridge had said about the scandal that would ensue if it became known that she had gained a fortune through winning the lottery. She had put herself in Joss's hands now.

'Well, your secret is safe, I promise. No doubt you will wish to avoid all those fortune-hunting adventurers who will want to capture your hand, heart and money,' Joss said, and the lightness of his tone eased Amy's tension. 'I fear you may be a little late, however. Your mother has already boasted—most discreetly, of course—of your good fortune. Only she has been suggesting that it is a bequest from an elderly relative, so I understand…'

Amy gave a little moan. 'I thought so! I asked Mama to keep quiet!'

'Impossible!' Joss tucked her hand comfortingly through his arm. 'It would be too much for maternal flesh and blood to keep silent. Lady Bainbridge told Mrs Vestey, who told Lady Bestable, who told half the company here tonight. It is the latest *on-dit*! Now, come and dance, Miss Bainbridge. You will find that life as an heiress is not so bad after all.'

Chapter Seven

Joss Tallant relinquished Miss Amy Bainbridge to the eager arms of Viscount Truscote and strolled over to the long terrace windows for a drink and some fresh air. The heat in the ballroom was becoming oppressive and he had no further desire to dance. Perhaps it was time to leave the genteel entertainments of Lady Moon's ball for less salubrious surroundings. A picture of Harriet Templeton came into his mind, but for some reason it seemed unappetising. Joss shrugged philosophically. No doubt Harriet would regain her appeal soon, but if not he could always find another mistress.

He replaced his empty glass of wine with a full one and stood watching the dancers. Amy was waltzing with Truscote, moving daintily and with grace. She might be small, but she was perfectly proportioned and danced divinely. She was looking up into Truscote's face with a confiding smile and it seemed she was enjoying the Viscount's company no matter what she had asserted before about finding little to entertain her at balls and parties. Joss felt a shaft of irritation pierce him. He put his wine glass down with a slap that showed scant regard for the delicate crystal. It was definitely time to move on. He felt bored and blue-devilled and had a fancy to drown the evening in brandy.

He could not be certain what it was that had prompted him to disclaim ownership of the lottery ticket. When Amy had first spoken, he had felt relieved to discover that his suspicions about her honesty had been groundless. This was so strange a reaction that it had held him silent for a few moments, for surely he should not have cared either way? He had dismissed the thought as she had carried on talking and had become intrigued by her attempts to find the rightful owner, charmed even by her determination to do the right thing. He had been less flattered by her instinctive assumption that he, along with everyone else, would have kept the money for himself. But then there was no reason for her to have a good opinion of him. And there was certainly no good reason why he should care if she did or if she did not.

'You seem to have played Pygmalion rather successfully this evening, Joss.' The Duke of Fleet had paused beside his friend and was also looking in Amy's direction.

'Miss Bainbridge is much in demand,' Fleet continued. 'Why put yourself to the trouble to bring such a plain girl into fashion?'

Joss met his friend's bland expression with a stony one of his own. He knew perfectly well what Fleet was up to and he was not about to give him the satisfaction of rising to provocation.

'I scarce think that my attentions will enhance Miss Bainbridge's reputation, Seb. The reverse is probably true.'

Fleet looked quizzical. 'Then why inflict your company on her if you think it will bring her into disrepute, old chap?'

Joss shrugged. 'I wanted to talk to her.'

'Was it worth it?'

'Decidedly.' Joss tried to crush the irritation that Fleet's conversation was engendering, but was only partially successful. 'Miss Bainbridge is not in the common way, which is good, for the common way bores me.'

Fleet frowned a little. 'Do you have no concern for her reputation?'

Joss shrugged again. 'No one comes to any harm waltzing with me in a crowded ballroom and any chaperon who believes otherwise has too vivid an imagination.'

'As long as you are not putting ideas into Miss Bainbridge's head with your attentions. It would be a pity to disappoint her. Unless…' Fleet paused. 'You did say that your father was suggesting matrimony?'

Joss laughed, although somewhere in the recesses of his mind the idea took root with surprising firmness. He tried to dislodge it. 'My father was suggesting progressive farming methods last week! His suggestions need not concern me, I am glad to say.'

Fleet shook his head. 'You're a cold fish, Joss. Fancy some Haymarket ware to warm you up?'

'Not tonight. I fancy a warm brandy bottle and a game of hazard at White's.'

Fleet nodded. 'I'll join you. It is better sport than this.'

Joss gave him a mocking look. 'Has Lady Spry lost her charm, Seb?'

'Not really, but she's too damned proper for me.' Fleet sighed. 'A widow with no inclination towards dalliance. My cursed luck!'

Joss clapped him on the shoulder. 'To White's?'

'Why not? If you have no desire to dance with the mousy Miss Bainbridge again.'

Joss had turned away but now he stopped, finding that he could not let that one pass. He felt so angry that he had to take a deep breath before he spoke. So Seb had found his mark. Damn him.

'I have not the least desire in the world to dance with Miss Bainbridge again,' he said coolly, after a moment. 'But as one who is at least a gentleman by title, I have to tell you, Seb, that Miss Bainbridge is *not* mousy.'

He turned on his heel and walked off. Fleet watched him go, a self-satisfied smile on his lips.

'A result at last,' he murmured. 'Joss, m'boy, this is going to be interesting.'

'I am so glad that your mama permitted me to be your chaperon tonight,' Amanda Spry said, as the new Bainbridge coach took them the short distance from Curzon Street to Portman Square, 'although I am sorry that she has the migraine. It is only a small party, not a ball, but I am sure that there will be many eligible gentlemen there tonight.'

Amy fidgeted nervously. She was aware that Lady Bainbridge had been swayed by this piece of information into letting Amanda take a role to which she was surely unsuited. Amy did not consider that she needed a chaperon, being one and twenty, but since she was obliged to have one it seemed silly that that person should be Amanda, who was twice as impetuous as she.

Amy stroked the pale blue silk of her new evening gown. She had chosen it because it matched her eyes exactly, and brought out the golden lights in her brown hair. She had stood before the mirror in her bedroom and had reflected that she actually looked quite pretty for once—but that was before she had seen Amanda, ethereal in apricot satin with a matching bandeau adorned with soft white feathers.

The carriage drew up outside the door. Amanda had told her that Mrs Wren was a widow of great respectability who gave marvellously entertaining parties. However, Amy was not long inside the house before she realised that Mrs Wren's parties were not the sorts of affair at which any débutantes would be present. The hostess set the tone in a clinging dress with a plunging décolletage that displayed to advantage a diamond necklace that Amy considered to be frankly vulgar. Mrs Wren's rooms were full of ladies and gentlemen chatting loudly and with a freeness of manner that was startling. The wine was flowing very copiously indeed and there was no lemonade. Even when the musical entertainment started the guests did not bother to lower their voices and Amy was irritated that the excellent singer was quite drowned out by conversation.

Amanda was soon dragged away from Amy's side to play a hand of whist and Amy took refuge behind a pillar where she sipped her glass of wine and wished that she had stayed at home. She had seen Richard across the room but her brother seemed disinclined to come and talk to her when he had a dashing blonde lady hanging on his every word. Amy, feeling shy and uncomfortable, resolved that she would not stay another minute. The party was threatening to turn into something rather less respectable, and at lightning speed. Yet even as she turned towards the door she was stopped in her tracks.

'Leaving so soon, ma'am? Why not come and have a li'l chat with me?'

Someone put their hand on her arm and Amy turned, repressing a shudder as the gentleman leaned closer and breathed stale wine fumes in her face. She could tell from the gleam in his eyes that he was drunk, but not sufficiently to be incapable. She backed away.

'Don't be coy,' the gentleman leered. 'You're a taking little piece! We should become better acquainted…'

'Thank you, sir, but I am waiting for someone,' Amy said, hoping that her desperation did not show in her voice. With the pillar behind her and the drunkard in front, her options seemed decidedly limited.

'Waiting for me, in fact,' a voice said briskly. Joss Tallant took Amy's arm and drew her close to his side. 'I do apologise for my shocking tardiness, my dear. Baverstock, you need not trouble the lady with your company any longer.'

The Earl of Baverstock muttered something and sidled away, and Joss drew Amy's hand through his arm and steered her towards a quiet alcove where they sat down.

'Of all the places where I might have expected to find you, Miss Bainbridge…' Joss said ruefully.

'I know!' Amy felt a little shaken. 'I believe that I was misled about the sophistication of the evening.'

'There is nothing very sophisticated about this crowd,' Joss said dismissively, looking around, 'but I take your meaning, Miss Bainbridge! Perhaps you should go home?'

Amy craned her neck for a glimpse of Amanda. 'I came here with Lady Spry. I do not suppose that I should simply abandon her.'

Joss laughed. 'Surely it is the other way about? Is she not intended to be your chaperon?'

'Yes, but...' Amy sought to excuse her friend '...it is not as though I need her protection.'

Joss raised his brows. 'Indeed? Were you enjoying Baverstock's attentions?'

Amy flushed. 'That was different, and, no, of course I was not! I am sorry, my lord—I should have thanked you for rescuing me.'

'It was a pleasure.' Joss gave her a slow smile. 'I have some sympathy with Baverstock, however, for you do indeed look most attractive this evening, Miss Bainbridge.'

Amy almost gaped. 'Come now, my lord! Not even my mother would allow that I looked more than tolerable! In such company—' She gestured at the painted ladies milling about them.

'You mistake your charm.' Joss stretched, giving her an assessing look that made her blink. 'In such a company as this it is precisely because you look fresh and innocent rather than jaded that you stand out, Miss Bainbridge. As for your mother, perhaps she should have spent more time telling you how charming you look, so that you would not lack the confidence to believe it!'

Amy looked at him in shocked silence. There had been an undercurrent in his voice that she did not understand. Their eyes met and then Joss sighed.

'I beg your pardon. I should not have said that about Lady Bainbridge.'

'No, but...' Amy was confused. 'I understand that you were only trying to make me feel better—'

'No!' Joss spoke so sharply that Amy jumped. 'That was *not* what I was doing, Miss Bainbridge! Why can you not believe me sincere?'

'I am sorry.' Amy was even more confused now. He

sounded exasperated, but beneath that she sensed a hurt that she did not understand. Surely the Earl of Tallant could not care about her good opinion? And why should it matter to him that she believe that he admired her?

She stared at him, her eyes narrowing thoughtfully. 'My lord—'

'I will go and find Lady Spry for you, Miss Bainbridge,' Joss said, interrupting abruptly. 'It is not in the least suitable that you should remain here any longer.'

Puzzled, Amy watched as he disappeared into the card room, to emerge an impressively short time later with Amanda. Amy wondered if he had summarily removed her in the middle of a rubber of whist.

It seemed so, but when Amanda reached her side, she was not the least inclined to leave the party.

'Amy,' she wheedled, 'I know that you wish to go home, but I would just like to play another hand. Please! And we need a fourth to make up the numbers, just for this rubber. Oh, please say that you will play!'

Amy groaned. She had no wish to disoblige her dearest friend, but playing whist, even for a nominal sum, was not her idea of fun. The evening was not far advanced but the behaviour was licentious, she was too hot and wanted to go home. She gave Amanda a look of exasperation. 'Mandy, you know I never play! Why not ask Lady Bestable if she will join you? She is a bosom bow of Mama's and I know she loves whist.'

'Lady Bestable is already playing,' Amanda said. 'We need someone else. Please, Amy…' Amanda put on her most beseeching expression. 'I know that you dislike to gamble, but there is no harm in this! We are not playing for more than pennies! And you were always lucky at cards. You know you were!'

'That is beside the point,' Amy said. She could feel

herself weakening and tried to strengthen her resolve. Amanda had always been deplorably persuasive, even in their schooldays. She had always managed to persuade Amy to some scrape against her better judgement. And now Amy felt like a killjoy, denying her friend some innocent entertainment. Perhaps she was making too much of her dislike of gambling, especially when it was a harmless game for a risible sum. Everyone gambled, after all. Perhaps, as Richard had implied, she was taking it all too seriously.

Amanda had taken her arm now and was propelling her towards the card room. It was even hotter in here. The curtains were drawn, blocking out both the darkness and any breath of wind that might have cooled the room but might also have scattered the cards. The air was thick with concentration and tension. Servants moved soundlessly between the tables, plying the gamblers with drink. Amy watched and found her stomach curling with the apprehension of memory. She could see her father's face, flushed and excited as he checked his cards, and she had to repress a shudder.

'Amanda, I don't think I want to do this…' she began, but it was too late to pull out without embarrassing her friend. Amanda was dragging her over to a table in the corner, where two ladies were already sitting. One was Lady Bestable and the other was a lady who looked vaguely familiar, although Amy could not place her. She had dark auburn hair, elaborately dressed, green eyes and a bored, lazy expression.

'Lady Juliana Myfleet,' Amanda said, performing the introductions, 'may I introduce Miss Bainbridge? Amy, Lady Juliana and I are friends from my come-out. The two of you have not met before?'

Lady Juliana shook her head. Her eyes were bright as they surveyed Amy from top to toe.

'So you are the little puritan who does not care to wager?' she murmured. 'How piquant that Amanda persuaded you to join us. Are we to play for pennies?'

Amanda blushed and Amy shot her a reproachful look.

'Amanda said that you needed a fourth to make up a game,' she said stiffly. 'However, if you are to play for high stakes I wish you would excuse me, ma'am—'

'No need, my dear, I do but tease.' Lady Juliana smiled her feline smile and cut the deck. 'This is a practice run for me. I shall do my serious gambling in a little while. Shall we start?'

Amy had played little in the last few years, but although she was out of practice she quickly remembered the mechanics of the game. She was partnering Amanda, who was a reckless rather than a skilful player and who often overplayed her hand. For all Lady Juliana's assurances, it was soon clear that she took the game extremely seriously and it was no surprise when she and Lady Bestable ran out easy winners. Amy, feeling that she had met her obligation to Amanda, was about to make her excuses and leave when a footman delivered a note to her friend and Amanda slipped away from the table with a word of apology. Mrs Wren immediately took her place. Their hostess wore a sharp, acquisitive expression. Her fingers, tapping the deck of cards, betrayed the tension of the dedicated gambler. Amy suddenly felt as innocent as a country girl in a brothel.

'Juliana, darling, we must have a game of vingt-et-un!' Mrs Wren exclaimed. 'Positively we must! I have been waiting all evening to play!'

'Very well, Emma,' Lady Juliana said, nothing loath. Her malicious gaze rested on Amy briefly. 'Lady Bestable, Miss Bainbridge—will you play?'

Vingt-et-un was the only game that Amy actually liked. It had been the first that she had learned, for her father had taught her as a child and had explained that it would be a useful way for her to learn to calculate. Amy had soon learned that each of the cards had a different value and that she had to get her hand to add up to twenty-one. Later she realised that her father's justification that the game helped her reckon figures better was nothing more than an excuse, but by then she was very good at mathematics so perhaps there had been some truth in his assertion. For that reason she thought she probably retained a small, nostalgic regard for the game. All the same, it was not enough to keep her at the table.

'No, I thank you. I have played enough for one evening.'

Mrs Wren pulled a face. 'Just like your dear papa, Miss Bainbridge! They always said that he did not have the temperament for the game. He proved it in the end, did he not?'

Amy felt a hot spurt of anger. She knew that Emma Wren was only trying to provoke her and on most occasions she would have allowed the insult to go over her head. Tonight she found she could not. Perhaps it was the memories that crowded in on her, or perhaps it was simply her dislike of Mrs Wren, but she found that she did not wish to retreat ignominiously.

'I do not believe that I am much like my papa,' she said coolly, looking Mrs Wren in the eye. 'Perhaps I shall play this one game…'

It soon became apparent that the ladies were now

playing for high stakes. Lady Juliana suggested an initial bet of ten guineas and proceeded to win the first game very quickly. This encouraged her to double the stake on the second. She was well in the grip of gambling fever by now, sitting forward, eyes a-glitter as she pounced on her hand of cards. Once again she beat the others to twenty-one, with Mrs Wren barely managing to conceal her hostility when she could only muster a total of nineteen points from her cards. Amy, for all her proficiency at the game, came in a poor third.

'You have the very devil's luck, Ju,' Emma was complaining. 'Damned if I can see why the Tallant family should be so prodigious good at cards! Give the rest of us a chance!'

Amy jumped at her words. She had had no idea of a connection between Lady Juliana and the Earl of Tallant, and she told herself that it made little difference, except to point out that she had vastly underestimated the level of skill and passion of her opponents. These were no middle-aged ladies playing patience to pass the long evenings. These were gamesters as dedicated as their male counterparts and as reckless. She had only herself to blame if she felt out of her depth. She should have followed her first instinct and kept well away.

Mrs Wren's spiteful gaze turned towards her again.

'I suppose one should not wholly dismiss you as a card player, Miss Bainbridge, since like Juliana you come from a gambling dynasty! Only your brother is not so lucky as Juliana's, is he? Nor so rich!'

Lady Juliana laughed. 'Let Miss Bainbridge be, Emma! She has not had so much practice as I have!'

'Another round?' Mrs Wren said eagerly. 'Let us make it the best of three.'

Amy hesitated. She cast a look at Lady Bestable, feeling in some way that her age must make that matron the safest of her companions, but her ladyship's eyes were riveted on the cards like a dog with a juicy bone.

'Let us make it an elimination!' Lady Bestable said. 'Double the stake—sixty guineas!'

Amy started to rise from her seat, then sat down again. She had sixty guineas and more, much more now that she possessed a fortune of thirty thousand pounds. But she certainly did not want to gamble her fortune away. She felt no thrill in the cards, only nervousness in the pit of her stomach and a strange, trapped feeling that seemed to be growing with each hand. The darkened card room and the eager thrill her companions took in the proceedings was horribly familiar. In her mind's eye she could see all those images that she had striven so hard to repress—she was a small child again, peering around the door of the library to watch her father and his cronies at play; she was a schoolgirl being driven away from the latest establishment when the money ran out; she was back in Whitechapel…

'I think little Miss Bainbridge does not wish to play,' Lady Juliana put in, in her sly drawl. 'Can you not take the heat, Miss Bainbridge?'

'Or perhaps she cannot…afford…to play?' Mrs Wren said, with deliberate innuendo. 'Although I do hear marvellous things about your prospects, Miss Bainbridge! Can you not share some of your fortune with us?'

Amy looked at her and reflected that she had seldom disliked anyone as much as she detested Emma Wren. It was neither noble, nor indeed, very mature in her to wish to humiliate her hostess, but the fighting spirit was suddenly there.

'I shall play,' she said, 'but I do not believe that I shall be sharing my fortune, ma'am.'

Lady Bestable cackled. 'That's the spirit, my dear!' She dealt the cards, her little eyes flashing with cupidity. Amy felt as though the ladies were already feeling the weight of her gold in their pocket and her resolve hardened, banishing the fear. She would show them that a Bainbridge could play and win!

It was Lady Bestable who was eliminated in the first, low-scoring round. Amy managed a score of fifteen, with Mrs Wren achieving eighteen and Lady Juliana sulking because she had only seventeen in her hand. Amy remembered her father saying that cards made a man disputatious and reflected that that was true of women as well. Lady Juliana looked as though she would like to knife Mrs Wren were only a weapon to hand.

Their game was attracting some attention now as word went round that they were playing an elimination and that the stakes were doubling each time. Some of the gentlemen drifted across from the faro table to watch. Richard was there, and a tall, fair man with a too-knowing expression, whom Amy had seen previously paying lavish attention to Lady Juliana. She felt acutely self-conscious. The stakes doubled again from sixty to one hundred and twenty guineas. Amy felt a little faint as she played her cards. She could not quite believe what she was doing and she wished she had been eliminated instead of Lady Bestable, who was sitting like a malignant toad at the side of the table and clearly resented the fact that she was no longer in the game.

A slight gasp went up from the crowd when Mrs Wren was eliminated in the second round. Mrs Wren herself did not look as though she could quite believe it. For a second Amy thought she was going to tear her cards across, but after a moment she controlled herself and gave Amy a sharp smile.

'A dark horse indeed, Miss Bainbridge! But you have not won yet.'

Richard nudged the fair man in the ribs. 'Always knew Amy had it in her! Gambling's in the blood, don't you think, Massingham?'

The fair-haired man laughed. 'In the Bainbridge blood for certain, Richard! But my money is still on Lady Juliana!'

Someone went into the outer room and fetched a ledger. To Amy's shock, she realised that they were taking bets now on the outcome of the game, on whether she or Lady Juliana would win. The most outrageous sums were being mentioned. She heard Richard wager a hundred guineas that she would triumph, and her nerve almost failed her on the spot.

Lady Juliana sat across the table from Amy, her green eyes glittering with excitement. 'Double or quits, Miss Bainbridge! The bet is two hundred and forty guineas. Will you accept?'

Richard was lounging against the doorframe, his face alight with a gambler's excitement. Amy met his eyes. She felt a little sick and her hands shook slightly. She could not believe what she was doing. The crowd pressed closer about the table.

Amy cleared her throat. 'I will play.'

Lady Juliana gave a crow of laughter. 'Oh, how we underestimated you, Miss Bainbridge! Let's play, then!'

Though, down to two players the game took much longer. Amy, keeping cards and discarding, was conscious of nothing but the flickering candlelight, the circle of avid watchers, and the frown between Lady Juliana's eyes as she faced her across the table. There was a buzz in her blood that was like excitement and wine; a part of her wanted desperately to escape but another part, the stronger, wanted equally desperately to win. The heat in the room seemed stifling and unreal—Amy told herself that none of it mattered; that soon it would be over like the dream it seemed to be.

'I do believe that Miss Bainbridge has won,' one of the gentlemen murmured as Amy, a little blindly, put her cards down on the table at the end of the game. 'A perfect vingt-et-un. Twenty-one precisely, Lady Juliana, unless you can match it?'

Amy's vision cleared. Lady Juliana was looking furious, a black frown between her brows. 'I have a twenty but not a twenty-one. Damnation! I cannot believe it.' She threw her cards down and they scattered like leaves in the wind. 'Do you care to play again, Miss Bainbridge—winner takes all?'

'No, thank you,' Amy said. Her mouth felt parched and she had a headache behind her eyes. The excitement had melted away as swiftly as it had come. 'I shall not play further.'

Lady Juliana's eyes narrowed. 'That is your right, of course, since the elimination is at an end. Alas, I cannot pay my debt immediately, Miss Bainbridge. You will take a promissory note?'

Amy knew the rules well enough not to decline. 'Of course.'

Lady Juliana's face broke into a sudden smile. 'Oh, no, I have a better idea! I will settle my debt of honour, Miss Bainbridge—by offering my brother in return!'

The crowd had started to break up, drawn back to their own tables and the promise of play, but they stopped at this new twist. A ragged laugh ran around the room.

'Good try, Juliana!' Massingham said humorously. 'Tallant is hardly yours to sell, though, is he?'

Lady Juliana's feline smile broadened. 'Oh, I do not know, Clive. If Captain Gramond can sell his sister in a game of faro, why can I not use Joss as my stake? He might be persuaded to help me...for one reason or another. You, there!' She turned imperiously to a footman. 'Fetch Lord Tallant! We shall see if he will come to my aid!'

Amy felt herself turn hot all over. Everyone was laughing and waiting to see the outcome of Lady Juliana's extraordinary suggestion. Amy closed her eyes and prayed fervently that Joss had already left the ball. She could not imagine facing him in this situation, and as for Lady Juliana's offer—well, that was quite ridiculous.

'I do not accept your stake,' she said, a little desperately. 'It was not what we originally agreed.'

Lady Juliana raised her eyebrows mockingly. 'Alas, my brother is not acceptable to Miss Bainbridge! Now, what shall we do?'

Mrs Wren leaned forward. 'Your brother is acceptable to me, Juliana!' she said with a meaningful smile. 'Miss Bainbridge—' she turned to Amy '—I will buy up your debt for three hundred guineas if you will turn Lady Juliana's offer over to me!'

Someone guffawed. 'Is Tallant worth that much, Emma?'

Mrs Wren flashed a wicked smile. 'That and more, so I hear!'

Amy felt her blush deepen. This was all getting far too complicated. When she had accepted Amanda's plea to play a hand of whist it had only been to oblige her friend, and now she had got herself into the most frightful fix. She had never intended to play for so long, or for such high stakes and she was starting to feel quite shocked at the gambling passion that had gripped her, albeit briefly. Besides, where had Amanda gone? It was dreadful of her to desert her like this! There was not a single friendly face in the room—even Richard seemed utterly unable to understand her distress—and the louche atmosphere was making Amy deeply uncomfortable. Massingham had paused to drop a kiss on Lady Juliana's pouting lips and Amy looked hastily away.

Richard came across and crouched down by Amy's chair. 'I think you must accept the stake or pass to Mrs Wren, Amy,' he said. 'It is a debt of honour after all and you cannot really refuse. Though it all depends on what Joss has to say to it, of course—'

'On what I have to say about what?'

A whisper ran round the room like the wind through corn. Amy turned in her seat. The Earl of Tallant had just come in, accompanied by the Duke of Fleet. She could see that Joss already had his coat on, as though he had been on the point of leaving when Lady Juliana's message had reached him. Amy wished with her whole heart that he had been less tardy. For a second her eyes met his and she saw a flash of some emotion there—surprise, perhaps, followed by a strange tug of empathy—before she dropped her gaze from his. Her heart was beating a swift tattoo.

'Joss, darling...' Lady Juliana stretched out an elegant hand '...the most dreary thing! I have just lost to Miss Bainbridge and do not have the means to meet my debt at the moment. I know that you could settle it for me, but then I thought that perhaps it would be more entertaining to use you to pay the wager instead. You must be worth at least two hundred and forty guineas—'

'They charge more in Covent Garden,' someone in the crowd put in.

'So if I promise you to Miss Bainbridge for a week,' Lady Juliana finished sweetly, 'would you do that for me to help me settle my debt? Please, Joss dearest...'

Amy, shifting uncomfortably in her chair, thought that Joss looked utterly unmoved by the plea. She held her breath, waiting for him to refuse. She was desperate to be out of there. The raffish atmosphere, the insinuations of the crowd, made her deeply unhappy.

'What does Miss Bainbridge have to say about this?' Joss asked. His amber gaze fastened on Amy and her heart missed a beat. His expression was unreadable.

'Miss Bainbridge doesn't want to take my stake,' Lady Juliana said with a mournful sigh. 'She finds you unacceptable, Joss.'

Joss inclined his head. Amy saw the flash of amusement in his eyes, the cynical twist to his lips before his customary impassivity returned.

'I see.'

'I find you more than acceptable, Joss,' Mrs Wren purred. 'I have already offered to buy up Lady Juliana's debt.'

Amy saw Joss's eyes narrow on her. She could read a definite challenge in them now. 'Thank you, Emma,' he said, his gaze never leaving Amy's face, 'but Miss Bainbridge has the prior claim. I regret, ma'am—' his bow to Amy was immaculate '—that you cannot decline my sister's offer. As it is a debt of honour you would give offence in the refusal...'

The chatter in the room died to silence.

'Debt of honour. Absolutely,' Richard Bainbridge said. 'You *are* honouring Lady Juliana's pledge then, Joss?'

'Absolutely,' Joss repeated, still refusing to take his gaze from Amy. She felt as though she was burning beneath it. 'It is my pleasure.'

Richard turned to his sister. 'Amy, I do not believe that you can refuse...'

Amy looked from him to Joss Tallant and back again. 'I see. Lady Juliana, your offer is accepted.'

Lady Juliana gave a crow of triumph. There were catcalls and lewd jokes that made Amy's cheeks burn.

'That little girl will learn enough in a week to fit her for Abbess Walsh's whorehouse!' she heard Juliana say to Clive Massingham in an undertone.

She stumbled to her feet, shaking Joss off when he put one hand on her arm to steady her. Her eyes were bright with unshed tears. She had gambled and won, and in the process she had betrayed her principles and made a fool of herself into the bargain. As for Joss... Amy cast him one searing glance as she hurried from the room. If she had made a fool of herself, he had connived at it. She would not forgive her own folly and she certainly would not forgive him.

Amy was barely in the carriage before she turned on her brother and all her pent-up feelings from the gambling session came pouring forth.

'How you could have let me do such a thing, Richard! I must have been mad! It was quite dreadful! Oh! For you to stand by when Lady Juliana made that monstrous wager—'

Richard raised a placatory hand. 'Amy, I don't know why you are making such a fuss! Juliana Myfleet was only joking and Joss decided to call her bluff. I have no doubt that you will have the money tomorrow rather than Joss himself.'

'Well, if that is the Earl of Tallant's idea of a joke, I do not want to be the butt of it.' Amy shivered and drew her cloak closer. 'Your friends and their exploits are too sophisticated for me, Richard!'

'You may be right,' Richard said unexpectedly. 'You should never have been playing cards with Lady Juliana, Amy, not an unmarried girl like you! Now if you were married of course, it would be different—'

'Which just goes to show how foolish society can be,' Amy said crossly. 'If I was married it would not make a jot of difference.'

'Except that you would have understood more of the jokes,' Richard said.

'I would still have no wish to gamble,' Amy said mulishly. 'It was the most dreadful experience.'

Richard shrugged. 'No one forced you to do it, Amy! Could've knocked me down with a feather when I saw you at the table! After all your high-flown sentiments…'

Amy shuddered. She felt sick and empty now, to think of what she had done. 'Richard, do not! I cannot bear it! It was so foolish of me—I wanted to show that odious Mrs Wren that she could not slight Papa and expect me to accept it so meekly! So I gave in to an impulse to play—' She broke off.

'And found that gambling fever can lurk in the blood of even the most innocent!' Richard finished, with a grin. 'And to think that I believed you were only there to oblige Amanda Spry!'

'I was originally!' Amy frowned. 'And that is another thing. Amanda vanished into thin air and left me to my fate! Oh, of all the miserable things for a friend to do.'

Richard shook his head. 'Seems to me that you are trying to blame everyone but yourself!' he said acutely.

'Besides, you won! I confess that I do not understand you, Amy—'

'Nor I you.' Amy huddled back against the seat. 'What a dreadful evening. I cannot understand how anyone can enjoy gaming. It makes me feel sick in the stomach.'

'Maybe you feel sick because you are shocked that you enjoyed yourself,' Richard said, with the same uncomfortable percipience. 'And before you deny it, Amy, think a little! Even if you did not enjoy the game itself, you liked administering a set-down to Mrs Wren. You enjoyed the winning!'

Amy did not contradict him. She stared out at the darkened streets. 'What a disastrous evening. And now I apparently have the Earl of Tallant for a week into the bargain, and I have no idea what to do with him!'

Chapter Eight

The morning following the ball was another glorious May day, but Amy awoke with a headache and a feeling that there was something very wrong. She rolled over in bed, opened her eyes, and immediately remembered her win at cards the previous night. A mixture of disbelief and guilt hit her hard, tempered by a very faint, stubborn pride. It was lowering to find that she had compromised her principles, that she was not immune to the lure of gambling. On the other hand she had no intention of playing again and so should just put the matter behind her. Except…except that there was the problem of the payment of the wager…

Amy got up and dressed slowly, going downstairs to breakfast late and alone. Lady Bainbridge had not risen and was no doubt still recovering from her migraine. Richard had mentioned going to White's the previous night and had probably not returned. It was bright and warm in the dining room, but Amy's spirits did not reflect the day. If Joss chose to come in person to pay the debt… But he would not. Amy was sure that Richard had been right and that she would receive the money that morning and that would be the end to it. She devoutly hoped that she was right.

Amy stirred some curd into her stewed apple and reflected that she must make sure that the household budget was increased immediately so that they actually had something appetising to eat for breakfast. That would mean supplementing their income from the thirty thousand pounds, of course, but since no one had claimed the money…

She stared at her reflection in the spoon's uneven surface. She had always been intrigued as to why it appeared upside down. Not that she would look much better the right way up. If she was about to spend her lottery winnings, then it could be argued that the most needy cause was still her appearance. She had bought several dresses now but she was aware that what she really needed was an entirely new wardrobe. Yet her heart was not in it. Looking good in the way that Amanda always did, for example, seemed unconscionably time-consuming. It was also expensive and she had already spent what seemed like an inordinate amount of money on the new carriage. What she really wanted to do was to give serious thought to her charitable causes. There were so many deserving cases.

Amy wrinkled up her nose as she tried to think of them. Climbing boys and street women and the people who had been rescued from drowning in the Thames and orphans and widows… Really, thirty thousand pounds was nothing when confronted with such a need for charity. She did not know where to start.

Feeling slightly better at the thought of some benevolent activity, Amy got to her feet. She had almost reached the dining room door when it opened and Patience, her face as disapproving as the sole of an old boot, stuck her head around.

'The Earl of Tallant is here to see you, Miss Amy. I have put him in the parlour. He says his business is most urgent.'

Amy jumped. Until now she had just about managed to keep at bay any thought of the outrageous wager that Lady Juliana had made. Now, however, she was forced to confront it and the prospect was not pleasant. She realised that she had been hoping that Joss would not honour the bet. The thought of seeing him again, and in such circumstances, was painful to her.

Her footsteps were slow as she crossed the tiny hall to the parlour door. She tried to console herself by thinking that Joss had only come to pay the money and explain that it was all a joke. She paused outside the door and brushed her old cambric dress down with a defiant gesture. She would take the money, of course—she could not really refuse a debt of honour—and then she would send him away with a flea in his ear for making her the object of a joke between himself and his sister. They might think that it was funny. She did not.

Nevertheless, she felt more than a little apprehensive as she opened the parlour door. Joss was standing by the window and the pristine austerity of his black coat and buff pantaloons made the small room seem even shabbier to Amy's eyes. This made her want to dislike him all the more but in this she failed miserably. He looked as elegant as ever—elegant enough to make her pulse race. She cleared her throat.

'Good morning, Lord Tallant.'

Joss bowed. 'Good morning, Miss Bainbridge. I apologise if I have disturbed you by arriving at this hour, but I did not wish to seem tardy.'

Amy frowned slightly. 'It is very early to call, but I assume… That is…' She realised she was making rather a hash of this and started again, somewhat bluntly.

'Have you come to settle Lady Juliana's debt, my lord?'

Joss smiled. 'Certainly I have, Miss Bainbridge. Did you think I would renege?'

Amy looked away from the mockery in his eyes. 'Oh, no, indeed. Of course not!'

'Good. For here I am at your service, Miss Bainbridge.' Joss bowed again. 'So, what are you going to do with me?'

Amy sat down rather quickly in one of the armchairs. 'Oh, but surely…I thought that you meant simply to pay? You cannot intend…to honour your sister's bet by…um…pledging yourself to my company for an entire week?'

Joss frowned. 'Certainly I intend it. You cannot know much about me, Miss Bainbridge, if you think I would fail to honour such a debt.'

'It was not your integrity I was questioning, but the nature of the payment,' Amy said, rubbing her hand across her forehead. The headache, lurking during breakfast, had returned with a vengeance. 'It seems so much easier to pay the two hundred guineas and have done with it.'

'May I?' Joss indicated the other chair and sat down. 'Well, of course it would be easier to pay, but I confess to a certain curiosity to spend a week in your company, Miss Bainbridge.' His gaze dwelt on her indignant face and he smiled a little. 'It might prove rather more amusing than merely handing over the money.'

'I am not an entertainment!' Amy said sharply. 'Nor do I consider this joke to be remotely amusing, my lord!' She fidgeted crossly with the frayed material on the arm of the chair, unravelling it even more. 'The next time that you and your sister design such a trick I beg that you will find an alternative dupe. I have no desire to provide you with diversion! Upon my word, you must be very bored to indulge in such behaviour!'

Joss laughed. 'I assure you this is no diversion, Miss Bainbridge, nor did Juliana and I design it for our amusement. She lost a bet to you. I am here to pay her debt because I wish to do so. That is all.'

Amy looked at him defiantly. 'Then you may go away again, my lord! The bet is cancelled. You do but waste your time here.'

Joss sat back in his chair. 'That seems a shame, Miss Bainbridge. Do you have no wish to spend a week in my company?'

'Certainly not!' Amy glared at him. The emotions inside her—a tumble of dread, nervousness and an edgy excitement—were not to be discussed with him. 'You are the last man I would wish—' She broke off, aware that she was about to be unpardonably rude. She took a deep breath. 'This is a foolish nonsense. I thank you for honouring your sister's pledge, my lord, but now I must ask you to go.'

Joss showed little sign of doing so. 'I am disappointed that I am not acceptable to you as a companion, Miss Bainbridge. In order to help me improve, perhaps you could give me a little advice. What is it about me that is particularly…inappropriate?'

Amy looked at him suspiciously. She was certain that this was just another way for him to amuse himself at her expense.

'I cannot believe you in earnest, my lord, but as you have asked... We have no interests in common and I am sure we should be bored with each other's company within an hour!'

Joss glanced at the clock. 'Let us put that to the test, Miss Bainbridge. If in an hour's time you find me tedious beyond bearing, then I shall go without further complaint. What do you say?'

Amy looked a little shamefaced. 'You make me sound very ungracious,' she said. 'All that I meant was that I feared we should have little to talk about.'

'Let us see, then.' Joss settled back. 'What do you imagine my interests to be, Miss Bainbridge?' He eyed her telltale blush with amusement. 'Dear me, are they all so shocking?'

'Yes...no!' Amy was thrown into confusion. 'I do not know, my lord.'

'But you must know, for you made a judgement that we had nothing in common. Take gambling, for instance, which I know you consider my chief pursuit. You were gambling last night, or we would not be sitting here. Therefore it must be something that we have in common.'

Amy looked at him. 'I thought you seemed a little surprised when you saw me in the card room.'

'I was. On the basis of our previous conversations I should say it was the last place that I would have expected to find you.'

Amy felt a little confused. 'Oh, I was only gambling last night because...' She hesitated. 'Amanda persuaded me to play a hand of whist and then Lady Juliana suggested vingt-et-un...' She met his gaze a little defiantly. 'I have to confess to all the wrong motives, I fear, my lord. Mrs Wren provoked me and I let my anger overcome my scruples. I was once quite good at vingt-et-un, you see, and I wanted to show her…' She hung her head. 'It does not reflect well on me, I know!'

Joss looked amused. 'You played for revenge, Miss Bainbridge? I would never have thought it of you!' He gave her a quizzical look. 'And did you get drawn in by the lure of the game? You did, didn't you! Admit it! The excitement of the cards is a fever in the blood—'

'I most certainly did not!' Amy said virtuously and untruthfully.

'So, how comes it that you were playing for doubling stakes, Miss Bainbridge?'

Amy bit her lip. 'I am not entirely sure,' she said. 'Someone suggested it and then I found myself swept along with the game… I kept imagining that I would be out in the next round, you see, but I had some luck and ended up winning.'

'Just like a country squire who finds himself winning at White's for the first time,' Joss said drily. 'Did it not go to your head, Miss Bainbridge? Were you not tempted to carry on playing and see where your beginner's luck might take you?'

'No, indeed,' Amy said feelingly, 'for I soon felt quite sick at the thought of what I was doing! That must be where I differ from the likes of Sir Humphrey, I suppose. I have no urge to try my luck further.' She looked him straight in the eye. 'Yet I do understand how an innocent might be lured into thinking that they might win and win…or, if they lose, that they only need gamble again to recoup their losses. There are always unscrupulous people leading them on.'

Joss shifted in his chair. 'Is that aimed at me, Miss Bainbridge?'

Amy shrugged. 'If the cap fits, my lord…'

'Well, it does not. It was your brother who put Sir Humphrey up for membership of White's, for example. You may acquit me of deliberately leading any man into gambling just so that I may fleece him. I am not so unscrupulous.'

Their gazes met and held, Joss's challenging, Amy's very straight. After a moment she said, 'I accept what you say, my lord, but at the very least it confirms that this is a topic which we do not have in common.'

'On the contrary, we may not see eye to eye but we have been enjoying a stimulating discussion for the past fifteen minutes! One need not always agree on a subject, you know. Sometimes it is more interesting not to do so!'

Amy smiled. 'I will concede that, but it does not make it a common interest.'

'True. So what else is there?'

Amy blushed. 'I do not know.'

Joss eyed her closely. 'Ah, I see that you are remembering I told you I was a rake and you are thinking that it must keep me quite occupied! That, alas, is probably not a topic for further discussion between us, at least not yet.'

Amy blushed crossly. 'I did not need you to tell me! Everyone speaks of it.'

Joss stretched. 'Now that *is* an interesting topic. Reputations. Why should we believe that everything we are told is true? That is tantamount to believing gossip!'

Amy frowned. 'In this case it is presumably true since you confirmed it yourself!'

'Yes, of course. But the wider discussion would be interesting. I am told that Miss Bainbridge is a reserved lady with scarcely a word to say for herself, yet I have found that manifestly untrue. You appreciate my example?'

'Of course,' Amy said, trying not to feel even the tiniest bit flattered by his words. 'This is nothing to the purpose, my lord. We were trying to establish that we had nothing in common.'

'You were trying to do that, I was not. I was looking for common ground. What else do you know of me?'

'You are a noted whip.'

'And do you enjoy driving?'

'Yes,' Amy said, incurably truthful, but feeling the ground opening up at her feet as she saw where this was going, 'although I have little opportunity.'

'Capital! Then I may take you driving in the park. That will wile away a few hours.'

'A few hours of what?'

'A few hours of our week together. But the time is not yet up. Are you bored, yet?'

'No,' Amy admitted, feeling the trap yawning wider, 'but...'

'But? Do you have some other objection to my company?'

'No...' Amy was struggling. She did indeed object, but she could not tell him why. It was not that she disliked Joss's company—the reverse was true, though she was at a loss to explain why. He should have been exactly the sort of man she disliked and despised, but oddly she found herself drawn to him. It made her most uncomfortable and it was the last thing that she wished to admit to him.

'I am encouraged that we have found at least one thing in common,' Joss continued. 'Perhaps we should make a list of all the activities we might indulge in together?'

Amy stared. 'A list?'

'You are familiar with the concept?'

'Yes, of course…' Amy made countless lists to help her manage her household duties.

'Or perhaps you feel there will not be sufficient items to put on the list?'

'It is not that.' Amy looked at him in reluctant fascination. 'It is simply that I cannot imagine you as a list maker, my lord. The idea seems absurd.'

'Why so? I assure you it is most useful. How could I possibly remember otherwise which gambling den to visit in which order, or which young lady I am reputed to have seduced?'

'Now you are funning me,' Amy said, shamefaced, 'and it is too bad of you.' She got up and went over to her walnut bureau, extracting her writing box. 'Very well, let us start.'

Half an hour later, Amy had ordered a pot of tea and cake for them and they had still not finished. The time had elapsed because the list was by no means without controversy.

'Driving in the park, or possibly riding,' she read out. 'Balls, parties, soirées and other social events.' She put the paper down. 'I am still not certain whether I wish to accept your escort to these events, my lord. Quite apart from my dislike of balls, there is the talk that would be consequent upon such action—'

'My dear Miss Bainbridge…' Joss made a slight gesture '…I thought that we had agreed that neither of us paid any regard to that sort of gossip?'

'Yes, but Mama will have a fit if I accept your escort to a ball!' Amy could not help giggling. 'Oh dear, it is not funny! Whilst I have no time for gossip, it is foolish to be careless of one's reputation!'

'Agreed, but we shall be behaving with perfect propriety.' Joss fixed her with a look. 'At the very least, agree to attending Lady Carteret's ball with me tomorrow night. Then, if you do not enjoy it, we shall attend no others.'

'Oh, very well.' Amy sighed and consulted her list again. 'Attend the exhibition at the Royal Academy. I confess that might be of interest. Attend the meeting of the Bettering Society.' She cast Joss a doubtful look. 'I cannot believe you will find that enjoyable, my lord.'

'Ah, but think how improving it will be for me, Miss Bainbridge!'

Amy frowned. 'I do wish you would not jest all the time. It is not for me to try to improve you.'

'Yet you currently *disapprove* of me.'

'Yes, well...you are dreadfully bad, but that is your choice.'

Joss grinned. 'How delightful you are, Miss Bainbridge! There will be no Spanish coin from you!'

Amy frowned. 'Coin! Oh, that reminds me! I have yet to decide what to do with my lottery winnings. I was puzzling over it when you arrived, my lord. There are so many good causes that I can scarce think which to address first. It is most perplexing. Perhaps *that* is a topic on which you might help me?'

Joss raised an eyebrow. 'You have decided to keep your winnings, then?'

'Well, as I cannot find the rightful owner of the lottery money, all I can think of is to give it away. Yet it is not that simple. I wish to weigh up the rival merits of the different charities and see which is most needy, but...' Amy wrinkled her nose up '...I do not have sufficient information.'

'Perhaps the Bettering Society might be the place to start? Or the Royal Humane Society? There must be plenty of people there who could advise you. Wait until after the meeting tomorrow. I am certain that we shall find you a good cause.'

Amy looked at him dubiously. 'Do you really intend to accompany me, my lord?'

'Yes, I do.' Joss smiled encouragingly. 'I know you will probably be ashamed to be seen with me, Miss Bainbridge, but please consider it an act of charity!'

Amy gave him a reproachful look. 'I asked you not to tease! Do you not think you will be hopelessly bored?'

'Not at all. I am certain that I will learn something new. Which reminds me—' Joss checked the clock '—are you bored now, Miss Bainbridge? We have been talking for almost two hours and we did agree that I would relieve you of my presence if you found it tedious.'

Amy avoided his gaze. 'I must confess...I am not bored, precisely...' She looked up to see Joss smiling at her in a way that made her feel very warm inside. She picked up her list and read an item almost at random.

'Attend a masquerade at Vauxhall Gardens—I do believe that you have added that one when I was not looking, my lord! How dreadfully improper!'

Joss twitched the list from her fingers. 'I admit it. I added it and it is quite improper but who knows you may find that you would like to attend? In fact, it may be that this week will be an education for both of us, Miss Bainbridge!'

* * *

'So what happened next?' Amanda enquired. She drew her friend's arm through her own as they strolled along the path in St James's Park. It was late afternoon and they had been shopping in Bond Street with Lady Bainbridge. Lady Bainbridge had declared herself fatigued by all the excitement and had gone home, but Amy and Amanda had wished to see how the preparations for the Regent's victory fête were progressing.

Amy giggled. 'After that I told him that I did not require his attendance for the rest of today as I would be going shopping with you and Mama. Do you know, Amanda, Lord Tallant even offered to accompany me to Bond Street, saying that he was quite an expert on the subject of female dress! Can you imagine the fuss that that would have caused?'

'I can,' Amanda said drily, 'and I do believe Lord Tallant told nothing but the truth. He is indeed a connoisseur of female charms!'

Amy blushed self-consciously. 'Oh, I know! I realise that he is the most dreadful rake! But our activities this week are going to be quite blameless, Amanda. Why, Lord Tallant is escorting me to a concert by the Charity Children of Westminster tonight. Mama and Richard will be there as well, so it is all quite innocent!'

Amanda raised her brows. 'Lord Tallant at a charity concert? Good God!'

'Yes, indeed, and tomorrow we go to a lecture at the Royal Humane Society! I have it in mind to give them a large donation from my winnings. So you see, Amanda, there is nothing scandalous about what we are doing!'

'Only the giving away of large sums of money,' Amanda said feelingly. 'That is quite disgraceful, Amy!'

Amy blushed. Although she had made up her mind to give most of the money to charities and she was quite determined to go through with it, the combined disappointment and disapproval of her family and Amanda was difficult to bear. Only Joss Tallant had not condemned her decision.

'You are aware that people will talk anyway if they see Lord Tallant dancing attendance on you?' Amanda was saying now, with a speculative glance at Amy's face. 'He never pays attention to any respectable female unless he wishes to seduce her! People will be saying that he has ruined you through this so-called debt of honour.'

Amy had already thought of this and some imp of obstinacy had refused to let it spoil her plans. Now that she had been persuaded to accept Joss's company, she was not going to be so poor-spirited as to be put off by a little gossip.

'I dare say people will talk scandal. There will be little for them to talk about, however, and what little there is will not be interesting. Oh, look—is that not a Chinese temple that they are building over there? The Prince's creations always have a grand design!'

They fell to discussing the victory celebrations.

'I did not tell you before,' Amanda said, 'but one of the reasons I came up from the country was to see all the victory festivities! I was last up in town in April for the visit of King Louis XVIII—I was in Piccadilly when the procession drove past, you know!' Her face fell a little. 'It was a sad disappointment, for the King is old and lame and the crowds were quite uninterested! I glimpsed the Duchess of Oldenburg as well, you know—she is a terrible fright and they say that the Regent and she took an instant dislike to each other!'

Amy herself read the newspapers when Richard took them, and so was quite aware of the visit to London of a whole bevy of princes and generals following the victory of the Allies in Europe. Unlike Amanda, however, she was quite indifferent to the phalanx of visitors. She knew that the Bainbridges were too unfashionable to receive invitations to any of the Prince Regent's private celebratory entertainments and had no wish to be crushed by the crowds who would wait for up to a whole day simply to see the famous pass by.

'I am quite beside myself at the prospect of seeing the King of Prussia,' Amanda continued. 'Czar Alexander will be visiting next month as well and he is reputed a vastly handsome man! I wonder if the Duke of Fleet could procure me an invitation to one of the Regent's dinners? He is an intimate of the Prince, after all. It is such a shame that half the fashionable world seems to have gone to Paris!'

Amy smoothed down her gloves. They were new and had flowers embroidered on the back and were really very pretty. She was beginning to feel almost part of the fashionable world herself. The Bond Street purchases, lavish as they had been, had not made a huge dent in the thirty thousand pounds. Amy reassured herself that there was still plenty left for her chosen charities.

''Tis a shame my aunt does not own a house along the Czar's procession route for I heard tell that people were asking fifty guineas to rent a window along the way!' Amanda said. 'Still, we may admire the preparations for the fête, I suppose! Look over there, Amy—they are building a Chinese bridge across the lake and a pergola and all manner of follies! The Prince is mad about Oriental fashions, you know, and so very extravagant, but I imagine it will be a magnificent party!'

Amy followed Amanda's pointing finger in the direction of the preparations, but rather than concentrating on the progress of the Prince's building work, her attention was caught by four gentlemen who were strolling towards them. She stiffened.

'Amanda, look! It is Richard—and the Duke of Fleet and the Earl of Tallant and Lord Parrish! Now what are we going to do?'

Amanda drew her breath in sharply. 'Oh dear, I do so hate having to cut anyone of my acquaintance dead! And especially your brother, my dear, let alone the Duke of Fleet. This is most delicate…'

It was not the gentlemen themselves who were the problem but the fact that each had his arm entwined about the waist of a personable young female. Amy stared—and felt herself blush. A strange feeling swept over her and a lump seemed to wedge itself in her chest, hard and hot and painful, as she watched Joss Tallant with his mistress.

'Ladybirds!' she said, in a stifled voice. 'Mama would have forty fits if she knew Richard was parading his *chère amie* in the park in the afternoon!'

'Lucky that Lady Bainbridge did not choose to walk with us this afternoon,' Amanda said, ever practical. 'A female's nothing but a fool if she expects men to be other than the way they are!' For a second there was a hint of bitterness in her tone that made Amy glance at her curiously, but then it was gone, leaving Amy wondering. She had thought Amanda's marriage had not been happy. Perhaps the late Lord Spry, whom Amy had met only once or twice, had been another such, who paraded his conquests with scant regard for his wife.

Her gaze was drawn back to the lady on Joss Tallant's arm and she gave a little, unconscious sigh. So this was how the Earl of Tallant spent his time when he was not attending upon her! Suddenly her lavender gown did not feel so stylish and Amy herself felt decidedly cross-grained. She and Joss had spent such a pleasant morning discussing their plans for the week, yet now he had obviously returned to his preferred entertainments. Amy, who had been at a loss to understand why he would wish to spend any time with her at charity lectures and visits, felt strangely humiliated. Her envious eyes took in every detail of the fashionable impure who graced Joss's arm. She struggled hard to overcome her ill temper, but was only partially successful.

'The…er…ladies are prodigiously pretty, are they not, Amanda? One can see the attraction!'

'The one with the Earl is Harriet Templeton,' Amanda said, lowering her parasol to conceal the fact that she was watching. 'She used to be an opera dancer, by all accounts, and now she has a part share in a very exclusive club in Covent Garden! But that is enough of this salacious gossip! Your Mama would be disgusted with me, discussing such matters with an unmarried lady!'

'I am no débutante,' Amy said, trying to sound cool, 'and I think I may stand the shock of knowing that such ladies exist! The question is—what are we to do?' The group was still strolling towards them and suddenly Amy felt a little panicky. Was she to ignore her own brother because of the company he kept? She had no idea how to deal with the situation. Yet it was on Joss Tallant rather than Richard that her gaze was still fixed and when Joss turned his head and looked at her, as though drawn by her scrutiny, she did not look away, and neither did he.

Amy was not sure what she had been expecting—that Joss would deliberately turn away to spare her embarrassment perhaps, or even that he might appear slightly abashed to have been caught in such a situation. Instead, he held her gaze with a steady regard that contained just the slightest hint of amusement and more than a little challenge. Amy's chin came up and she gave him back look for look. She saw his smile deepen and the hot, angry feeling inside her welled up and threatened to spill over. Then she turned away, finding it quite easy to cut him dead after all.

Amanda took her arm and led her down a little path off to the left, and in a moment the danger was past and the gentlemen and their ladies, laughing and chattering, had passed on by. Amy was shocked and a little breathless to find that she was trembling.

'Whatever was that all that about, Amy?' For once Amanda's voice had lost its light tone. 'I hope you are not developing a *tendre* for the Earl of Tallant! I was worried about it as soon as I heard about this foolish debt! Lud, he is the last man on earth for an innocent miss to tangle with!'

'I assure you that there is no such danger,' Amy protested, trying to quell her shaking. 'I barely know the man and what I do know of him does not dispose me to like him!'

'Gracious, what has liking to do with anything? One can look once and...' Amanda shrugged airily. 'What I cannot understand is that *he* was staring at *you*!' Her gaze skimmed her friend thoughtfully and Amy could not help but laugh.

'I know! You are wondering what a man like the Earl

of Tallant, with the beautiful Miss Templeton hanging on his arm, could possibly see in me!' she said, with a hint of bitterness. 'Well, Amanda, I beg you not to trouble yourself. I am persuaded that you are making too much of this. The Earl has no romantic interest in me and I...do not think of him in that way at all!'

Her friend looked unconvinced. 'Yet you will be much in his company during this week—'

'And the rest of the time he will be following his own inclinations,' Amy said lightly, 'as we have just seen.' She took a deep breath to steady herself. It seemed ridiculous, but seeing Joss Tallant like that had, just for a second, felt like a betrayal. Amy had enjoyed his company that morning but now she felt disappointed and resentful. She knew it was ridiculous, for she had no claim to him, but it felt suspiciously as though she was about to cry. It felt loweringly as though she was jealous...

She stole a look at Amanda's face. Her friend did not seem much happier to have witnessed the Duke of Fleet with his *chère amie*. She gave Amanda's arm a little shake.

'Shall we take some tea at the rotunda? I have had quite enough of gawping at the sights for one day!'

Amanda smiled a little sadly. 'A good idea, Amy. There is nothing so reviving to the spirits as a hot cup of tea!'

Chapter Nine

'Did you enjoy the lecture, Miss Bainbridge?' Joss asked, as he tooled his curricle through the park the following afternoon. It was a cooler day, grey with a chilly edge to the breeze, so the crowds were fewer and Amy had been obliged to wrap up warmly in her new pelisse. They had been to a lecture given by Dr Thomas Hardiment, a notable fundraiser, at the Royal Humane Society and afterwards Amy had resolved to donate a large sum for the funding of the Society's work. She intended to speak to Mr Churchward about it the following morning. She sighed. There was something very worthy about charitable giving, of course, but the lecture had been dry and a little depressing.

'I am sure that Dr Hardiment does a marvellous job,' she said now, in answer to Joss's question, 'but for my part I found his lecture a little tedious. All those graphic descriptions of resuscitation, for example! Perhaps the fault is in me for being so squeamish, but I did not care to know the detail.'

'The good doctor is certainly fond of his subject,' Joss said with a grin, 'but I fear that not everyone has your delicacy, Miss Bainbridge. I do believe that there are plenty of people who relish the grisly details of illness and death!'

'The same people who would enjoy a public hanging, I suppose,' Amy said ruefully. 'Oh, I dare say I am too nice in my opinions and the Society does a great deal of good work.' She turned to look at him. 'I do hope, my lord, that you do not feel you are suffering from an excess of charity? Remember that it was your idea to accompany me!'

Joss shot her a grin. 'My dear Miss Bainbridge, I beg you not to concern yourself! I found the Westminster Orphans' School concert to be most entertaining last night! Some of the children could sing very sweetly; as for that angelic child who played the harp—I am persuaded that the orphanage would not give her up even if twenty people offered her a good home, for she is far too talented for them to lose!'

Amy frowned at him. 'Upon my word, you are a dreadful cynic, sir!'

'You know that I am right. Charity is a business as much as any other.'

Amy looked troubled. 'I do not like to think of it in that way, my lord. There is no question that the likes of Dr Hardiment do a most useful job—'

'Oh, indeed, I would not dispute that. But it is also their task to raise funds and promote their work. There is no harm in it. Someone needs to persuade the idle rich to part with their money to help the deserving poor!'

Amy frowned all the harder. In some ways she hated to hear Joss speak like this and yet there was an uncomfortable truth somewhere in what he was saying.

'Do you think, then, that a great many people make donations to salve their consciences?' she asked.

'Assuredly. It makes them feel as though they are doing some good.' Joss turned and looked at her. 'They *are* doing good, Miss Bainbridge. So everyone wins.'

'Yet it feels more satisfying to actually do something to help, does it not?' Amy sighed. 'Something active, I mean.'

Joss smiled at her. 'Which is why you pay visits to the old and sick as well as giving so generously to the work of the Society. You are a positive paragon, Miss Bainbridge!'

'Oh, do stop teasing!' Amy looked at him. 'I suppose that you do nothing useful with your time, my lord?'

'You suppose correctly. Nothing other than entertaining myself. That seems useful enough to me.'

Amy shut her lips in a tight line. It was at moments like this that Joss irritated her almost beyond reason for she was certain that the flippant exterior hid something deeper. She had been willing him to tell her that she was wrong and to recite a whole list of the useful causes in which he was involved. Yet she knew that he would not. Joss had always been quite open about his selfish lifestyle and just because in some irrational way she wanted him to be a better person, it did not make him so.

'Would you like to hear about my activities, Miss Bainbridge?' Joss was saying now. 'I drink and play cards excessively, I read the newspapers, attend the races, go to balls and routs, visit my friends, drive in the park and, of course, do other unmentionable things as well! That is my idea of gainful employment!'

Amy refused to reply. She knew he was trying to provoke her and she was well aware of his unmentionable activities. The incident in the park the previous afternoon had remained unspoken between them, as though it had never happened. When Joss had arrived in Curzon Street to accompany the Bainbridges to the charity concert Amy had been careful not to enquire into his afternoon's activities, but the memory of Harriet Templeton hanging on his arm still made her feel sore and scratchy.

'I assume, then, that you did not enjoy the lecture,' she said crossly. 'Perhaps Dr Hardiment's words left you quite cold?'

'It is the manner of these philanthropists that offends me, rather than their message,' Joss said, with a lop-sided smile. 'I fear that their paternalistic attitudes remind me rather too strongly of my father. They always appear to think that they know what is best for everyone.'

Despite herself, Amy's attention was caught. It was the first time that Joss had ever referred to his family. 'Is the Marquis very dictatorial? He never comes up to London, does he?'

'No, never. He prefers the country. And to disapprove of me from a distance, of course. It is the way with fathers, I suppose.'

'Dear me.' Amy tucked back the tendrils of hair that were being tugged from her bonnet by the wind. 'No doubt you give him plenty of which to disapprove.'

'I do. As does Juliana. It is difficult to know which of us is more of a disappointment to him.'

There was no hint of expression in Joss's voice but for some reason Amy was sure that he was more upset than he showed. She looked at him thoughtfully. 'Does that not…distress you?'

'To be estranged from my father?' Joss flashed her a smile. 'Not really. He cannot disinherit me. He could cut off my allowance, I suppose, but that would reflect badly on the family honour…'

'I was thinking along personal rather than mercenary lines,' Amy persisted. For all Joss's flippancy, there was some other feeling there. 'Would you not prefer that there should be some affection between the two of you?'

Joss raised a cynical eyebrow. 'My dear Miss Bainbridge, what an extraordinary idea! I believe that there was once some affection between my parents and look where that got them!'

'I see.' Amy thought that she understood. She remembered that the Marchioness of Tallant had decamped many years ago with one of her lovers, leaving her children behind in the care of their unbending father. 'Is your mother still alive?'

'I believe so. I have not heard otherwise.' Joss's tone was careless. 'She has lived in Italy these twenty years past and I lost count of the string of her lovers. Meanwhile, my father and I only speak when he wishes to upbraid me or to try to persuade me into marriage.'

'That sounds melancholy. Have you no wish to oblige him?'

Joss shot her a look. 'Not in that, no. A love match is out of the question and to marry for convenience seems equally empty to me, although I expect I shall bring myself to the point one day.'

Amy shivered in the spiteful little breeze. It seemed a very grey day indeed. 'I remember you telling me before that you thought romantic love to be sentimental. Just because your parents were unhappy does not mean—' She broke off, unhappily aware that she was in no position to preach. She had no experience to draw on. Her father had undoubtedly made her mother unhappy, but in a different way, yet, despite that, the love between Sir George and Lady Bainbridge had never been in question.

'I agree that it would be foolish of me to dismiss the idea out of hand simply because my parents were unhappy.' Joss had slowed the horses and his voice slowed as well. 'I am not so shallow, Miss Bainbridge, for all that I might seem so. Even so, you cannot be surprised that it might make a man wary. To me, the idea of finding happiness in marriage seems as remote as flying to the stars. Yet I am not so much of a cynic to deny that others have found it. Even my sister at one time seemed exceptionally happy with her husband...'

Amy wrinkled up her face. His words were bleak but he was right—they lacked his customary ring of cynicism. He did not deny the existence of love, only doubted that he would find it. That seemed sadder in a way.

'Do you know, Miss Bainbridge,' Joss said slowly, 'my parents both gave me the same piece of advice on the same day? It was the day my mother left and I remember it well, for all that I was only seven years old. My father told me that love was for fools. My mother said the same. I suppose I took it to heart.' He looked at Amy and she saw that there was a strange, dazed look in his eyes before he blinked and it was gone. 'Good God,' he said in tones of deep disgust, 'I cannot believe I have become so mawkish! I never told anyone that before. It must be all these charitable thoughts that have unmanned me!'

They drove for a little in silence.

'Did you never wish to marry, Miss Bainbridge?' Joss's voice was his own again, cool and a little hard. 'It is surely the ultimate aim of every young lady?'

'Of most, I suppose,' Amy conceded. A dimple touched her cheek as she smiled. 'Unfortunately no one has asked me, my lord—apart from Mr Hallam, of course! But, yes, when I was younger I wanted to marry. I was quite desperate to find a husband! I thought that would give me a settled home.'

'Your father's changing fortunes must have been most disturbing,' Joss said. His voice had softened a little. 'I can see that a quieter existence might prove attractive.'

'Oh, yes! I was mortified that I had moved about so often, you see. Governesses never stayed for long—we could not afford them—and I went to so many seminaries for young ladies that I do believe I could write a guidebook! My education was somewhat neglected as a result and I did not have the chance to learn all the ladylike accomplishments. I never learned to play the piano, for example, as I had nowhere to practice. So when I failed to attach a husband I was convinced that this must be the reason!'

Joss laughed. 'If you ascribed it to a lack of discernment on the part of the gentlemen, Miss Bainbridge, you would be closer to the truth.'

Amy smiled. 'Thank you. That is a very pretty compliment, sir. However, it does not matter now, for I am a lady of independent means and have achieved the security I craved! To my mind that is much better!'

'There might be other reasons for marriage,' Joss observed, after a moment. 'The society, the companionship, the shared interests. It is sometimes lonely being on one's own.'

'That may be true,' Amy said, 'though it surprises me to hear you say so, my lord!'

They had reached Curzon Street and now Joss helped

Amy to alight, swinging her down from the phaeton in a manner that never failed to take her breath away.

'I will see you tonight at Lady Carteret's ball, Miss Bainbridge, but what do we do tomorrow?'

Amy hesitated. She had planned to go to Whitechapel the following day, to take a hamper of food and children's clothes to Mrs Wendover and to visit the School for Ragged Children. She had already decided that it would not do to ask Joss to escort her. That would entail an explanation of her connection with the Wendover family; besides, it was one thing to accept a gentleman's escort to the Royal Humane Society and quite another to drive to Whitechapel alone with him. She tried to imagine Joss leaving his elegant phaeton outside Mrs Wendover's lodging house and was almost betrayed into a giggle. It would be minus its wheels in five minutes—unless, of course, Joss bribed an entire gang of street children to guard it.

'I am not sure,' she said, hastily composing her face. 'I do believe that I shall visit a friend in the morning, and perhaps we could go to the Royal Academy in the afternoon?'

'That sounds most pleasant,' Joss said, taking her hand. His perceptive gaze scanned her face. 'I do believe though that you are keeping something from me, Miss Bainbridge! Who is this mysterious friend that you do not wish me to meet?'

'Oh...' Amy felt herself blushing and pulled her hand away. 'It is...an old school friend who lives in reduced circumstances, my lord. I would not wish to overwhelm her with too many visitors!'

'Very thoughtful of you! It is not that you are ashamed of me, reprobate that I am?'

Amy stared. 'What an absurd idea, my lord! It is

simply...I only thought...' She hesitated on the brink of disclosure. It would be the utmost folly to confide the truth in Joss, for he could not be anything other than shocked to know that she had once lived in a lodging house in a Whitechapel rookery. She turned away.

'As I said, my lord, my friend has very limited means and I would not wish her to feel obliged to entertain us.'

Joss pressed a kiss on her hand before letting it go. 'I can tell when you are being sparing with the truth, Miss Bainbridge, but no matter! I will look forward to seeing you later.'

He stood watching as Amy went in at the door. Bond Street and a little lottery money had wrought quite a change. Her saucy blue straw bonnet matched the elegant pelisse and fitted her neat figure to perfection. Beneath the hat her hair was brown and glossy, feathering her cheeks in wind-blown tendrils. She looked thoroughly enchanting. As she reached the door, she turned and gave him a very sweet smile and for some reason Joss felt as though a hand had squeezed his heart. It left him feeling slightly breathless.

He gave the horses the office to move off. It had been an interesting afternoon and he looked forward to seeing Amy again that night at Lady Carteret's ball. It was refreshing to speak with her for she had decided opinions and was not afraid to voice them to him. He smiled to himself a little ruefully. Perhaps that was what led him to play devil's advocate with her sometimes—it was interesting to provoke her to discussion. She was so utterly unlike any other lady of his acquaintance.

That reminded him of Harriet Templeton. When he had left her bed that morning she had been quite sulky at the thought of not seeing him for the entire day. It had cost him the promise of a pearl necklace and a trip to Vauxhall to buy back a smile, and it all seemed damnably like too much hard work. He knew that he was tiring of her—the signs were unmistakable and had been for a while. Yet for some reason he was reluctant to end their association just yet, as if the thought of ridding himself of Harriet would leave him too exposed. He remembered Fleet's suggestion that he should marry Harriet to scorn his father. She would look magnificent in the Tallant diamonds, but the thought of her as Marchioness of Tallant was otherwise repugnant to him.

Marriage… Joss frowned. He could scarcely believe that he had told Amy the tale of his parents' separation and far less that he had mentioned their advice to him. He had thought such childhood memories were long forgotten. Yet perhaps they did remain to colour one's judgement. Certainly Amy had been most affected by George Bainbridge's fecklessness. But now the spectre of genteel poverty was banished and she had all the security she needed. Perhaps, now that she was an heiress as well, she would attract a suitor who pleased her.

The warm feeling that Joss had experienced whilst thinking of Amy vanished abruptly at the thought of a suitor who might catch her interest. The idea certainly did not please him. He could not imagine that any future husband of Amy's would countenance for a moment the continuation of their visits and conversations. Yet they were only meeting so frequently to fulfil the terms of the debt of honour. At the end of the week the arrangement would cease and Amy would be free of his company. Feeling thoroughly grumpy now, Joss turned the phaeton in the direction of Covent Garden. Thinking about Amy was proving too problematical and he did not wish to question why. On the other hand, Harriet would be delighted to see him and that was not complicated at all. All the same, he knew that he was running away.

'Amy, I have been thinking.' Richard Bainbridge had caught his sister at the foot of the stairs as they waited for Lady Bainbridge to join them for the Carteret ball. Richard's fair, good-humoured face was creased with worry and this, together with the unusual information that he had been thinking, made his sister vaguely apprehensive.

'Yes, Richard? Whatever is the matter?'

'It's Joss Tallant.' Richard leaned a hand against the newel post and surveyed his sister with severity. 'Dash it, Amy, it just won't do, you know. Yesterday you were closeted with the fellow for nigh on two hours and today you vanish with him for a whole day! It makes me uncomfortable!'

Amy raised her brows. 'I thought that Lord Tallant was a friend of yours, Richard?'

Richard looked affronted. 'What has that to do with the price of fish? Joss is a friend of mine, but he ain't suitable as a friend of yours!'

Amy shrugged. She felt irritable. 'You know there is no harm in it! Besides, you did nothing to stop the wager at the time.'

Richard shifted uncomfortably. 'I thought that Joss would simply pay up. I never imagined him squiring you around Town in this devilishly attentive manner! People will talk, you know!'

'People always talk,' Amy said crossly. 'Dear Richard, I know that you have my best interests at heart, but you more than anyone must see how baseless your fears are! I know it is indelicate to mention it, but what would Lord Tallant be doing with me when he has Miss Templeton to…entertain him?'

Richard blushed. Amy found this rather endearing. 'Amy! You should not…I cannot…'

'Amanda and I saw you all together, remember?' Amy said with brutal candour. 'You, Parrish, Fleet and Joss Tallant in the Park with those ladies.'

Richard recoiled. The sound of Lady Bainbridge's tread could be heard on the landing above and he threw a hunted look over his shoulder.

'For God's sake, do not mention this in front of Mama, Amy! She would have an apoplexy!'

'Why?' Amy raised her brows in mock ignorance. 'Surely she knows you have an actress in keeping—'

'Amy!' Richard backed away, rather as though she was an unpredictable dog that might bite at any moment. 'You know full well why you should not speak of it! Besides, Mama would be furious to discover that I had Kitty Maltravers in keeping! Papa was cheated at cards by Kitty's first protector and Mama never forgets something like that.'

Amy gave a snort of laughter. 'Oh, Richard, I am sure you are more worried about that than ever you are that I might be in danger from associating with the Earl of Tallant…'

'Now there you are wrong,' her brother said virtuously, straightening up as Lady Bainbridge, in emerald green and a startlingly large diamond necklace, started to descend the stair. 'I have your interests firmly at heart! By the by, if you think that Joss's amorous interests are focussed on Miss Templeton these days, you are far out! Why, he barely seems interested in the girl. I believe it will not be long before Miss Templeton is looking for another protector.'

'Truly?' Amy felt her heart lift in a most inappropriate and telling way. 'Not, of course, that it is any concern of mine… Mama!' She turned to Lady Bainbridge, grateful for the distraction. 'You look magnificent tonight! And those diamonds—I had no notion that you possessed anything so fine.'

'All paste, my dear,' Lady Bainbridge said, patting her chest fondly as she approved her reflection in the hall mirror. 'I tried to pawn them when we fell upon hard times, but I fear the pawnbroker was not interested! He said they were too gaudy!' She frowned and checked her reflection again. 'I cannot imagine what he meant!'

'I say, Amy,' Richard whispered, as they waited for the new carriage to be brought round, 'can you lend me a monkey, just for tonight? My pockets are to let.'

'How much is a monkey?' Amy asked innocently.

Joss arrived at Lady Carteret's ball very late in the evening and Amy, noticing him the moment that he walked through the door, thought that he looked slightly tousled, which in no way detracted from his startlingly attractive appearance. She watched as he greeted his hostess with a gallantry that had her ladyship blushing and smiling and made his way by very slow and slight degrees to Amy's side.

At first she had assumed that this casual approach was designed to quash any gossip. They had agreed earlier that Joss should not escort her to the ball, but Amy had thought that the arrangement had at least involved Joss arriving tolerably early and dancing with her a couple of times. He was the one who had added balls, parties and masquerades to her list, after all. They were not her preferred mode of entertainment. As the evening had wound on and he had failed to appear, Amy found that she had every dance spoken for. To start with she had thought to save one for him; now she was glad that she had not.

She was not sure how she knew, but when he finally bowed over her hand she immediately realised that he was out of temper and that the easy camaraderie that had been between them only that afternoon had vanished. A slight frown creased her brow as she studied him. Joss's dark auburn hair was casually dishevelled and he wore his clothes with a careless distinction. Some instinct suggested to her that he looked as though he had just got out of bed. And as she stared, her mind transfixed by the idea, she realised that it was true and, further, that he had not been alone. She blushed scarlet with mortification, snatched her hand away and muttered something incoherent.

'Would you care to dance, Miss Bainbridge?' Joss asked, sounding to Amy's ears as though the very thought bored him to death. She gave him a tight smile.

'Thank you, my lord, but I fear all my dances are taken,' she said. 'Here is Lord Holles come to claim me for the boulanger. Excuse me, if you please.'

Joss bowed. His face was studiously blank but there was an edge to his voice. 'Some other time then, Miss Bainbridge?'

'Perhaps,' Amy said, with an equal edge to hers.

She did not remember much about the boulanger other than that from her place on the floor she could see Joss and Richard making their way to the card room. That seemed to make everything worse, as though Joss was deliberately doing everything he could to anger her by arriving late, acting in an offhand manner and then heading straight for the gaming tables. When Amy told herself not to be foolish and that she had no right to censure his behaviour, it only served to make her feel worse. She could not understand why she felt so upset. She had known all along what manner of man he was, and, if he chose to go directly to visit his mistress after he had spent the afternoon with her, that was his concern. She was not interested in his sophisticated games. It was not as though she had any romantic claim to him.

Nevertheless, there was a hot pain in her chest and tears burned behind her eyes. She had known that the debt of honour was a foolish idea from the very start and she decided that it would be better to finish it now, before it was really started, and have done with the pretence.

The dance ended and Amy accepted Lord Holles's arm back to her mother's side. The poor man had been doing his best to be agreeable and she realised that she had not taken in a word that he had said to her. All that she could think was that she would speak to Joss at the next opportunity and tell him that their plans for the rest of the week were cancelled. That way she need not see him again.

Joss was faring little better than Amy. He had not enjoyed his time with Harriet, despite the strenuous efforts to do so that had made him late for Lady Carteret's ball. Their physical encounters had always been satisfying before, even if he had never found Harriet a particularly stimulating companion in other ways, yet he had found the last few hours utterly unfulfilling. He was bored and irritable and had found it almost impossible to work up any enthusiasm for their lovemaking no matter how he tried, and Harriet's failure to notice this seemed only to serve to emphasise the gulf between them. Afterwards she had prattled on about trips on the river and the projected visit to Vauxhall, until Joss had been desperate to escape her company. When she had flung her arms about him as he left and pressed her scented body against him, he had felt physically repulsed.

All in all it was enough to put him into a very bad mood and for some obscure reason it had seemed to be the fault of Miss Amy Bainbridge. He had enjoyed his afternoon with her so much that it had made the following hours seem even more disappointing. Then, when he had finally caught up with Amy what seemed like hours later, she had greeted him very coolly indeed and promptly gone off to dance with some other gentleman. For his part, Joss had headed for the card room in habitual fashion, only to find that he could not concentrate on the game of hazard that was in progress. He emerged a short while later, prompted by the need to discover whom Amy was dancing with next.

He was not amused to see that it was Clive Massingham who was plying her with lemonade and attention in equal measure under the approving eye of Lady Bainbridge. There were a couple of other young ladies present and a gaggle of younger sons whom Joss cynically identified as hanging out for a fortune. Amy was looking rather pretty, he thought, in another of Madame Louise's confections, this time of pale pink gauze embroidered with tiny rosebuds. There were matching flowers on the bandeau that held back her ringlets and her hair gleamed golden brown in the light. She looked tiny and delicate and she also looked extremely cheerful and not at all reserved. Joss's hands clenched in an involuntary movement as he saw Amy laughing with unrestrained enjoyment at one of Massingham's anecdotes. He detested Massingham. The man was a fortune hunter and a libertine and Joss knew it was hypocritical, but he deplored Massingham's lack of morals. He could hardly bear to be near the man—the fact that Massingham had been lover to both the Marchioness of Tallant and now to her daughter Juliana made Joss feel sick.

He was also surprised to see Lady Bainbridge countenancing Massingham's attentions to Amy when it was well known that the man had an unsavoury reputation. As for Massingham himself—thirty thousand pounds would never be enough for him. Joss knew that he had refused to marry Juliana because she did not have enough money to tempt him.

'You're looking very grim, old fellow,' Sebastian Fleet commented as he passed Joss the glass of wine that he had thoughtfully procured for him. 'I would have thought that a few hours with the lovely Harriet would have put you in a better humour!'

Joss shrugged irritably. 'I was just reflecting that Clive Massingham was a rather inappropriate suitor for Miss Bainbridge. I wonder that her mother allows it.'

Fleet raised his brows. 'Surely Lady Bainbridge would be *aux anges* to see her nestling married off to anyone who offered. Miss Bainbridge may have a fortune now, Joss old boy, but it don't make her any less reserved—or less plain.'

Joss's jaw tightened. Somewhere, not far below the surface, he felt violence bubbling up inside him.

'It may be, Seb, that your taste only runs to the more obvious-looking female! Miss Bainbridge has a certain distinction.'

Fleet smothered a grin in his wineglass. 'I stand corrected. Clearly you have more discernment than I.'

Joss found he could not stop himself even though he

knew Fleet was deliberately goading him. 'Miss Bainbridge is charming, Sebastian.'

'You must be grateful to Lady Juliana for the debt of honour,' Fleet said, a twinkle in his eye, 'if it has given you the opportunity to ascertain as much!'

Joss gave him a darkling stare. He put his empty wineglass down with controlled force.

'This ball is boring me. I believe I shall go.'

Fleet's smile grew. 'To White's, old fellow? Or to Covent Garden, perhaps?'

Joss paused. Neither of Fleet's suggestions held the slightest appeal and he realised with a strange pang that he was not at all sure where he would go or what he would do. A part of him wanted to stay at Lady Carteret's ball simply to be near Amy, but at the same time the thought of watching her dancing with other gentlemen irritated him almost beyond measure.

Even as he hesitated, Fleet touched his arm to draw his attention to the tableau across the room.

'I did not realise that Juliana was a particular friend of Miss Bainbridge?'

Joss turned. His sister had indeed come up to the group about Amy and was engaging in conversation that seemed most amicable, although her gaze was dwelling on Clive Massingham with a possessive intensity. Joss frowned. Surely Juliana did not imagine Amy a rival for Massingham's affections? It seemed absurd. Yet a vague sense of unease possessed him; he started across the room towards them and as he did so Juliana's drawling tones floated over to him.

'Lud, Miss Bainbridge, I had no idea that you were such a secret gambler—and such a successful one! First you lift over two hundred guineas from me at play, and then I hear that this mysterious fortune of yours is a lottery prize! We should be calling you the lottery heiress!'

There was a sudden lull in the conversation all around, as though all ears were out on stalks. Like everyone else, Joss had his gaze fixed on Amy's face and saw the colour fade from her cheeks before her chin came up sharply and an angry gleam came into her eyes. She spoke quietly but with emphasis.

'Thank you, Lady Juliana, but I should prefer no such soubriquet.'

Her eyes met Joss's and he saw the hurt and anger there before she turned away with contempt. Joss felt his own anger start to burn. He caught Juliana's arm in an iron grip and pulled her unceremoniously towards an alcove.

'That was not well done, Juliana.' He wanted to shake her and only just managed to restrain himself. 'Sometimes your spite shocks even me, sister dear!'

Already word of Amy's lottery win was rippling away from the group, a frisson of excitement accompanying the whispered words as such a prime piece of gossip was passed on.

Juliana pulled a face. She shook his hand off her arm. 'Lud, what is it to you, Joss? I heard a piece of gossip and thought to tease a little, that is all—'

'You thought to damage Miss Bainbridge's reputation! You must know that Lady Bainbridge has put it about that the money was inherited.'

Juliana shrugged. 'I do so dislike dishonesty, don't you, Joss? If little Miss Bainbridge wishes to be courted for her money, all well and good, but at least let it be known where that money has come from!'

Her green gaze searched his face for a moment and then she smiled, her lazy smile. 'Lud, you do look angry, my dear. Can it be that you are developing a *tendre* for the innocent little Miss Bainbridge? How piquant! I declare that that would be a greater piece of gossip even than the lottery winnings!'

Joss's eyes narrowed. He was shocked at the anger he felt inside; anger with Juliana for her malice, mixed with the most astonishing desire to protect Amy from such spite.

'You will not spread such gossip, Juliana!'

'Shall I not?' Lady Juliana arched an elegant eyebrow. 'How so?'

'Because you are scarcely lily white yourself. I would not wish you to...damage...yourself in the process. A story about Miss Bainbridge could lead so very easily to a disclosure about you...'

For a moment they stared furiously at each other, then Juliana lowered her gaze. A bright spot of colour burned in her cheeks. 'Bah, you are an odious wretch sometimes, Joss! You would do it, too!'

Joss bowed slightly. 'I would. You see, Juliana, little Miss Bainbridge, as you call her, is indeed a genuinely innocent girl, whereas you and I inhabit the sort of world that has nothing in common with hers, except superficially. I suggest that you leave her alone.'

Juliana smiled. 'Oh, I will, brother dear. Just as long as you do. You could damage her reputation far more than I ever could.'

Joss held her gaze. He knew she was right and he also knew he could not afford to give her any advantages.

'Which is why I shall be keeping well away from her myself,' he said coldly. 'There is no truth in your suspicions, Juliana. None whatsoever.'

Chapter Ten

Lady Bainbridge, close to indulging in a fit of the vapours, had wanted to retire from the ball immediately when the word of the lottery win was out, but Amy had refused to retreat in ignominy. It was not that she felt there was any further enjoyment to be obtained from the evening; on the contrary, it had been a disappointment from start to finish and the fact that everyone was talking scandal about her only served to confirm her poor opinion of society. However, she had a task to undertake and it was one that her anger would enable her accomplish. Tomorrow would be too late. She wanted to give the Earl of Tallant a piece of her mind.

It had to be Joss who had told Lady Juliana about the lottery win and she was furious with him for it. First they had hatched their stupid joke, calling it a debt of honour, and then they had humiliated her at the ball for good measure. If ever a brother and sister were kindred spirits, Amy thought angrily, it was those two. They deserved each other.

She could not see Joss anywhere in the ballroom and thought that he might have left. There was no trace of him in the card room or the refreshment room, although there were plenty of prying eyes and sly smiles from those people who watched her. Her fury increasing by the minute, Amy was about to call her hunt off and retire, when she saw Joss just coming through the terrace doors. He appeared to be alone. She hurried across the ballroom and caught up with him before he had taken more than a few steps inside, planting herself directly in his path.

'Lord Tallant!'

'Miss Bainbridge?' Joss's tone was measured in comparison with her own and he sounded coolly bored. The thought made Amy's temper soar. Now she was well served for even thinking for a moment that they had established some kind of innocuous friendship. She had stumbled well out of her depth and should withdraw—but not until she had told him what she thought of him.

'I wish to speak with you, my lord.' Amy kept her tone steady although her pulse hammered hard. 'Immediately!'

Joss looked amused at her vehemence. He made a slight gesture. 'Please do so.'

'Not here!' Amy said, glancing around. The crowd in the ballroom was thinning a little because of the lateness of the hour but there were still plenty of people present and many of them were looking their way.

'We cannot step outside without causing further speculation,' Joss pointed out. 'If you wish to speak with me now, Miss Bainbridge, it will have to be in public.'

Amy glared at him. 'I am surprised that you scruple at causing further scandal, my lord! Perhaps you should have thought of that before you told your sister that I had won my fortune on the lottery. I asked you to keep that a secret and I trusted you to do so!'

Joss's eyes narrowed. 'Am I to understand that you

believe that *I* told Juliana that you had won the thirty thousand pounds? Why should you think such a thing?'

Amy threw a quick glance over her shoulder. Now he sounded almost as angry as she.

'It must be you! Who else?'

Rather than answer, Joss took her arm and drew her out of the long terrace windows. He did not stop at the balustrade, but hurried her down the steps and on to the spruce-flanked lawn at the bottom. A full summer moon rode high in the sky so it was not entirely dark, but Amy shivered in the cool breeze. Already the ballroom seemed a long way away.

'Oh! Why did you do that? I thought you just expressed a wish to avoid scandal?'

'I judged that it would cause more scandal for us to quarrel in public than for us to take a small walk,' Joss said, through shut teeth. 'However, I am not detaining you, Miss Bainbridge. If you wish to return to the ballroom you may do so at once.'

Amy surveyed him in silence for a moment. Her anger had ebbed as soon as she had thrown the accusation at him and now, although he had not refuted it, she found that she no longer wished to argue with him.

'Were we quarrelling?' she asked in a small voice.

'Assuredly. And we shall continue to do so if you accuse me of breaking your trust.'

Amy frowned slightly. 'So you did not tell Lady Juliana?'

'I did not.' Joss's tone was uncompromising. 'As for who the culprit might be, there could be a number of possibilities. Lady Bainbridge, perhaps, or your brother or even Amanda Spry. I suppose you told her the truth of your situation?'

'Yes, but—' Amy had started to feel quite regretful.

Perhaps she had jumped to conclusions. She probably owed him an apology, except that now Joss had started to speak it was difficult to offer one. She realised that he was very angry—she had never seen him like this before.

'Then there were the gentlemen you were accosting at Lady Moon's ball when you were trying to find the owner of the lottery ticket,' Joss continued. 'Hallam and Dainty may have been too slow to realise what you were about, but Sebastian Fleet is no fool!'

'No,' Amy said, 'but—'

'But what?' Joss's body was tight with tension. Amy could feel it emanating from him in waves. 'None of the other suspects are as likely as I am? Is that what you wished to say, Miss Bainbridge?'

Amy felt the need to justify herself. 'I am sorry. It is simply that Lady Juliana is your sister and as the two of you had already colluded over Lady Juliana's debt to me, I thought…' Her voice faded away then strengthened. 'I thought that it was all part of some jest at my expense…'

'I see.' Joss's voice was very polite. 'You thought that I had conspired with Juliana to make fun of you, despite the fact that I had already assured you that was not true, and you also believed that I had told Juliana about the money.'

Amy shivered again. 'You make it sound very foolish of me.'

Joss shrugged. 'It merely proves that you do not trust me.'

Amy swallowed what felt like a huge lump in her throat. She did not understand why the stark words should make her feel miserable but they did. Nor could she deny them for that was exactly what she had said to him only a few minutes previously. It was too dark to see his expression, but she was certain that she had hurt him in some way although the idea seemed manifestly absurd. She made a slight gesture.

'I am sorry if I made a mistake...'

'Under the circumstances, it is probably better that we cancel the rest of the arrangements for this week and that I pay the debt in full,' Joss said formally. 'You will have your two hundred guineas tomorrow morning, Miss Bainbridge.'

'Oh, no!' Amy said quickly, feeling that matters were going from bad to worse. 'That is, if you prefer it that way.'

'It is not what I prefer,' Joss said, still with immaculate courtesy, 'but rather what you favour, Miss Bainbridge.'

Amy made a slight, helpless gesture. 'I accept that I have misjudged you, my lord. I have no wish to make matters worse by insisting on receiving the money in lieu of your company! Besides, it is Wednesday tomorrow! We have already spent two days together—'

'Are you suggesting that I should be granted some kind of discount, Miss Bainbridge?' Now there was violence in Joss's tone. 'A concession for services already rendered?'

Amy put her hand on his arm. 'Please! I do not wish to quarrel with you! I should have thought what would happen...'

There was a silence, but for the breeze in the night-scented pines. Then Joss put his hand over hers where it rested on his sleeve. His touch was warm. His tone had softened.

'Do you trust me, Amy?'

Amy caught her breath. 'Yes.'

'And do you wish our...arrangement...to be at an end?'

'No.'

She did not. Ten minutes previously Amy had vowed to tell him that she never wanted to see him again, but now she realised just how much she had hurt him with her accusations—and how much she would suffer if she were to deny herself his company. It was a matter that required some careful thought, for it was telling her something very significant about her feelings. Except that she could not think about it now. Now she was aware of nothing except Joss's hand on hers, the sound of his breathing, the expression in his eyes. All her senses were focussed on him. At the back of her mind was the faint belief that she was getting herself into the most dreadful danger, but it was a distant thought and it did not really trouble her. She made no move away from him.

Joss bent his head and kissed her. For a moment Amy was acutely aware of the touch of his lips on hers, their warmth, their gentleness. Then the effect of the kiss and the shock that it was Joss kissing her hit her simultaneously. Her knees weakened and his arms went about her, drawing her closer.

The feel of his mouth on hers was unfamiliar and a little frightening, for Amy had never been kissed before. Despite the strangeness she felt no urge to withdraw from the embrace and after a moment her fear receded, drowned by the delightful sensations that were flooding her body. A rush of warmth swept through her and she was shaken by the sweetest pleasure she had ever felt, and when his tongue touched hers with a featherlight caress she shivered all the way down to her toes.

Joss drew back, but he kept an arm about her.

'I am sorry.' His voice was a little husky. '*Now* do you wish our arrangement to be at an end, Amy?'

Amy blinked and moved away from him. She felt a little cold. The stars settled back into their courses and the outlines of the trees came back into focus, yet she had the strangest feeling that something had changed irrevocably.

'I…don't know.' She frowned a little. 'Why are you sorry? A rake does not apologise.'

She saw Joss smile and the sight of it gave her a strange, warm feeling. 'That's true when he plans a seduction. I did not plan this, Amy.'

'Oh!' Amy stole a look at him. 'Then what do we do now?'

She saw Joss's smile deepen and her heart lurched, but he did not take her back in his arms, which was the answer she really wanted.

'That depends on you,' he said. 'If I have offended you and you do not wish to see me again, we should settle the debt and have done with it. Otherwise I think we could continue as we were before—and forget that this evening ever happened.'

Decidedly this was not what Amy wanted. Her heart sank a little and with it went all the lovely warm feelings that the kiss had engendered. Joss's words seemed eminently sensible but it was not sense that she wanted now. Nevertheless, she knew that he was right. She had been missing from the ballroom for far too long, she was with the most notorious rake in London and common sense rather than starry-eyed romance was what was needed here. To Joss a kiss might be no great matter; to Amy, who had just received the first, heart-stirring embrace of her life, it was a different thing entirely, but she could still see the disparity in their positions.

'I think that your payment of the debt of honour should continue,' she said, as briskly as she could. 'We are engaged to see the exhibition at the Royal Academy tomorrow afternoon, remember, and on Thursday we are to visit the St Boniface almshouses.'

'I will see you tomorrow afternoon, then.' Joss took her hand and pressed a kiss on it. Amy could detect nothing in his voice except good humour and it lit a spark of rebellion in her. It was not fair that he should be so calm when her senses were still humming with awareness. If he could be cool, so could she. She pulled her hand from his grasp.

'Good night, Lord Tallant.'

'Good night, Miss Bainbridge.'

Amy went slowly up the stone steps and slipped in at the ballroom door. The light seemed very bright. The ballroom was still full of chatter and over by the door Richard was supporting a tottering Lady Bainbridge out into the hall. It was time to go home. And nothing had changed.

Joss caught up with his sister Juliana as she was about to step into her carriage. She was not alone. She was leaning on the arm of Clive Massingham and it was obvious that they were leaving together. Equally obvious was the fact the Juliana did not care who knew, whereas Massingham looked slightly nervous to see Joss approaching them, though he soon covered it with his customary truculent expression.

Joss hesitated for the merest split second. 'Juliana, a word with you, please.'

Juliana yawned widely. 'Not now, Joss, not again!

Can you not see that I am anxious to reach home—and my bed?'

Massingham laughed at the innuendo. Joss's expression tightened. 'Yes, now! It will take but a moment.'

Juliana turned a pettish shoulder. 'Lud, you become more like our father every day! I declare, Joss, you will be spoiling your bad-boy reputation if you turn into a moralist!'

Joss gave Massingham a look of calculated dismissal. 'What I have to say is private, Juliana. Perhaps you and Mr Massingham may meet up again later?'

Juliana laughed. 'Oh, very well. You had better come with me in the carriage, Joss. Clive, darling…' her voice sank to a throaty purr '…I shall be all of five minutes…'

'I will count on that.' Massingham took her hand and pressed a kiss ostentatiously on the palm.

Juliana gave a pleasurable shiver. 'Forgive me if I embarrass you, Joss,' she said with evident insincerity.

'Your behaviour does not offend me in the least, Ju,' Joss said coolly, 'but the company you keep is beneath you. What you see in Massingham—'

'Can you not imagine?' Juliana allowed him to help her up into the carriage. 'And I had heard that your imagination was so very…vivid…as well, Joss dearest, when it comes to matters of the heart! I hear that Harriet Templeton speaks so highly of you! But not recently. Recently I'm told she says your mind is distracted, darling…'

'We were speaking of you and Massingham, I believe.' Joss's voice was hard.

'Oh, yes.' The undertone of amusement had returned to Juliana's voice. 'Are you concerned about his past relationship with our mother, Joss? He says that I am better than she—'

Joss's fist hit the smooth leather of the seat with a smothered crash. 'That is enough, Juliana!'

'Oh, very well. I do but tease.' Juliana's eyes flashed. 'Which reminds me—when are you to marry little Miss Innocence? What a change that will be for you, Joss! So much purity—I declare, it quite goes to one's head!'

'I infer you are speaking of Miss Bainbridge?' Joss said coldly. 'I have warned you before, Juliana—'

'Oh, I will not speak of her to anyone else, of course, but you can confide in me, Joss.' Juliana gave her feline smile. 'Is she not the sweetest little thing? Too good for you, my dear!'

'Precisely,' Joss said, through shut teeth. 'I can never aspire to marry Miss Bainbridge, Juliana—'

'Stuff! Why ever not? When you are in love with her as well…'

'My feelings are beside the point here. Miss Bainbridge should marry someone who can make up for the sufferings she has already endured. A reputation besmirched by years of gambling and womanising is scarcely much to offer, is it? Why, it is asking almost as much as acceptance of years of financial ruin!'

'Lud, you are in love with her!' For a moment Juliana's voice had softened to something that Joss remembered. 'You are too honourable, my dear. Just because George Bainbridge made his womenfolk suffer, it does not mean that Miss Bainbridge would find you an unacceptable suitor—'

'Miss Bainbridge has exactly the right opinion of my gambling, Ju—she deplores it. Now—' Joss clamped down on his temper with an effort '—may we speak instead of the matter in hand? I wish to know who it was told you of Miss Bainbridge's lottery win.'

Juliana laughed. 'Then you will have to go hang, my

dear, for I cannot tell you. I may need to use that source again sometime!'

'Was it Richard Bainbridge? I have yet to learn that he is in your thrall, but it may be so.'

'No,' Juliana said consideringly, 'it was not he. Though you do give me an idea, Joss. If Massingham fails—'

'Fails to do what?' Joss's voice had an edge to it. 'Offer you marriage? You'll be waiting a long time there, Ju!'

It was too dark to see his sister's face but, though she took every pain to erase the hurt from her voice, he knew her too well. He heard it and understood it.

'Lud, I am not hanging out to be Massingham's wife! No, a better title is all that could capture me—' Her voice broke and she hurried to cover it up. 'But I will never tell you my informant, Joss, so you need not press me.'

Joss knew she would not. But the field was narrowing. If not Richard, then possibly Lady Bainbridge herself, or the Duke of Fleet, or even Amanda Spry…

'I see you have taken up with Lady Spry again,' he said carelessly. 'Does it remind you of the old days?'

Juliana gave him a sharp look. 'You'll not catch me that way, Joss! No, Amanda Spry and I cannot be friends now. One grows apart from one's girlhood friends.'

'I see.' Joss said slowly. 'Perhaps seeing her reminds you too much of Myfleet? You were all friends once, were you not? He was a good man, Juliana—'

'The best.' Joss heard the edge of tears in his sister's voice. 'But now I have Massingham, remember? I fear I shall have to ask you to leave now, my dear. You are tedious dull tonight, and if there is one thing that I cannot bear, it is to be bored.'

'Amy dear, you seem most distracted this morning.' Lady Bainbridge's faintly querulous voice made Amy jump and she dropped her bread honey-side down on the carpet. There was just the two of them for breakfast and for most of the meal Lady Bainbridge had kept up a lament about the events of the previous night—how could the spiteful Lady Juliana ever have heard the truth, what sort of wicked rumours would be circulating that morning, what was to become of them all now...? Amy had barely noticed her diatribe, for she was struggling with difficulties of her own. Shortly she would have to face Joss in the daylight and pretend that the previous evening was forgotten, yet she did not feel the same about him and, more confusingly still, she was not even sure what she *did* feel.

'I beg your pardon, Mama,' she said. 'I was thinking about what to do—'

'Precisely!' Lady Bainbridge looked triumphant. 'We must come up with a plan. I knew I should not have worn the yellow slippers yesterday, for yellow is a most unlucky colour and I should have known something bad would happen. Oh, that wretched Juliana Myfleet! She always was a wicked girl and now she has ruined things for you, Amy. Ruined! You will not catch a respectable husband now, for *ton* society cannot look kindly on a fortune derived from gambling. Not in a woman!'

The blatant double standard in this jerked Amy out of her preoccupation.

'Well, that is the biggest hypocrisy I have ever heard!' she said indignantly. 'Fortunes are won and lost at the tables all the time, yet no one condemns the gamblers! Not that I wish to catch a husband, Mama, as I told you from the first!'

Lady Bainbridge chose to ignore this. 'It may be hypocrisy, but it is the way of the world. To win the lottery is *not* respectable. Oh, to think that I told all those people about Aunt Bessie's legacy and now they are all laughing at me. It is too much!'

Amy privately thought that her mother had already been halfway to believing in the late Aunt Bessie and her legacy, and would probably soon say that the rumours were not respectful to her memory. She knew that Lady Bainbridge must be suffering. Her mother had always been so concerned with society's opinion, a fact that had given her much mortification when George Bainbridge had embarrassed her with his financial disasters. This new gossip would be most hurtful to her, whereas Amy was tempted to tell all the scandalmongers to go hang.

'I think we shall just have to ignore the gossip, Mama,' she said. 'If we carry on as though nothing has happened—'

Lady Bainbridge looked horrified. 'Oh, that is not to be thought of! I could not possibly walk into another ballroom now. No, Amy, I have plans for us to retire from town at once. If we go to Nettlecombe for a space, matters may settle down and we may return next season. Of course you will be older by then, and there are those who already think you at your last prayers, but it cannot be helped. No, I am decided! We leave for the country at the end of this week.'

Amy made an exasperated gesture. 'Mama, I cannot bear for us to appear to be running away from this. It is not that important.'

Lady Bainbridge looked outraged. 'Of course it is important! We *are* running away.'

Amy sighed. It was the old pattern repeating itself, of course, for her mother had had only one way of dealing with the scandals that had surrounded her life. Whenever George Bainbridge had been financially embarrassed, his wife had suffered an equivalent social embarrassment. They had removed Amy from her schools and her friends, they had moved to different lodgings, they had retired to the country, all to save face as well as save money. Amy could not be surprised that her mother was reacting this way now. She made a last appeal.

'Mama, I have so many plans that I do not wish to put off. Why, Amanda and I were going to attend the victory celebrations in St James's Park.'

Lady Bainbridge shuddered. 'If you wish to be cut dead by all of our acquaintance, Amy, then pray remain in town. I shall be going to Nettlecombe as soon as I may arrange it!'

Amy could see the tears in her mother's eyes. She felt the exasperation swell up and stifled it. To argue now would only upset her mother further. She patted her hand instead.

'Very well, Mama. We shall go to the country if you wish it.'

Lady Bainbridge's blue eyes swam with tears. 'Thank you, my love. I confess that will set my mind at rest.' She frowned a little. 'There is something else that concerns me, however—that most unsuitable young man, brother to that hateful Juliana Myfleet. There has been talk, Amy—'

Amy stood up abruptly. She had been prepared to humour her mother on other points, but she did not want to talk about Joss. It felt like trying to walk on a twisted ankle.

'I collect that you mean the Earl of Tallant. He is suitable enough to be a friend of Richard's—'

'Oh, yes, but that is quite different, for he is rich and if Richard can win from him… But for you, my love it is quite another matter. Though I suppose,' Lady Bainbridge said, diverted momentarily, 'he is vastly handsome…'

'Well, you need not worry, Mama.' Amy moved towards the door. 'Since we shall be leaving London soon I shall have no more opportunity to see him.'

'No more you shall!' Lady Bainbridge said, brightening. 'That is all right then!'

'I am going to visit Mrs Wendover this morning,' Amy said, pausing with her hand on the doorjamb. 'I thought to take some food and some clothing for the children and books for the school.'

'That is kind of you, my love,' Lady Bainbridge said. She looked up sharply. 'You had better take Patience with you. Oh, and you had better procure a hack! Do not take the carriage to Whitechapel, not when it is so new! I could not bear for it to be damaged!'

'I wondered whether you had seen this,' Amanda Spry said, reluctantly holding out a sheet of paper to her friend. It was the evening and Amy, out of deference to Lady Bainbridge's wishes, had cancelled her attendance at a musicale and chosen instead to spend a quiet evening at home with her friend. Yet even here, it seemed, gossip pursued her. She took the scandal sheet from Amanda's hand and perused the doggerel written there:

Little Miss B
Who lived retired
To gambling and marriage
Never aspired
Now tempted to sin
By a lottery win
She plays for high stakes
With the greatest of rakes.'

'Oh dear.' Amy put the sheet down gently. Her first impulse had been to thrust it into the fire before Lady Bainbridge saw it, but now she scanned the rhyme again. 'I am not entirely clear what they are lampooning me for? Is it for the lottery win or for the time I am spending with Lord Tallant?' she sighed. 'Both, I suppose.'

Amanda's blue eyes scanned her face thoughtfully. 'You do not seem much concerned, Amy! If it were me I should have left town already! I cannot bear people speaking scandal about me.'

Amy shrugged with an assumption of ease. 'It will die away when the next *on-dit* comes along! I know I am considered an original and society so dislikes someone who does not fit in! Give that person a fortune and...' She shrugged again. 'It is easy to see why I am unpopular.'

Amanda was still watching her with concern. 'And what of Lord Tallant's part in this? He does not seem concerned that he has made you an object of scandal.'

'That is putting it far too strongly.' Amy spoke firmly. 'Just because I have chosen to spend some time in Lord Tallant's company should not give rise to speculation!'

Amanda gave her a pitying glance. 'Perhaps it should

not, but it has! A rake of Lord Tallant's reputation accompanying you to charity concerts and almshouses! Half the people are saying that he has been making a game of you and the other half that he must be hunting your fortune—'

She broke off at the angry flash in Amy's eyes. 'I beg your pardon, Amy. That was unpardonably rude of me.' She spread her hands in a gesture of appeal. 'It is simply that I am worried about you! Lord Tallant—'

'There is nothing scandalous between Lord Tallant and myself, Amanda,' Amy said, feeling herself blush. If only her friend realised how desperately Amy wished the reverse were true! Ever since the previous night, Amy had found her thoughts returning to Joss's kiss with tiresome repetition. She had been so tongue-tied in his company that afternoon that it had been fortunate they had been looking at an exhibition of art, for it gave her the excuse to keep quiet as she contemplated the pictures. Certainly Joss did not appear to have noticed anything different in her demeanour and he had seemed quite preoccupied himself.

'It will all blow over,' she said again, with more composure than she was feeling. 'It only requires a Countess to run off with her footman and I shall be quite forgotten!'

'I envy you your hardihood,' Amanda said. 'What if it *were* something truly scandalous, Amy, such as your sojourn in Whitechapel when you were a girl? How would you feel if that story got out?'

Amy raised her brows. 'Living in Whitechapel is hardly a scandal, Amanda, although it is not something that I would wish to be common knowledge. In the end I would have to say that if people wish to speak of it, let them do so!'

Amanda shook her head. 'I believe that you are deliberately misunderstanding me! There must be something that you have done in the past you would not wish people to know! Everyone has their secrets.'

Amy searched her mind for something so reprehensible that she would fear it coming out. Her memory remained obstinately blank. She shook her head.

'No. I fear that I have led a very dull life. No one could blackmail me for my fortune!'

A tinge of colour came into Amanda's cheeks. 'So you are to go to Nettlecombe. I think that I shall leave town when you do, Amy. It will not be so much fun without you.'

Amy stared. 'Why ever should you do that? You know that you adore the balls and parties and you have plenty of friends here.'

Amanda sighed. 'I do not have many real friends, Amy, only acquaintances.'

'But surely...there is Emma Wren and Lady Juliana—'

Amanda met Amy's eye. Her own were bright with some emotion that Amy could not identify. 'Oh, stuff! They are no friends of mine! Emma is too fast for me—her behaviour gives me quite a disgust! As for Juliana...' Amanda's voice slowed. 'Well, we were friends once, perhaps, but that was in the days when Lord Myfleet was alive. Juliana was different then. She was not so hard. Now...' Amanda sighed. 'I declare she is quite another person!'

'Perhaps she is unhappy,' Amy said. She did not wish to think kindly of Lady Juliana after the way that she had behaved towards her and yet something prompted her to be generous. Perhaps it was the echo of Joss's words: *My sister at one time seemed exceptionally happy with her husband.* If Edwin Myfleet had not died, matters might well have been very different.

'Perhaps so.' Now there was a hard edge to Amanda's voice. 'She is not the only one, however.'

Amy put her knotting to one side and took Amanda's hands in hers. 'Mandy, I had no idea…'

'It does not matter.' Amanda, whom Amy had always thought of as elegant to a fault, now gave a most inelegant sniff. She snatched her hands away and stood up hurriedly. 'It is nothing to the purpose. Excuse me, Amy, I must go home. I have the headache.'

'Oh, but—' Amy was at a loss, wanting to help her friend and yet realising that Amanda did not want to talk. 'I will see you before we leave town?'

'Of course.' Amanda gave her a watery smile. 'Excuse me,' she said again. 'I fear that the megrim always makes me tearful.' Upon which blatantly untrue note she went out, leaving Amy to wonder what on earth could be the matter.

Chapter Eleven

'You are fast ruining my bad reputation, Miss Bainbridge,' Joss said resignedly, as Amy leaned out of his phaeton to hand him a pile of blankets, a hamper of food and a bag of medicines. 'Yesterday I was delivering school books for the orphans of St Boniface and today I am visiting in Windsor! Whatever next?'

'It is most kind of you, my lord.' Amy passed him the remainder of the pile of provisions. 'I am persuaded that Nurse Benfleet will be very grateful. We must not stay long, however. I did not tell Mama what I was doing and I simply must be back before evening or she will be fretting herself to flinders.'

She felt Joss's gaze upon her and willed herself not to blush. There were several practical reasons why she had not told Lady Bainbridge of the trip to see Mrs Benfleet. Firstly was the undeniable impropriety of driving to Windsor with Joss, even with a groom in attendance. Amy had considered this, but had decided it could not be allowed to matter. Mrs Benfleet had been ill and needed her help, and that was the most important thing. Then there was the fact that her mother had warned her not to see Joss any more. Amy knew that this would not be possible beyond the end of the week, for their move to Nettlecombe was now fixed for the following day. Selfishly, she wished to make the most of her time with Joss before then, storing up the pleasure of his company against the future.

As Joss helped her down from the curricle his touch was impersonal and he took his hand away at once. Amy deliberately avoided looking at him. The worst of her self-consciousness had faded now, for Joss was treating her in exactly the same way as he had done before that fatal night in Lady Carteret's garden. He was charming but somehow remote.

Amy had been first relieved at Joss's attitude and then, once she had overcome her shyness, she had been frustrated. Inside her something had changed, her feelings had shifted, and when she looked at Joss sometimes and caught him looking at her, she thought he must feel the same. Yet there was a reserve in his manner that told her more plainly than any words that he would not kiss her again, that he would not come any closer, and Amy, to her shock, found that she wanted to shatter his cool resolution.

She picked up the pile of blankets and made her way up the stone-flagged path to the door of the cottage. Joss had dismissed the groom to take the curricle to the nearby inn until it was needed, and he followed her with the hamper in one hand and the medicines in the other. Amy smothered a smile. She had to applaud the uncomplaining way in which Joss had accepted the terms of the debt. It was difficult to imagine such a man visiting orphans or attending charitable lectures under any other circumstances. Yet he had accepted it all with a good grace.

'Miss Amy! Whatever are you doing here! Bless my soul, what a surprise!'

Mrs Benfleet, a round, motherly body in a white apron and lace cap with lavender ribbons, looked understandably surprised but pleased to see them. She hugged Amy warmly, then ushered them hospitably inside. The cottage was spartan but clean as a new pin and its ceiling was so low Amy feared Joss would hit his head on a beam.

'I am much better, thank you,' Mrs Benfleet replied, in answer to Amy's anxious questions about her health. 'That last package of medicine you sent was just the trick. Pure poison to taste, so I could tell it was doing me good!'

'You always used to say such things to me when I was a child,' Amy said, smiling.

'Yes, well, look at you! It must have worked. You look as fresh as a flower, child!'

Amy saw Joss smiling and blushed. 'I am sorry, I forgot—this is a...a friend of mine, Bennie. Lord Tallant—Mrs Benfleet.'

Amy saw Nurse's eyes open very wide as Joss took her hand. 'My word, Miss Amy!'

'Yes, well, anyway...' Amy hurried on for sudden fear that Mrs Benfleet was about to comment on either Joss's title or his indisputable good looks or possibly, even more embarrassingly, ask his intentions.

'We cannot stay more than a few minutes, Bennie, nor do we want to tire you out, but we brought you a few more bits and pieces to help pick you up. Some honey and some tonic wine—'

'I should be mortally offended if you don't take a bite of luncheon with me,' Mrs Benfleet said. 'There's a nice ham in the larder, and bread and apples and milk enough for three.'

Amy cast a quick glance at Joss under her lashes. It was impossible to imagine him sitting down to any kind of repast in this cottage.

'We really must not—' she began.

'A splendid idea, Mrs Benfleet,' Joss said, smiling. 'Thank you very much. May I help you with anything?'

'That's the spirit,' Mrs Benfleet said approvingly, leading the way into her tiny kitchen. 'You go out into the garden, Miss Amy,' she called over her shoulder. 'It's nice and warm over by the apple tree.'

Amy went. The pocket-handkerchief of a garden had a bench against the south-facing wall and it was hot with summer scents and the buzzing of bees. She sat down and closed her eyes. The sun beat against her closed lids. She could hear the murmur of voices from the kitchen. So Joss was actually speaking to Mrs Benfleet, not merely helping to carve the ham or to carry things for her. Amy frowned a little. Perhaps she had been unfair to Joss in imagining he would feel awkward or out of place in such a setting. Whatever his other faults, snobbery was not amongst them.

'Over there, if you please.' She opened her eyes to see Mrs Benfleet advancing with a loaded tray and Joss carrying a table, which he placed in front of them beneath the apple tree.

'I was just telling your young man that he ought to try my homemade cider.' Mrs Benfleet beamed, handing the tray over as Amy hastened to grab it from her. 'Oof, that's better!' She subsided on the bench. 'Sometimes I forget I've been poorly and try to do too much. Move up, Miss Amy! There's room for three!'

Amy shifted along the bench so that there was space

for Joss to sit down. It was a tight squeeze and she was acutely conscious of the press of his thigh against hers. Once or twice his hand brushed hers as they passed the food around. Mrs Benfleet was chattering now, regaling Joss with stories of Amy's childhood. The sunshine, Joss's proximity and, most of all, the cider were all starting to make her head swim. She yawned widely, and then jumped, opening her eyes wide. It would never do to fall asleep. 'Oh, pray excuse me!'

'You sleep if you want to, my lamb,' Mrs Benfleet said comfortably. 'I'm sure your young man will help me to tidy all away when we've finished.'

'He is not my young man,' Amy said sleepily. She turned her head and her hair brushed Joss's shoulder. Suddenly the urge to rest her head there seemed overwhelming. She straightened up quickly.

'Is there anything else that you need me to send you, Bennie?'

'No, my pet, you've been more than generous.' Mrs Benfleet smiled mistily. 'Though where you found the funds for it I just don't know!' She turned to Joss. 'A crying shame it's been, my lord, to see Miss Amy scrimp and scrape to make ends meet in that house—'

'Bennie,' Amy said pleadingly.

'I know I speak out of turn,' the nurse said defiantly, 'but it was a shocking thing, my lord, the way that Miss Amy was dragged from pillar to post by that papa of hers. How Lady Bainbridge tolerated it, I'll never know! But that's marriage, I suppose. For better, for worse. I'm fortunate that my Sam was nothing if not steady, God rest his soul! That was my idea of a marriage—good companionship! Ah, well.' She hauled herself to her feet and bent to kiss Amy. 'You doze out here for a while if you like, Miss Amy. I'll be going in for my rest now, but I do thank you for coming.'

Amy watched through closing eyes as Joss carried the lunch tray back inside. She felt a very strong resistance to going back to London. The warmth and the peace of Mrs Benfleet's garden were so soothing after the bustle of the city. Perhaps it would not be so bad to return to Nettlecombe after all. She had always loved the country…

'Amy?'

Amy opened her eyes. She thought that it was the breeze touching her skin, but now she realised that Joss was crouching down next to her and that he had brushed the hair away from her face with gentle fingers. For a moment she stared into his eyes. Such tenderness… And as she stared, she received a revelation as shocking as a dousing with cold water.

The afternoon sun struck across Joss's face, lightening the amber of his eyes. Amy seemed to see him in extraordinary detail. His hair, slightly windswept, was the deep, dark red of autumn leaves, thick and glossy. He narrowed his eyes against the sun and she could see the shadow of his eyelashes, spiky against his cheek. He smiled again and Amy's heart seemed to skip a beat then start to race, so that the blood tingled around her whole body and all her senses tightened with anticipation. In that second, Amy realised that not only did she desire him with a longing that was as shameless as it was strong but that, more importantly, she loved him, and that everything else seemed to dwindle into unimportance in comparison.

She looked at him for what seemed like hours whilst the exultation swept through her and left her shaking, then reality returned and she blinked and sat up hastily.

Somehow, she had no recollection of quite how, she had slid down on the bench and had been dozing with her head against the armrest. Her bonnet was all squashed and her face felt hot.

'Oh, Mama will be beside herself! I have been out in the sun for hours without my parasol!'

Joss traced the line of her cheekbone with one finger. 'You certainly look a little pink. Perhaps you will get freckles—'

Amy gave a squeak. She was not vain, but better that he should suspect that than think that she was red in the face because of his touch.

'I suppose we must go back now.' She started to stand up and Joss put a hand under her elbow to help her rise.

'Yes, indeed. If you would care to wait here, I shall go to the Rising Sun to fetch the phaeton.'

'No,' Amy said, remembering that there was something she needed to tell him. 'I will walk with you. It will help me to wake up.'

They went back through the cottage. From upstairs came the rhythmic sounds of Mrs Benfleet snoring. They exchanged a look like conspirators and tiptoed out.

They walked a little of the way down the track to the village in silence. The sun was still high and Amy tried to keep into the dappled shadows. The birds were calling in the trees and the road was dry, baked hard in the sun. Joss strode easily along beside her. Amy smiled as she thought about the gentlemen of fashion who tottered about St James's, leaning on their sticks, complaining if they got a speck of dirt on their boots or if the breeze ruffled their neck cloth. Joss was not like that. Whatever his debauchery amounted to, it had hardly affected his physical or mental condition. There was a tiny frown between his brows and he seemed abstracted and Amy remembered that he had said he did not like the country. No doubt this bucolic sojourn was exactly the sort of thing he did not enjoy.

'Thank you for bringing me here today,' she said hesitantly. 'It was very good of you, for I recall that you do not enjoy the country.'

'It is simply that the country has held few attractions for me in the past,' Joss said. 'The hunting and shooting is all very well, I suppose, but I have always valued the entertainments of town above such things. Perhaps I was mistaken, however. It is very beautiful here.'

The warm breeze feathered across Amy's skin. 'I meant also to thank you for your kindness to Mrs Benfleet. I had no intention of staying for luncheon—indeed, when she invited us I thought that you would surely refuse—'

She broke off. Joss looked amused.

'My dear Miss Bainbridge, you have a very poor idea of my manners!'

Amy frowned. 'Yes, but there is a difference between accepting something because one's manners are good and accepting with a good grace, with genuine willingness, if you like…' She bit her lip. 'Oh dear, I have offended you—'

'Quite right. I like Mrs Benfleet enormously and it was no great effort of will on my part to stay and enjoy luncheon with her. Why should you think otherwise?'

Amy made a slight gesture. How to convey to him that the thought of a Corinthian like Joss sitting down to lunch in a cottage garden was quite absurd?

'I suppose…because it would not be your choice of entertainment… I thought—'

'You assumed that I was a snob.' Joss's tone was even. 'Admit it, Miss Bainbridge.' He smiled. 'I believe that, paragon of virtue that you are, you may actually be at fault here.'

There was a pause whilst Amy wrestled with herself. 'I suppose so. I beg your pardon.'

Joss's smile broadened. 'It does not matter. You will know me better in future.'

Amy's heart sank a little. That gave her a very neat opening to tell him of the plan to go to Nettlecombe and the fact that they would not be seeing each other at all in the future, but just for now she did not wish to spoil things. The day had been so enjoyable, warm and bright, with Joss's sole company to enjoy, and she was loath to spoil it.

'I suppose that it was rather improper of me to request that you escort me here today,' she said slowly, following this train of thought out loud, 'but Mrs Benfleet has been ill and I wanted to visit her...'

'And it was easier to ask me than to hire a carriage.' Joss was laughing. 'Besides, this whole week has been an education for me, Miss Bainbridge, as well as an opportunity for you to start using your lottery money to do good!'

Amy's eyes flew to his. She stopped walking. 'I do wish you would not say things like that! I told you before that I had no wish to improve you. It is not my place to do so. Anyway, I have the oddest feeling that I will find that you already give away half your income to charity, or that you fund schooling for rescued climbing-boys and have simply not told anyone.'

The smile vanished from Joss's face. 'You are quite mistaken. In fact, as usual, you give me too much credit. I have been a selfish creature all my life and have never done anything to oblige anyone else. I beg you not to think so.'

Amy frowned. 'You have been very obliging to me this week.'

Joss's expression softened. 'That is different. I have a duty to repay my sister's debt and…' his gaze lingered on her face '…I find it very easy to be obliging to you, Miss Bainbridge. I think that I would probably do anything you asked of me.'

Amy caught her breath. The blood fizzed beneath her skin as though she had heatstroke. She dragged her gaze from his and started walking again, quite quickly.

'I must tell you, my lord, that the end of the debt tomorrow coincides with my departure from town,' she said. 'Mama intends for us to remove to Nettlecombe. She is most upset by the fuss that there has been about my lottery prize and would prefer to withdraw from town altogether.'

Joss caught her arm to slow her down. 'A moment, if you please, Miss Bainbridge. May we discuss this properly rather than on the run?'

Amy reluctantly slowed. There was a disused field gate to the left-hand side, beneath the shelter of a spreading horse chestnut tree. She drew into the shade and leant against wooden bars. They felt sun-warmed against her back.

'What do you wish to discuss, my lord? It is a foregone conclusion.'

'I see. Lady Bainbridge wishes to run from the speculation and you are humouring her?'

Amy blushed. 'For my part I would happily face it out, but Mama is not made of such stern stuff. She has been made very unhappy by all the gossip and she feels that if we were to go to Oxfordshire the scandal might fade away.' Amy shrugged. 'It seems a small price to pay to make her happy and I have always loved the country.'

'I see,' Joss said again, in an odd tone. 'So, we are not to meet again.'

'I suppose not.' Amy put out a hand. 'It is probably for the best. This debt has caused a great deal of talk—almost as much as the lottery win—and it will be good to let the gossip die down.'

Joss's gaze was intent on her face. 'Do you mind all the talk?'

'No, but then I am always being told that I have no society sensibility. Where there is no smoke I cannot see that there can be a fire.'

'Yet I suppose I must bear some responsibility.' Joss shifted slightly. 'I accepted the debt and caused a great deal of talk, all for the pleasure of your company, Miss Bainbridge.'

Once again Amy felt her heart leap. 'Indeed, you have been so very obliging, my lord.'

'So you said already. Well, as I have discovered the country anew today, perhaps I should come to visit you at Nettlecombe. Would you invite me, Miss Bainbridge?'

Amy gave him a small smile. 'Yes, of course.'

She could not believe that Joss would venture as far as Oxfordshire just to visit her. Why should he? With all the sophisticated delights of the town about him he would soon forget their rather strange association.

'So this is to be our final enterprise,' Joss said, with a slight smile. He leaned one hand against the top of the gate and smiled at her. 'As this is probably the only privacy we shall have before you leave, I want to tell you that I have enjoyed your company very much, Miss Bainbridge, and shall be sorry to see you go.'

'Thank you, my lord.' The sunlight falling between the shifting leaves was bright enough to make Amy blink. She swallowed hard, surprised by a sudden empty feeling inside. She felt small and lost. This was ridiculous. Here was Joss taking a light and charming farewell quite in keeping with their relationship, and here was she wanting…what? If only she had not tumbled so disastrously into love with him. In some ways it had been inevitable given the attention that he had paid her and yet in others she had thought herself quite safe. Intent on disapproving of him so heartily, she had barely noticed as her censure had slowly given way to enjoyment of his company. From there innocent delight had slid into something deeper and she was utterly lost.

'I hope that I have…ah…fulfilled all the duties required of me,' Joss continued. The sun was in Amy's eyes and she could not see his expression. 'If there is anything I have failed to do, then you have but a little time to rectify the omission.'

'Well, I…' A picture flashed through Amy's mind, a vision of the garden at Lady Carteret's ball. 'There is one thing.' Her voice sounded strange even to her own ears. She cleared her throat. 'You could…kiss me goodbye.'

As soon as the words were out she shrank back under the horse chestnut tree, seeking its cooling shade on her hot cheeks. She did not dare to look at Joss. She was seldom so forthright, but he had asked what else he could do for her and she had given an honest answer. As the silence stretched to several heartbeats, Amy wished fervently that she had lied.

'Once again you surprise me, Miss Bainbridge.

Surely that is something we have already done—if you remember?' Joss's voice was light, unreadable, but there was something in his tone that made Amy start to burn, shade or not. She knew instinctively that he was not going to refuse her.

She raised her chin. 'Strictly speaking, my lord, that is incorrect. It was an action that you took of your own accord. It was not one of the stipulations of the debt. Besides, this is a kiss goodbye, which is different.'

Their eyes met. Joss's were very dark, but there was a smile lurking in the depths and it made Amy's toes curl.

'So, what would you like me to do?' His voice was smooth. 'As this is part of the debt and is therefore your call, Miss Bainbridge…'

'I would like you to come here.' Amy's voice was no more than a shaky whisper. Her legs felt weak and she was trembling. When Joss obligingly crossed the small space between them and came to stand directly before her, she thought she might give up breathing altogether.

'And now?' Joss's tone was very soft.

Amy cleared her throat. 'Must you make this so difficult for me?'

'I am sorry.' Joss smiled. 'Will this do?'

It was not a question that Amy could answer immediately. He kissed her with a thoroughness that left her breathless, his hands smoothing her body's curves against the hard length of his to a devastating effect. Amy felt the liquid heat race through her, kindled by his touch. She drew back with a gasp, leaning against the rough bark of the tree, relieved at the support its sturdy trunk provided.

Joss did not speak, only looked at her.

'Yes,' she gasped, 'that will do very well.'

Joss laughed. 'For you perhaps, Amy.' His tone was husky. 'Now I find that I need something on my own account.'

Amy's gaze was riveted to his and she jumped when his fingers touched the back of her neck, drawing her gently forward so that her lips met his again. A soft groan escaped her. The kiss was light and teasing at first, but still the heat returned to her body with an aching intensity that shocked her, yet somehow drew her on. She kept quite still allowing the sensuous excitement to course through her as his lips and tongue explored hers in ways she had never even imagined. Her hands came up to Joss's chest, to curl against his jacket, then slid of their own volition around his neck so that she could entangle her fingers in his hair and kiss him more deeply. It was only when Joss's hand slid from the nape of her neck to caress the hollow at the base of her throat then move lower still, that Amy recoiled, abruptly shaken back to reality.

She could not let this go any further, no matter how strongly she desired it. Already she could not bear the thought of leaving him. She did not want to set off for Nettlecombe with her heart broken and her future in tatters.

She stepped back, out of his embrace. 'Joss, please—'

Joss looked as though he was awakening from a dream. He removed himself abruptly from her proximity, putting at least three feet between them. 'Forgive me, Amy. I had no wish to frighten you.'

'I was not afraid,' Amy said tremulously, 'but it did not seem such a very good idea after all.'

She knew she was not expressing herself at all well

and then she saw the expression on Joss's face, the lightning flash of pain in his eyes that was gone so swiftly it seemed almost as though she had imagined it. She put out a hand to him.

'Oh, Joss, I am sorry—I did not mean it to sound like that! Only you must see the folly of it! I am to leave London and you…' Her voice trailed away. She could not speak for him, she did not even know whether there was any equality in their situation. For her to be in Joss's arms was the sweetest thing, but for him? This was a man whose relationships with women were never sincere in the sense she wanted. She had to be a fool even to dream of it and in future her memories would be all she had.

She saw Joss's expression harden slightly, saw all emotion wiped from his face and he stood back to allow her to precede him back on to the track. It was only five minutes to the inn and from there it would be a swift journey back to London. And that would be that. She could go to Nettlecombe with a memory to warm her of the time that she invited the most notorious rake-hell in London to kiss her. It had been an adventure. The whole week had been an adventure. And yet… Amy avoided looking at Joss as the outskirts of the village drew near. And yet it suddenly seemed too late to avoid a broken heart. If she was honest—and she always was—she knew that Joss Tallant had stolen her heart and soul.

'There you are, my love!' Lady Bainbridge was sitting by the fire in the parlour at Curzon Street and was feeding what looked like a large quantity of papers into the flames. Amy paused on the threshold. The room was like a furnace for the fire was roaring fit to set the chimney on fire and all the windows were closed. Amy's head, which had ached incessantly on the silent journey back to London, now felt as though it was about to explode. She had seldom felt so miserable in her life.

She had said a formal goodbye to Joss at the corner of the street. Under the interested eye of his groom he had thanked her for her company during the week and wished her well for the future. Amy had been equally cool and courteous. And, despite his previous assurance that he would visit her at Nettlecombe, Amy had thought it unlikely that she would see Joss again.

'Mama, what are you doing?' she asked mildly, striving not to take her pent-up misery out on her mother. 'Those look like letters—'

'They are, my dear! So useful.' Lady Bainbridge beamed. 'Now we do not need to use up any more coal!'

'It is quite warm enough to do without a fire,' Amy observed. 'Besides, Mama, we can afford the coal now. There is no need to scrimp and scrape any longer.'

Lady Bainbridge looked downcast. 'I fear I cannot stop, my love. I have got into such a habit now. Besides, who knows how long the money will last? Which is why you should not be giving it away to any of these people.'

Amy came up to the table and picked up the top letter from the pile that was being consigned to the flames.

'Dear ma'am,' she read, *'I here as you as won some money and was wondering if you could spare some for me. I am a widow woman and my little ones need food and medicine—'* She broke off abruptly. 'Mama, what is this?'

'Begging letters,' Lady Bainbridge said with a shudder. 'Now that the truth is out, people have been dropping letters in all day. This one here—' she thrust it under Amy's nose '—this is from Lady Belmarsh! She has signed it Mrs Otter and thinks I will not realise the real author, but I recognise the way she writes her letters! The "T" gives her away! To think that she has sunk to this!'

Amy frowned. 'I cannot believe... And you are burning them all! But there may be some genuine cases of hardship amongst them!'

'Undoubtedly, my dear.' Lady Bainbridge picked up another handful and stuffed them into the grate. The flames roared and the edges blackened. 'There are always genuine cases, but how to tell? Are you to spend all your days checking who is needy and who is not? Besides, there are those such as *this*—' Lady Bainbridge shuddered '—who do not deserve to be heard!'

Amy glanced down at the letter in her mother's shaking hand. *'You scheming bitch, that money should be mine—'* she read. She pushed it away, revolted. 'Oh, Mama!'

'I know!' Lady Bainbridge threw her a tearful look. 'Another good reason for us to leave London!'

Amy's shoulders slumped. 'I suppose so. I will go and start packing my bags.'

'Oh, I forgot!' Lady Bainbridge paused, her hands full of paper. 'Amanda Spry is waiting for you in the dining room. She says that it is urgent and she has been waiting a considerable time. I offered her tea in here with me, but she said she would wait in the cool. I suppose it is rather hot in here...'

Amy went back out into the hall, breathing the cooler air with gratitude. The door of the dining room was half open and she went in. Amanda was sitting on one of the hard chairs, her head down her, shoulders drooping. She looked as abject as Amy felt. Amy hurried forward.

'Amanda, I am so sorry to have kept you waiting so long! Would you—?'

She broke off as her friend raised her gaze to hers. Amanda's pretty face was swollen and tear-stained almost out of recognition. Amy went down on her knees on the carpet and clasped both of Amanda's hands.

'Amanda! Whatever has happened? What is the matter?'

Amanda burst into a fresh bout of sobs. She sounded as though she was almost exhausted with crying and she had already shredded her sodden cambric handkerchief between her fingers. Then she had started on her gloves. Amy could see that she had unpicked a whole seam.

'Oh, Amy, I am in such trouble and I need your help!'

Amy frowned. 'Well, of course, I will do whatever I can, but, Amanda, you must tell me—'

'Twenty thousand pounds!' Amanda said wildly. 'I need twenty thousand pounds at once, Amy! Please say you will help me! If you do not, I shall be ruined!'

Half an hour later, Amanda was tucked up in Amy's bedroom and Patience was fussing round with warm milk and a soothing draught of laudanum. Amanda was almost transparent with exhaustion and could barely keep her eyes open. Amy had already sent a reassuring message to Amanda's aunt explaining that Lady Spry would be staying with her that night and that there was no cause for alarm. Now, with the evening drawing on, she came to sit beside the bed and took Amanda's hand in hers.

'There now. Everything is organised and all will be well. You need do nothing except sleep and cease this worrying.'

Amanda's hand clung to hers. 'The money—'

'It will be yours. Do not worry about that now.'

Two small tears seeped from beneath Amanda's eyelids as though she were too weak to cry any more. The hair clung to her forehead with sweat. Amy thought it very likely that she was developing an ague.

'Oh, Amy, I have been such a bad friend to you,' Amanda wailed. 'You have been so kind and I have not even told you what the money is for!'

'You need not.' Amy pushed away the terrifying thought of parting with twenty thousand pounds and told herself stalwartly that she would still have ten thousand to stand between her and penury. Amanda was her dearest friend and she could not—would not—let her down, even if it meant that her own circumstances were reduced.

She patted her hand, anxious only that Amanda should not completely exhaust herself. 'Tomorrow will be soon enough to sort everything out. Now, take your draught.'

'No.' Amanda pushed her hand away. 'I must tell you everything first. I must!'

'Very well,' Amy could tell that her friend was so agitated that she would not rest until she had unburdened herself. 'Do not neglect your milk, though!'

'Very well.' Amanda took a sip. 'Where to start?'

'Where is the beginning?'

Amanda frowned. 'I am not sure.' She put the cup down with a rattle and knitted her hands together. 'I fear that I am being blackmailed.'

Amy stared. The idea seemed manifestly absurd.

'Amanda, who could want to blackmail you and more to the point, about what?'

Amanda looked away. 'I…I suppose that I must tell you everything.' She looked back at Amy. 'I have had an anonymous letter demanding twenty thousand pounds to prevent the release of certain…letters…to the *ton*. Love letters. Do you understand me, Amy? If I do not meet the blackmailer tonight and make arrangements for payment, he will publish my letters in all the scandal sheets. I shall be utterly ruined!'

Amy frowned. 'Amanda, if the letter is anonymous—'

'Oh, I know what you will say!' Amanda made a wild gesture that almost knocked her cup of milk over. 'If it is anonymous, how can I know the identity of the blackmailer? But you see, Amy, there is only one person who knows about the letters…and he has sent me one just to prove that he is in earnest.'

Amy tried to work this out. 'But who would do such a thing?'

Amanda sighed, closing her eyes. She was parchment pale. 'Let me tell you the whole story and then, perhaps, you will understand. I do not want you to think badly of me…'

'Of course.' Amy patted her hand.

'I never wrote to you much about my marriage, did I? That was because I was so unhappy that I had no wish to talk about it. I allowed my mother to choose my husband for me, and Frank Spry was the man she chose. He…' Amy shuddered '…he was not kind to me.'

Amy sighed. 'I am sorry, Mandy. Did nobody know?'

'No, no one. I was so far away, you see. Frank was a gambler and when he was in his cups he would be free with his fists. He swiftly ran though my fortune and after that treated me with contempt. When I discovered that I was breeding he was furious—another mouth to feed, he said, when there was not enough for the two of us. We quarrelled and he…' Amanda shook her head. 'No matter. I lost the child and Frank was pleased, actually pleased!' Her defiant gaze met Amy's again. 'After that, well…I could never care for him again and I took a lover.' She gripped Amy's hand again. 'Please do not hate me!'

'Oh, Mandy!' Amy's throat closed. 'As if I could!'

'I know most people would be obliged to condemn me.' Amanda twisted uncomfortably in the bed. 'And it was not as though I truly loved him, which makes it so much worse! But I was unhappy and it was part misery and part revenge—' her voice rose '—and part just wanting to do *something*—' she screwed up her face '—anything to show my defiance! So I had an affair and I wrote the man some indiscreet letters, and Frank found out…'

'Oh, no…' Amy grimaced. 'What happened?'

'Frank was set to banish me when he fell into an argument over some card-sharping and died in a duel. So I was a widow and thought all safe. I had parted from my lover some time before and had thought…' Amanda plucked at the blankets '…that he had gone abroad. Alas for me that he has returned—and that he still has my letters! Even then I was slow to believe…I thought him a gentleman and not one to sink so low as blackmail!'

A cold breath touched Amy's heart. 'Who was he, Amanda?'

'It was Clive Massingham.' Amanda peered at her

friend. 'Why, Amy, you look as white as a sheet! Whatever did you think?'

Amy took a huge, shaky breath. Not even to herself could she admit that she had thought—just for a split second—that it might be Joss Tallant. She had known that she distrusted Joss's reputation and deplored his relationships with women, but to have doubted him so far was a shocking betrayal.

'I thought it might have been Sebastian Fleet,' she said.

Amanda smiled tiredly. 'No. Oh, Fleet admires me and might wish to make me his mistress, but I have more sense than that now! No, I have learned my lesson the hard way, but it seems that, despite that, my sins will find me out!'

'If it were only your word against Massingham's—'

'But it is not. He has the letters.'

'Of course. He has proved it.'

Amanda nodded slowly. 'As I said, the blackmailer has sent me one of the letters. To help me make up my mind quickly, he said.'

Amy sighed. 'And you are to give him your reply tonight?'

'Yes. That was why it was so urgent that I see you. I am to go to an address in St James's later this evening.' Amanda struggled a little as she tried to get out of bed and sank back with a sigh. 'Oh, I feel so exhausted! I could think of nowhere to turn for the money except to you, Amy, although I knew you would despise me! But I have to pay or else Massingham will distribute my letters about the *ton* and I shall be ruined! Truly, I think I should kill myself!'

'Don't speak like that, Mandy,' Amy said quickly. 'I will keep your assignation with the blackmailer and tell him that the money will be his as soon as I can arrange it. There is nothing for you to fear. You must stay here and rest.'

Amanda's gaze clung to hers. 'You are so good a friend, Amy, and I have been so poor a one to you!'

'Stuff!' Amy went over to her wardrobe and started to rummage through. She needed a dark cloak and a hat with a veil. 'Remember when we were at school and the others were always horrid to me because of my father being a gambler? I was lonely and miserable and you were always the one who defended me!'

Amanda looked as though she was about to cry again. 'I suppose that was so. Yet there is something else that I must tell you. It is nothing to do with this case—nothing at all—but you ought to know...'

Amy's hand stilled. She took the cloak from the wardrobe and came to sit down again. 'What is it?'

'It is Juliana Myfleet.' Amanda sniffed. 'You have remarked before that Juliana and I were friends in my first season. It was the year before you were out. Juliana was such fun but...' she smiled sadly '...she gambled even then, and even though she was unmarried. It was scandalous, of course, but there... Anyway, when I came back up to town this spring I was determined to avoid her, but she sought me out.' Amanda shrugged. 'Once again she tried to involve me in high play, but I have little money now and more sense. I accidentally let slip to her that you had come into a fortune and that was why she inveigled you to gamble with her that night. Not just that—I deliberately left you alone at the tables with her so that she could try to fleece you! I am so sorry, Amy.'

Amy's eyes narrowed. 'Amanda, were you the one

who told Lady Juliana that I had won the money on the lottery?'

Amanda evaded her gaze. 'Oh, Amy!'

'Did you?'

'Yes!' Amanda burst out. 'I am sorry. I owed her money—a trifling sum—but she said that she was willing to trade it for information about your fortune! The only thing I could think to tell her was that you had won thirty thousand pounds! Oh, I cannot bear it!'

Amy sighed. 'It does not matter. I knew that it had to be one of you. I thought it might have been Richard, for Mama is indiscreet but fears society's disapproval too much to let such a matter slip. The only other person who knew was the Earl of Tallant and for a while I suspected him because I thought he might be in league with his sister over that foolish debt!'

Amanda gave a watery laugh. 'I doubt it, Amy! Joss Tallant keeps his distance from Juliana these days.'

Amy looked at her sharply. 'Why, what can you mean?'

Amanda hesitated. 'This is not really my secret to tell—you shall have to ask Lord Tallant about it, and…' she gave Amy a sweet smile '…perhaps you should, since I suspect you have feelings for him.'

'Amanda!' Amy said quickly. She was blushing. 'I am to ask him what?'

'Ask him why he took the blame for his sister's gambling debts all those years ago. Ask him why he allowed his father to believe it was *his* fault, not Juliana's, and why he has never told the truth about it.' Amanda yawned. 'Lord, I am so tired…'

'Yes, but—' Amy grabbed her arm and almost shook her. 'How do you know this? Everyone says that it was

Joss who incurred those debts that almost brought the Tallants down. Why, it is common knowledge—'

Amanda shook her head, still yawning. 'As I said—I was Juliana's best friend in her first season. She confided in me. She was different in those days, Amy.' Amanda sighed. 'There was something softer to her then, more gentle. She knew that she would be utterly disgraced if it all came out and she was desperate to marry Myfleet. 'Tis a pity he did not live—he was a good man and would have been a steadying influence. But Juliana was afraid that he would not have her if he knew… Ask Lord Tallant what happened next. I think he will tell you. All I can say is that no breath of scandal ever attached to Juliana's name and it was Joss who was banished in disgrace…' She slid down in the bed. 'Thank you so much, Amy. I am so sorry…'

It was only a few minutes before the laudanum took full effect and Amanda was asleep, but Amy sat beside the bed for much longer. Deliberating on Amanda's unhappiness and the ways to prevent blackmail, she also thought of Juliana Myfleet and her love for a good man, and of Joss Tallant, who might well prove to be a better man than ever he had been painted.

Chapter Twelve

Joss knew that he was in deep trouble. He had known it for a long time, but had refused to face up to it. He had known it when he had accepted Juliana's wager purely for the pleasure of spending time in Amy's company, he had known it when he had paid off Harriet Templeton and admitted to himself that he had no desire to set up another mistress, and he had known it when he had kissed Amy in Lady Carteret's garden. The only thing that he had not done was acknowledge the truth to himself, indulging instead in a whole range of activities designed to distract his thoughts from their one inevitable conclusion. Now, as he made his farewells to his gambling cronies at a scandalously early hour, Joss was conscious of nothing other than a relief that he had finally admitted the truth. He was in love with Miss Amy Bainbridge and he wanted to marry her.

The thought was shocking, exhilarating and nerve-racking all at the same time, and he had no very clear idea how it could possibly have happened. Since it had, however, he realised that he had two distinct options: to ignore the malaise and hope that it was of short duration or to act on his impulses, ask for an interview and put his fate to the touch. It was a terrifying thought because he did not flatter himself that Amy would accept him.

Outside White's it was raining. The cold night air helped to clear his head, although the thoughts that followed were not encouraging ones. As he walked, Joss enumerated them in his head. Amy thought him a gambler, a wastrel and a womaniser. She hated gambling because of her father's excesses. She would never, never give herself to a man who had the same weakness. Against his will, he remembered her words when they had discussed marriage:

'I am a lady of independent means and have achieved the security I craved. To my mind that is much better…'

He could hardly fool himself that his prospects were bright and yet it only served to strengthen his resolve. He wanted Amy Bainbridge with an ardour that made a mockery of all his previous experience. He wanted to make love to her and he wanted to protect her with the same passionate intensity, and now that he had belatedly admitted to himself that he loved her with all his heart, he had not a hope in hell of suppressing his feelings.

Amy, with her quick wit, shy but astringent, sweet and kind… Amy, small, soft and yielding in his arms… Joss almost groaned aloud. If he had been able to go around to Curzon Street and demand an answer at once, he would have done so. As it was, he suspected he was in for a long, wakeful night.

It was raining. Somehow Amy had not been expecting that and she stood in the darkness outside Number 12 St James's with the raindrops dripping off the brim of her hat and pooling on her cloak. She felt damp and miserable and her wet veil kept sticking to her face.

The blackmailer was not at home and now she was uncertain just what to do.

It had not occurred to her that he would not be there. Either Amanda had got the time or the place wrong, or this was a deliberate attempt to keep her waiting and make her more on edge. Amy suspected the latter. She had no desire to huddle on a street corner until Massingham deigned to return, but equally she did not want to leave Amanda to her fate. It was a dilemma.

She retreated on to the pavement and viewed the dark windows of Number 12 dubiously. Richard had not been at home when she left, or she would have asked him who lived there just so that she had some confirmation of Amanda's suspicions. She felt conspicuous and vulnerable, despite the thick darkness, and when someone touched her arm she almost screamed.

'Miss Bainbridge, it is you. I thought so, but I could scarce believe it! What the *devil* are you doing here at this time of night?'

There was an edge of furious exasperation in Joss's voice and he took her arm in a tight grip. Amy shook him off.

'Oh! It's you!' She looked at him doubtfully. 'Do you live here?'

'I live just across the road. What are you doing loitering in St James's, Miss Bainbridge?' Joss's gaze skimmed her in the gloom. 'And dressed like a shady widow as well? Good God, if I did not know better I should say you were visiting a gentleman—'

'I am.' Amy's teeth were beginning to chatter and a raindrop edged its cold path down her neck. She saw Joss's gaze whip round incredulously and she started to laugh. 'Oh, not in the way that you mean! May we discuss this inside? I am rather cold and wet.'

Joss took her arm again and turned her firmly in the direction of Curzon Street. 'No, we may not! That would be utterly improper. I am taking you home immediately.'

Once again, Amy freed herself. 'That would be quite pointless for I should only be obliged to turn round and come straight back. I cannot believe that the greatest rake in London is debating morality with me in the street at midnight! Please, my lord—'

A couple strolled past them and gave them a curious look. Joss gave an irritable sigh. 'Oh, very well! Come along!'

He hustled her across the road and in at the door. Amy looked about her with interest. Joss's chambers were a mirror of the man himself, stark and austerely decorated. Everything was in excellent taste, but it lacked a spark of warmth, as though Joss deliberately strove to eliminate emotion in his surroundings as much as in his life. Glancing at him, she saw that he was watching her and was immediately obliged to revise her opinion. There was enough heat in his gaze to scorch her. Amy turned hastily away, the danger of stepping into the rooms of a notorious rake hitting her just a little too late.

'Belton, a bottle of brandy, if you please, and some wine for Miss Bainbridge.' Joss was divesting himself of his cloak and hat and passing them to the valet, who had materialised silently in the corridor in front of them. Amy started to feel a little better. There was nothing more respectable than a servant.

'Once you have brought the drinks you may retire,' Joss continued.

'Certainly, my lord,' the valet said.

Amy bit her lip. 'Oh dear, how perfectly scandalous this is! Perhaps I should not have come in—'

'Of course you should not.' Joss ushered her into a drawing room where a cheerful fire burned and the candles were already lit. 'You are here now, however. Would you care to give me your cloak and that rather extraordinary hat?'

Amy started to struggle out of her disguise. Belton came into the room, set down a tray with the drinks and unobtrusively slipped out again.

'How well your valet copes with such disreputable goings-on, my lord!' Amy smothered a yawn. The warmth of the room made her feel sleepy. 'No doubt he has had much practice!'

Joss did not look amused. 'No, indeed. Belton and I live a very quiet life.' He scrutinised her. 'Amy, you look as though you should be on stage at Drury Lane rigged out in that garb! What *is* that ridiculous contraption on your head?'

Amy unpinned the black felt hat and looked at it sorrowfully. It had drooped in the rain and the veil was dripping water. 'It is dreadful, is it not? At least Mama was never fond of it!' She broke off as she realised that Joss's attention was focussed on her hair rather than the hat in her hand. The shining strands were tumbling straight about her shoulders but she could not see why that should be responsible for his slightly stunned expression. She flicked it back a little self-consciously.

'I suppose I look a fright! Would your valet be good enough to dry my cloak?'

'Of course.' Joss seemed to shake himself and took the soaking black cloak from her outstretched hands. He was careful not to touch her and Amy suddenly understood. A burning blush washed over her as she acknowledged that she was alone with Joss in his rooms at past midnight. It was, as he had said, utterly improper. Yet a small, traitorous tickle of excitement ran down her spine at the thought.

'I would not have expected you to be home at this hour, my lord,' she said, accepting the glass of wine that he passed to her. 'I thought that you would be gambling at White's, or—' She stopped, blushing harder. That was what one got for allowing unruly thoughts to get away.

There was a glimmer of a smile in Joss's eyes. 'I fear that you have improved me even if you did not desire to do so, Miss Bainbridge,' he said slowly. 'I am home so early because I find that you have ruined my concentration at cards. As for the rest…' his smile deepened '…I fear that holds little interest for me either!'

'Oh, well…' Amy attempted to achieve a coolness to match his own although she knew she was looking pink and flustered. 'Perhaps you will find some new pastimes in a little while.'

'Perhaps so.' Joss's gaze held hers intently for a loaded moment, and then he moved away, his manner becoming briskly businesslike. 'That is nothing to the purpose, however. Come and sit by the fire and tell me what is going on.'

Amy took a sip of her wine. It was warming and strong and she started almost imperceptibly to relax.

'It is a little difficult…I am here on behalf of another lady, you see. Oh!' She looked up as a thought struck her. 'Perhaps you could tell me who lives at Number 12, my lord? It is most important that I find out.'

'I could tell you,' Joss said, swirling the brandy in his glass, 'but not until you tell me the whole story.'

Amy frowned. 'That is not fair play! I am keeping a

secret for another lady and am not at liberty to disclose the whole!'

Joss shrugged. 'You will not get something for nothing, Miss Bainbridge! Is the gentleman expecting you or will he be surprised to find the assignation kept by a different lady? I should warn you to be careful!'

Amy laughed. 'It is not that sort of assignation, my lord. I am here to assure the gentleman that...' she hesitated '...that he will receive his money in good time.'

'A blackmailer?' Joss's tone hardened. He sat forward in his chair, resting his elbows on his knees. 'Then I should also counsel you not to pay, Miss Bainbridge, for blackmailers are seldom satisfied with a single sum. He will return and bleed you dry.'

'I know.' Amy screwed up her face. She had already thought of this, but could see no immediate solution. If Amanda did not pay, she would be ruined; if she did pay, no doubt she would be called upon to do so again and again. 'I have told my friend this, but...'

Joss sighed. 'Your friend? Amy, are you sure that it is not you who are being blackmailed?'

Amy pulled a face. 'Of course not! What reason could anyone have to blackmail me? I have no secrets!'

Joss shrugged. 'If you say so, I believe you. It is just that when someone alludes to a mysterious friend, it is usually themselves they are referring to...'

'Oh, I know!' Amy took another draught of the wine. 'I realise it sounds most odd and unconvincing!' She hesitated. 'If I trust you with the whole—'

A light flickered in Joss's eyes. 'Would you do so?'

'Yes, I think I would,' Amy looked undecided. 'I feel a little disloyal all the same.'

Joss straightened up. 'Perhaps I can make matters easy for you. I would guess that your friend is Lady

Spry and she is being blackmailed about some indiscretion, but because she has no money you have decided to help her pay—'

'Stop!' Amy held a hand up. 'You are correct in all particulars, my lord, and I can see that there is no point in withholding the truth from you! Amanda is in desperate straits and I have sworn to help her.'

Joss shook his head. 'You are not helping. The blackmailer will not accept a single payment, Amy. You know he will not! Whatever Lady Spry's secret, he will hold it over her head until she pays and pays again! It would be easier for her just to tell him to publish and be damned.'

Amy looked away. 'Like his Grace of Wellington? She cannot. She will be ruined.'

Joss made a slight gesture. 'What is it—a love affair? It might be uncomfortable for her, but she will live it down. She is a widow and cannot be ruined by so commonplace an indiscretion—'

'You do not understand. It was whilst she was married to Frank Spry and he threatened to banish her.'

'Even so—' Joss frowned '—Spry is dead and whilst such rumours would be unpleasant—'

'There are *letters*,' Amy said, with emphasis.

There was a silence.

'I see,' Joss said at length. 'That does make it considerably more difficult.'

Amy gave a slight laugh. She pushed the hair back from her face, where it was drying in silken strands. 'Difficult! If you could have seen her, Joss! She said that she would kill herself if the letters were ever to become public!'

'So you agreed to help her. Of course. How much money is he asking?'

Amy looked down. 'Twenty thousand pounds.'

'Two-thirds of your fortune. Amy, you said that now you had the money you felt secure at last—'

'It is nothing,' Amy said quickly. She swallowed hard. 'I have thought about this, Joss. Amanda has been a good friend to me. Besides, I shall still have ten thousand pounds—less the sum I have already spent…'

Joss said nothing. His face was shadowed and still. 'And the name of the blackmailer?'

Amy stared. 'It is Clive Massingham. Surely you knew? I thought… If he lives at Number 12…'

'No one lives there presently,' Joss said. 'It has been empty, which I suppose makes it a useful address for a blackmailer to take.' He stretched and stood up. 'I will go and see Massingham, Amy, and retrieve your friend's letters for her. In the meantime I suggest you return and reassure her that all is well. I will get in touch with you as soon as I have them.'

Amy got slowly to her feet. She felt relieved but puzzled by his offer of help. '*You* will go to see Massingham? But why?'

'To help you, of course.' Joss raised an eyebrow. 'He is not the sort of man with whom you should be arranging a midnight rendezvous. It will also save you wasting your winnings on him. He will never be a good cause.' He smiled. 'Now you should go home, Amy.'

Amy was watching his face. 'Yes, in a little… How will you make Massingham give up the letters if you do not pay him? He will not be persuaded easily!'

Joss's expression hardened. 'I think I can persuade him, though perhaps Lady Spry should be prepared to leave town for a little until the matter dies down.'

'I had thought of that,' Amy said. 'I plan to take Amanda to Nettlecombe with me for a space.'

Joss's face softened. 'I do not understand it, but it seems you must for ever be helping waifs and strays, Amy—'

Amy met his eyes very directly. 'It is not my sole prerogative, is it, Joss? What about yourself?'

Joss had been moving towards the door, but now he paused. 'What do you mean?'

Amy held his gaze. Now that the moment had come for her to ask for the truth she felt acutely nervous. 'Why, I mean that you are going to a deal of trouble to help me now, but that is nothing compared to what you did to help Lady Juliana.'

Joss's jaw tightened. She saw a muscle move in his cheek. He walked slowly over to the fireplace and laid his arm along the mantel, resting one booted foot on the fender. He looked relaxed, but Amy knew he was not. The tension in him was as taut as twisted steel.

'Who told you about that, Amy? I cannot believe that Juliana—' He broke off. 'It was a long time ago and no doubt you have heard a garbled tale.'

Amy moved across to him. She touched his arm very lightly. There was anger and gentleness in his eyes, warring for mastery, and it made her heart contract.

'I heard that you took the blame for all of Lady Juliana's gambling so that she should not be ruined and might marry Lord Myfleet. Is my informant wrong?'

For a long moment Joss stared down into her eyes, then he pulled away. His tone was clipped. 'No, she is in the right of it! Lady Spry, I presume? Juliana swore she had never told anyone, but I did not believe her!' He took an angry pace across the room. 'Damnation, of all the things that I did not wish you to know—'

'I do not understand,' Amy said tremulously. His anger shook her. 'I do not understand why you took the blame and allowed your father to banish you, and I do not understand why you did not wish me to know—'

Joss was looking furious. 'Oh, you understand well enough, Amy! I took the blame out of misplaced chivalry, in the same way in which you wanted to save Lady Spry from Massingham!' His tone was savage. 'Juliana is my little sister and she was a different girl then. Oh, she was wild, and she gambled too hard, but she was gentler—she could have been so different if our childhood had not been as it was!' Joss brought his fist crashing down on the mantelpiece. 'Juliana came to me in tears and told me that she had made huge losses at the gaming table. I confess that when she told me the sum I was shocked. She was in despair—Myfleet was on the point of proposing and I knew she was head over heels in love with him. I also knew that if the scandal of her losses came out our father would send her away and ruin it all for her. Myfleet would have forgiven her, but our father never would! He was always unbending and she...she had lost eighty thousand pounds! She almost brought the family down! To my father the dishonour was more important than anything else!'

Amy sank back down into her armchair. 'But how did you fool him?' she whispered.

'It was simple enough.' Joss shrugged indifferently. 'My father never comes up to town. Juliana had some hen-witted female as chaperon—the woman could not control her and knew nothing of her antics. And I was a young man about town who gambled sometimes... No one thought it strange that I should have incurred such losses.'

'But your father sent you away...'

'Yes—' Joss gave her a grim smile '—but Juliana married Myfleet and was happy and I thought...' His face twisted. 'I thought it might make up for all the callous indifference that our father had shown her over the years. I still believe that, if Myfleet had not died, Juliana would be quite different...'

Amy went across to him. 'But what about you, Joss?'

'What about me? I was luckier than Ju—he always suspected that she was not his daughter, you see. Whereas I had my father's attention, his good opinion—'

'Until you deliberately threw it away.'

Amy saw him flinch. 'It does not matter. It was all a long time ago.'

'It does matter!' Amy felt a surge of rage so powerful that she was shaking. 'Surely Juliana could tell your father the truth now? It could not hurt her after all these years! Whereas you have borne his disapproval and dislike unnecessarily for all this time—'

Joss moved away from her. His voice was cold, forbidding her to trespass further. 'It would make no difference now.'

Amy made an impotent little gesture. 'Do you not care?'

Joss gave her a sideways look. 'Not any more. Now...' his tone eased '...it is time that you were going.'

Amy stood her ground. 'You have not told me yet why you did not wish me to know.'

Joss stopped. 'I was afraid you would interpret it as a noble gesture, my dear, and I wished to avoid that above all things.'

Amy was stung by the contempt in his tone, though whether it was for her or for himself, she could not tell. She went up to him and put a hand on his arm. 'Well, and so it is a noble gesture—why deny it? What you did for your sister was truly generous and shows the essential goodness of your character.'

'It shows nothing! This is *exactly* what I knew you would say!'

'Then why make yourself out to be worse than you truly are—?' Amy stopped, at a loss.

'I shall tell you why!' Joss grabbed her arms. For a moment Amy thought he was about to shake her, but he just held her in an iron grip, his fingers biting into her flesh. 'One noble deed does not make a hero, Miss Bainbridge, and it is naïve and foolish to think otherwise.' His furious face was heart-stoppingly close to hers. 'Every other thing that you have heard of me, every stupid and dangerous and arrogant thing—the gambling, the women—everything is true. Probably it is worse than you have heard. *That* is why I cannot have you believing me to be good.'

He let her go as swiftly as he had grabbed hold of her. 'Now will you leave?'

'No,' Amy said. Her voice was shaking and distantly she realised it was because her throat was thick with tears. 'I will not go until I understand what you are trying to prove to me.'

With an infuriated groan, Joss wrenched her into his arms.

'Amy, you try me past endurance! Not two hours ago I was resolved to offer you marriage, but now I am indebted to you for showing me why it can never be! What can I do to make you see that we can never be together? Our worlds are so utterly different—'

'You do speak a deal of nonsense, Joss,' Amy said clearly. Her heart had leapt at his words, but now she schooled herself to calm. She raised her hand to his cheek and felt the stubble rough against her palm. Inside she was trembling but she knew she could not let it show. Any uncertainty on her part now would compound his own agonising doubts and then she could never break through them. The only way was to show absolute confidence, when inside she was terrified. This was the biggest gamble of her life.

'I am tired of being on a pedestal,' she said. 'I have made mistakes and misjudged people and thought that I knew best. I do not want to be treated like a saint!' She pressed her fingertips against his lips. 'I want you, Joss.'

Amy felt Joss go very still. After such a declaration it would have been impossible to withdraw, even had she wanted to do so. Her hand fell to his chest, pressing against the smooth material of his jacket. Would he never move, never speak? She loved him so much that she could feel the desperation and longing rise within her in a devastating tide. She had gambled now—was she about to lose it all? She could not help the lone tear that slid down her cheek.

Joss bent his head and captured it, his lips following the salty trail to the corner of Amy's mouth. She was shaking like a leaf now. His lips brushed hers, the lightest of contacts, and she shivered and opened to him, the desire burning through her as the kiss deepened.

Joss swung her up in his arms and took two strides over to the sofa, where he sat down with her on his knee. Amy slid her arms about his neck and held tight. She found that she liked their new position; she turned her head and pressed her lips against his throat, inhaling the scent of his skin overlaid with the spice of sandalwood. Excitement flared inside her. She felt as though she was on the edge of some precipice, about to step into thin air, but in the knowledge that she could fly.

Tentatively she parted her lips and touched her tongue to his skin, tasting, marvelling. She heard Joss groan, and then one of his hands came up to tangle in her hair and he turned her lips up to his again, plundering her mouth with his own. The world spun, ignited by their mutual passion.

When Joss finally broke the kiss and drew back, his breathing was ragged and his eyes dark with desire.

'Amy, believe me, I want nothing more than to keep you here with me and make love to you, but it must not be—'

Amy leaned forward and kissed him again, her teeth closing over his bottom lip, biting gently. Joss smothered another groan.

'Amy, damnation…'

Joss could feel his self-control slipping perilously. He had been fighting this ever since she had stepped into the room. When she had removed her ridiculous hat, the sight of her hair loose about her shoulders had transfixed him. When she had taken off the cloak he had wanted to ease her out of every other item of clothing that she was wearing. He had barely been able to concentrate on what she had been telling him about the blackmail attempt because all his senses were focussed on her and the devastating need that possessed him. He had thought that if he could only get rid of her, finish the discussion and send her home, he might at least have some chance of getting through the encounter with Amy unscathed. Then Amy herself had turned that upon its head and now…

His hands tightened about her waist, drawing her against him. He let her pursue the kiss, his senses tightening as she took the initiative and tentatively touched her tongue to his. Joss could feel her breasts crushed against his chest and his entire body clenched in anticipation. He eased her bodice down and her left breast, small and perfect, fell into his hand. He rubbed his fingers over the taut nipple and felt Amy tense in his arms.

'Oh, my goodness! *Joss…*'

She sounded dazzled and profoundly intrigued. Joss bent his head to take her nipple in his mouth. Amy stifled a small scream.

'Joss! Oh, please…'

In the firelight her skin was flushed warm and pink, too tempting to resist. He could see the dawning passion in her eyes, their topaz blue dazed and slumberous with desire. He kissed her again, his hand cupping her breast, and tumbled her beneath him on the sofa.

'Amy…' He brushed the shining hair back from her face. 'Sweetheart…you know what will happen if you stay…' In about ten seconds, he thought wryly, if I do not find my self-control. He drew away from her. 'You must go home.'

Amy reached up to slide her arms about his neck. 'I know.' Her words were a whisper. 'I love you, Joss.'

It was almost his undoing. He brought his lips back to hers, sliding his tongue into the intimate depths of her mouth, kissing her with all the pent-up desire that possessed him. Then, carefully, he drew away. His fingers were shaking as he helped her to rearrange her dress and to get to her feet.

'This is not how I want it to be between us, darling. Not some midnight tryst in my rooms with your reputation in ruins if it were to ever come out. No!' He warded her off when she would have come into his arms again. 'Grant me this, please. If I am to have you, then it must be done properly. I must ask your brother's permission and speak to you in form and…' he hesitated

'...give you the opportunity to think about it in case you wish to refuse me...'

He saw the tender laughter in Amy's eyes and felt his heart leap.

'Very well, Lord Tallant,' she said demurely. 'In that case you had better escort me home.'

The streets were wet and dark, with a cool rain still falling. It felt like tears against Amy's cheek and she ducked under the shelter of Joss's umbrella to keep dry. She gripped his arm tightly and pressed close to his side, comforted by his proximity. Their earlier passion had melted into companionable warmth but under it a current of excitement still ran strongly. Every so often Amy would glance up at Joss's face and, even though it was dark and shadowed, she could see the faint smile that curved his lips. She felt so intensely happy that she could not stop herself smiling. She knew that she would not be able to sleep.

At the door of Number 3 Curzon Street, Joss turned to her very formally and kissed her gloved hand.

'I will go to see Massingham now and I will bring Lady Spry's letters for her in the morning. Then, perhaps, we may talk, Miss Bainbridge?'

'I should like that,' Amy said shyly.

Joss smiled and bowed, then turned and walked away. Amy watched him until the shadows swallowed him up and the echo of his footsteps died away.

A light still burned in the house and Marten came out into the hall when she opened the door. He showed not a flicker of surprise to see Amy returning alone at that hour of the night, informed her that Sir Richard had yet to return and wished her goodnight. Amy climbed the stairs slowly. The euphoria that had filled her in

Joss's company had settled to a simmering of excitement now and the ache of unfulfilled passion had eased. She felt precious and, in a strange way, fiercely proud of Joss.

Patience had had the foresight to make up a bed for her in the small, spare room, and as Amy slid between the fresh, lavender-scented sheets, she thought of what Joss had said about Juliana, and about his relationship with his father. So much unhappiness and misunderstanding…

Amy was too tired to think properly but she knew there was one more thing that she had to do, one more wrong to be righted. Joss would deal with Massingham, but in the matter of Juliana's debts he would never tell his father the truth. Amy turned over on to her side, pressing her hot cheek against the cool pillow. She suspected that were Joss to discover what she intended, he would do everything in his power to prevent her. Which meant that she would have to leave London early and go to Ashby Tallant alone. On that thought, to her vague surprise, she fell asleep.

Chapter Thirteen

After Joss left Amy he did not, as she might have supposed, go back to Number 12, St James's but went instead to an elegant house in Cavendish Square, where a slightly flustered maid showed him into the drawing room and informed him that her mistress was from home but was expected back soon.

Sure enough, not five minutes had elapsed and Joss's glass of brandy was almost untouched when the front door banged and there was the sound of angry footsteps on the hall tiles, followed by the murmur of the maid's voice.

'Lord Tallant is here to see you, ma'am —'

'Joss is here? At this time of the night?'

The drawing-room door was thrust unceremoniously open and Juliana Myfleet swept in. Joss thought that she, too, looked flustered for one brief moment, then her expression changed to chagrin and finally amusement.

'Joss, dearest,' she said coolly, 'I scarce expected to see you tonight! Whatever can have brought you here?'

Joss smiled. 'May I pour you a glass of wine, Ju? You will need it if you have been out in the rain. I always say it is so time-consuming owning two properties. One is called out at all times of the night!'

Since Lady Juliana was even now shaking the raindrops from her black cloak, she did not waste time on denials. She gave her brother a faint smile.

'A glass of port would be welcome, I thank you, Joss. But I repeat, what do you do here?'

'I came about a business matter,' Joss said. He poured for his sister and took the glass over to her by the fire before resuming his seat in the other armchair. 'Your business, to be precise. I fear that you have had a wasted journey, Juliana.' Then, when she made no move to reply: 'To Number 12 St James's.'

Juliana's gaze flickered slightly. 'I do not understand you, my dear—'

'I think that you do.' Joss's tone was very even. 'Lady Spry did not arrive for your assignation, did she?'

'I know nothing of a meeting with Amanda Spry.' Juliana gave a petulant little shrug. 'The apartment in St James's belongs to Massingham. He uses it for certain…business arrangements. It is so much more convenient. I was awaiting him there but he—' She broke off.

'He failed to arrive. I understand that Massingham is normally to be found in Covent Garden these days, enjoying the company of Miss Templeton. Why do you tolerate it, Ju?'

Juliana gave a slight shudder, so imperceptible that Joss almost missed it. 'Massingham's *amours* do not trouble me. A woman is a fool if she expects a man to be faithful and that little bitch was always for sale to the highest bidder! You know that, Joss! You were the one who left the vacancy!'

Joss put his brandy glass down gently. 'I am less

concerned with Massingham's *amours* than I am with your business affairs, Juliana. If you needed money, why did you not ask me, instead of trying to extort it from Lady Spry? That was needlessly cruel.'

They stared at each other for what seemed an hour. There was no sound but the crackle of the fire and the pale hiss of the candles burning down. Joss refused to break the silence and Juliana's composure smashed.

'I did not ask you because I detest being your pensioner, Joss, and I knew…' She swallowed a sob. 'I knew that you would not give me the money if you found out why I required it! Massingham and I are to go to Paris, but we cannot do so without the funds to support us and I knew you detest Massingham and would never pay! For once…' she gave him a self-deprecating smile that wobbled slightly '…I did not wish to lie to you and pretend that this was a gambling debt…'

'You mean that Massingham will not take you for love alone?' Joss's face twisted. 'Juliana, the man is worthless. Have done with this!'

'No!' Juliana's glass smashed on the marble fireplace. She jumped to her feet and swung round on him, the tears streaming down her face. 'I love him, Joss! Was that what you wanted to hear? You have driven me to say it. I love him without pretence or illusion and I still want him! If he will not take me without fortune, then fortune I must have!' She scrambled for a handkerchief. 'I do not expect you to understand.'

Joss handed her his handkerchief. His heart felt heavy. He knew that he had to let her go, had to help her, even against his better judgement. 'I do understand, Ju. I understand better than you might imagine.'

Juliana stared at him. 'Because of Miss Bainbridge? The cases are not the same.'

'No, they are not, but loving Amy has made me see that one cannot always control love as one might choose,' Joss sighed. 'If Massingham is what you want, Juliana, then I will give you the money to go with him. Now, come here.'

She came to him and he hugged her in much the same way as he had done when they were children. He rested his chin on the top of her head and spoke quietly.

'How did you come by Lady Spry's letters, Ju?'

He felt a shudder go through her. 'I found them. Clive had kept them all, bound in pink ribbon. Pink ribbon, for pity's sake! And I was so angry, Joss, so angry and jealous that I took them all. I was going to destroy them, to burn them all, but then Amanda Spry came up to town and I suddenly thought to have my revenge on her and gain something out of my loss...' She freed herself and scrubbed her cheeks viciously. 'I do not believe that Clive even knows that I have them.'

Joss shook his head. 'So much hatred, Juliana. And Lady Spry did not even have the money to give to you.'

'No, but I knew that she was thick with Amy Bainbridge and that Miss Bainbridge *did* have the money.' Juliana looked up and gave her brother a glimmer of a smile. 'I suppose I should have guessed that Miss Bainbridge would come to you, Joss, but I underestimated two things: the fact that she trusted you and the fact that you loved her. If anyone had asked me I would never have imagined it, not in a thousand years! I do not believe that I know my own brother well at all...'

Joss smiled and moved away. 'You know me well enough. I will give you your twenty thousand pounds in return for Lady Spry's letters—all of them, Ju.' There was a warning note in his voice. 'And I will wish you godspeed and say that no matter what happens I shall always want to see you again—'

'Enough!' Lady Juliana had regained some of her brittle composure and stepped away from him. The malicious gleam was back in her green eyes. 'You grow maudlin, Joss! If this is the effect that love has had on you I shudder to think what a doting husband you will make and I am glad I shall not be here to see it! Now, I will fetch the letters and I shall be obliged if I may draw on your bank…' She wafted towards the door. 'You are too good to me, my dear. It is a shame that you have been unfairly damned as the black sheep of the family, but I fear that when my latest exploits are known I shall inherit that role. I shall hope to bear it with fortitude.'

It was mid-morning of the following day when Joss reached Curzon Street and the rain of the previous night had gone, blown away by a fresh breeze. It felt like a day for new beginnings.

As Patience let him in to the house, he became aware of a certain tension in the atmosphere. The sound of Lady Bainbridge's voice came to him from behind the parlour door, rising and falling like a peal of bells.

'It is all very well for you to say that, Richard, but we were supposed to remove to Nettlecombe today and now that Amy is missing—'

Joss quickened his step. For a split second he had the most dreadful conviction that Amy had fled to the country because she regretted the events of the previous night. She did not want to marry him—she would never want to do so. She would never even want to see him again… He shook his head to dispel the images, remembering a little grimly that he had once told Amy that his family history was bound to make him wary of marriage. What he had failed to grasp, he thought now, was how inextricably his happiness had become bound up in Amy. She could break his heart so easily, but he had to have the faith that she would never do so. It seemed a monstrously difficult lesson to learn and he had only just started.

Lady Bainbridge, Richard and Amanda Spry were assembled in the parlour and the addition of another person made the room seem rather small. Richard was lounging by the window and looking irritated, Amanda was sitting with her hands clenched in her lap and looked very pale and Lady Bainbridge, her hair in drooping ringlets, her face creased with worry, was waving a piece of paper in her hand.

'She says in her note that she has had to travel to the country unexpectedly and will meet us at Nettlecombe this evening!'

'There you are then, Mama!' Richard said heartily. 'There is no mystery—' He broke off as he saw Joss and a look of relief crossed his face, though whether it was for the distraction or because he thought the newcomer might help Joss was not sure.

'Good morning, Joss! Perhaps you might be able to shed some light on this as you've been seeing a lot of Amy recently—' Richard broke off again, evidently aware of his infelicitous choice of words and his mother's frown. Joss came forward and bowed over Lady Bainbridge's hand, smoothing her ruffled temper with his most charming smile.

'Good morning, ma'am. Lady Spry…' He bowed to Amanda before straightening up and turning to his host. 'Do I understand that Miss Bainbridge is from home?'

'She has gone to Oxfordshire,' Lady Bainbridge wailed, brandishing the note, 'and she has travelled post! Post! It is so much more expensive!'

'Come now, Mama,' Richard said, with an apologetic look at Joss, 'you know you would prefer Amy not to travel alone on the common stage.'

'No,' Lady Bainbridge conceded, 'but I do not understand why she must go jauntering off in this manner at all!'

Joss caught Amanda's eye. It was clear that Lady Spry suspected that Amy had gone off on some errand connected with the blackmailer, but that she did not dare disclose her suspicions. If Amy had arrived back in Curzon Street too late to see her friend and had set off that morning whilst it was still early, Amanda might even now be labouring under the belief that the blackmailer was still at large. Joss gave her a reassuring smile.

'Before I forget, Lady Spry, I was commissioned to give this to you by Miss Bainbridge.' He passed her an anonymous brown parcel. 'Something that she has...procured for you, I believe. You will find that it is all there. I am to tell you that there was no charge.'

The colour flooded into Amanda's cheeks, changing her from tense and strained to pretty and animated once again. 'Oh! Thank you, sir!'

'A pleasure, Lady Spry.' Joss bowed and turned away. 'Lady Bainbridge, I beg you not to worry. I believe that Miss Bainbridge may have gone to Ashby Tallant to see my father. Would you like me to find her for you?'

Richard and Lady Bainbridge exchanged a look. 'To see your father?' Lady Bainbridge echoed faintly. 'But Amy does not even know the Marquis!'

'I feel sure it is an omission she is about to remedy,' Joss said, a little grimly. 'We had a conversation yesterday that leads me to suspect that Miss Bainbridge would wish to speak with him urgently. With your permission, I will ride to Ashby Tallant and find out for myself. Then I can escort Miss Bainbridge to Nettlecombe once the matter is settled.'

Lady Bainbridge looked understandably perplexed. 'Well, if you are certain, my lord…'

'Of course, ma'am.' Joss turned to Richard. 'You are in agreement?'

Richard was looking relieved. 'Of course, old fellow! Only surprised that you want to be bothered! Still, it saves me trouble. I'm already late for a game at the Cocoa Tree—' He caught his mother's admonishing look and broke off.

'If I might delay you a little longer,' Joss said smoothly, a twinkle in his eye, 'there is something rather particular I wished to ask you. It might also explain why I…er…would be bothering to follow Miss Bainbridge…'

He saw the light dawn in Richard's eye, heard Amanda catch her breath, and allowed himself a grin.

As Richard ushered him out of the room, Joss heard Amanda turn to Lady Bainbridge with the excitement vivid in her voice:

'Oh, Lady Bainbridge, is it not wonderful! Amy is to be a Countess!'

'Well, dear,' his future mother-in-law said, 'one should not refine too much upon these things, but it is more than I had ever expected for Amy! And it will be so much cheaper to have her off my hands at last!'

Richard closed the door very firmly and turned to Joss, offering his hand.

'Welcome to the family,' he said.

* * *

Amy had been impressed by her first view of Ashby Tallant. The lime avenue was very fine and the frontage of the house, red brick with a great hall and a tower at one end, was most imposing. Even in his most prosperous times, Sir George Bainbridge had never possessed a house like it and Nettlecombe, the only remaining Bainbridge property, was on a considerably smaller scale. Nevertheless, Ashby Tallant did not appear to Amy as a comfortable family home.

The liveried servant who answered the door informed her that the Marquis was out in the gardens but that if Miss Bainbridge would not mind waiting, someone would be sent to fetch him at once. She was escorted into a drawing room decorated in blue and faded gold. It was cold and dusty and Amy, perching on the edge of one of the hard chairs, felt a little over-awed as the chill seeped into her bones.

The house was quiet as the grave and the long wait gave her plenty of time to think. When Joss had confirmed the story that Amanda had told her, her first and overwhelming reaction had been fury—fury that Joss had taken all the blame for Lady Juliana's misdeeds and that the Marquis was so cold and censorious a character that he had never forgiven his son. The long journey from London had given her time to try to compose herself and she had admitted to herself that it was her love for Joss that had prompted such furious indignation. She could not bear to see him hurt any more and that alone obliged her to tell the Marquis the truth. She had no notion what her reception might be or whether it would make any difference at all, but she felt she had to try. At the back of her mind was also the thought that Joss would probably be quite angry with her for interfering, but she refused to think about that. Her stomach rumbled with hunger—it was past the hour for luncheon—and she could not repress a sneeze.

The door opened.

'His lordship will see you now, Miss Bainbridge,' the footman intoned.

The hall was a vast affair of white stone and dark wood, and on the other side of it the footman opened a door and stepped aside for her to enter.

'Miss Bainbridge, my lord.'

The Marquis of Tallant was standing before the huge fireplace, leaning heavily on a gold-topped cane. Amy had been uncertain what to expect but now the sight of the Marquis surprised her; he was stooped and his face was pulled with pain and his hair was white, but his eyes were the same amber as those of his son, and burned with the same fierce light.

'Miss Bainbridge,' he said, and his voice was beautiful, smooth as polished leather, 'this is a great honour.'

'I fear it is a great intrusion, my lord,' Amy said, suddenly feeling the whole weight of the Marquis's age and authority, and wondering how she would ever have the courage to blurt out her tale. 'I must thank you for seeing me.'

The Marquis gestured her to a chair. 'No imposition, Miss Bainbridge. We have never met, but I do believe that I knew your father once. Your family has property over Nettlecombe way, I believe? You have a great look of George Bainbridge about you.'

'Do I?' Amy was so startled that she was distracted from the purpose of the visit for a moment. No one had ever likened her to her father. Richard, with his glowing fair looks and blue eyes had always been the obvious comparison.

'You have his spirit,' the Marquis said, on a sigh. 'I see it in your eyes. Would you care for some refreshment, Miss Bainbridge? I suspect that you have travelled a long way.'

Amy was tempted. 'Well, I confess I am a little sharp set, my lord. I left London very early and I was not sure how long the journey would take...'

'It must have been urgent, then,' the Marquis said. He gave the bell pull a sharp tug.

'Ah, Watson, a tray of food for Miss Bainbridge and...some wine?'

'Just a little, if you please,' Amy said, blushing. 'I am not accustomed to strong drink.'

'A small glass,' the Marquis instructed, 'and some canary for me.'

There was a short silence after the servant had left the room. Amy was aware that she should state her business and even more conscious that if she did so and the Marquis took exception to her words, she would be out of the house without any time for refreshment at all. She bit her lip as she tried to think of the best way to broach the subject. The Marquis, who had been watching her expressive little face, limped across to the other armchair and eased himself down.

'Take your time, my dear. I always say that there is no point in rushing an important matter.'

Amy gave him an agonised look. 'Oh, my lord, it is simply that I am fearful of what you will think.'

'Then do not be. I doubt that I could think badly of you and I shall certainly not turn you off before you have had your wine!'

Amy stifled a laugh. 'My lord, you say that now—'

'Allow me to help you to overcome your scruples,' the Marquis said. 'Does this matter concern my son, perhaps?'

Amy stared. 'Why, yes, but…how did you know?'

The question was not to be answered for a moment, for the footman reappeared with a tray laden with bread, cheeses, honey, ham and fruit for Amy and a glass and bottle of canary for the Marquis. By the time that everything was served and Amy had obeyed the Marquis's instruction to eat, the barriers had been broken down further.

'It is always a mistake to tackle high emotion on an empty stomach,' the Marquis said, watching with amusement as Amy attacked the food with enthusiasm. 'I always feel that food gives one an appropriate sense of proportion.' He took a sip of canary. 'As to how I knew—well, I cannot go to London much these days—confounded ill health, you know—but there are those who keep me informed and they told me that my son had recently abandoned his usual pursuits in favour of spending time with a certain young lady of… impeccable quality. You, my dear. I confess that I was delighted to hear it.'

Amy looked up and blushed. 'Oh, well, yes, but it was not as you might suppose.'

The Marquis raised an ironic eyebrow. 'Indeed? I had thought that perhaps Joss had taken to heart my strictures about taking a wife…'

Amy blushed harder. 'Yes…well, no! You see, Lord Tallant only spent time with me because his sister made a bet… Oh dear, this is difficult…I had not intended to tell you so much…'

The Marquis's sardonic smile melted into one of genuine charm. 'My dear Miss Bainbridge, why do you not simply tell me the whole? You will probably find it easier to come to the point if you tell the whole tale from beginning to end.'

'Yes, my lord.' Amy was also beginning to realise that it would not be possible to tell half a story. Nor did she wish to. The Marquis was so very different from the image that she had in her mind that she was certain he would charm the truth from her by one means or another. He was just like his son.

'Before I begin, my lord,' she said impulsively, 'I wish you to know that I am aware of the…the lack of sympathy that there has been between you and your son.' She saw that he was looking at her inscrutably and hurried on. 'Oh, I know that this is none of my business and that in speaking thus I am guilty of the greatest impertinence, but I had to tell you! What I will relate must surely make you see that you are mistaken in Lord Tallant and that he is—essentially noble!'

The Marquis raised his eyebrows. 'Noble? I might say that you are coming it a bit strong, Miss Bainbridge, but I fear you would call me out! Your tale will speak for itself, I am sure. As for my opinion of you, nothing can alter the esteem in which I hold you.'

Amy smiled tremulously. She was not clear how the Marquis had come to have such a good opinion of her in such a short time, but she was fearful that she might lose it soon. Nevertheless, the story had to be told. She suspected that she might have given away something of her feelings for Joss in her last impassioned outburst, but that appeared to in no way have impaired his father's view of her. Maybe that was the key to his approval—he was so pleased that his son had apparently attached himself to a respectable female that he was willing to give her a certain latitude. On that thought she took her courage in both hands and plunged in.

She left nothing out. She told the Marquis how she had first met Joss at the house in Curzon Street, how she had won the lottery, how Joss had accepted Juliana's debt and spent the week doing good deeds. When she related that he had escorted her to the concert given by the children's charity choir and had gone to visit the St Boniface orphanage with her, the Marquis was overcome with a fit of coughing and Amy was afraid that he might choke.

'I can only assume that my son holds you in even higher esteem than I do, Miss Bainbridge!' the Marquis said, when he had regained his breath.

Amy saw the twinkle of humour in his eye and it disconcerted her. She hurried on to relate how Joss had given her his help in dealing with the blackmailer, omitting nothing but Amanda and the blackmailer's identity. Finally she reached the story of what had happened when Joss had saved Juliana seven years before, and at last she saw the Marquis become very tense and still, and he did not speak until she had finished.

When she had finally run out of words there was a long silence in the room. Amy felt exhausted and her heart was racing, but she also felt a tremendous relief that she had done what justice demanded. Her only remaining concern was the effect upon the Marquis. He seemed to have shrunk in his chair, turned in upon himself, shrivelled and aged. Impulsively she left her own seat and went across to kneel by his.

'I am sorry, my lord, so sorry to have had to shock you like this, but I thought that the truth must be told—'

'You did the right thing, Miss Bainbridge.' The Marquis's voice was no longer smooth but scarred and old.

'My only doubt is how I could have not realised this sooner. Oh, Joss was as wild as any other when he was young, but he had never given me serious cause for alarm. He gambled a little and I suppose there were women, but...' he sighed '...he was never excessive in his behaviour. Never before. But then this happened and his excesses bordered on madness and I felt him slipping away from me, and I could not get him back.' His voice faded, then strengthened. 'Truth to tell, I did not try. I was so angry and disgusted by his behaviour and every new outrage seemed to confirm my initial disappointment—that he had gambled away eighty thousand pounds, brought disgrace upon us and almost ruined the family in the process!'

Amy put her hand on his. 'My lord, do not distress yourself—'

'As for Juliana,' the Marquis said, 'there I failed even more badly.' His tone was bleak. 'I could never love the chit in the same way as I loved Joss, for I knew she was not mine. Yet that was not her fault—it should not have mattered. I should not have let it matter!'

Amy closed her eyes to stop the tears squeezing from beneath her lids. She had had no very high opinion of Juliana before and, even when Joss had spoken for her, Amy could find little sympathy in her heart. Nevertheless she could understand the bond between Joss and his sister—and understand the Marquis's agony.

'It is never too late,' she said quietly.

They sat for a little, very still, Amy's hand clasped in his, and then the Marquis stirred.

'So,' he said, and his tone had strengthened now, the authority showing through, 'it seems I have grossly misjudged my son, and the rest of the world has done so too. Yet...' he smiled down at Amy '...you have seen proof of his wildness, Miss Bainbridge. You must admit that Joss is not blameless—'

'No.' Amy got to her feet. 'Indeed, Lord Tallant said the very same thing himself. Yet when one can understand the reasons…'

'One can also forgive?' The Marquis's mouth twisted. 'If you can do so, Miss Bainbridge, I shall find myself profoundly grateful to you—'

He broke off at the sound of a horse been ridden hard up the drive, then lay back in his chair with a contented sigh.

'Ah, that will be my son, I think, come in good time. How excellent to have my suspicions confirmed!' He saw Amy's look of curiosity and gave her a smile. 'It is quite evident that you love my son, Miss Bainbridge—so evident that I do not scruple to speak of it. Logic suggested to me that if he had one iota of the same feeling for you, he would follow you to the ends of the earth, let alone to Ashby Tallant! It makes me very happy to see that I am right. Oh, Miss Bainbridge—' his voice halted Amy when she was already halfway to the door, looking for somewhere to hide '—you shall oblige me by staying here with me. I imagine that Joss will wish to speak to you too!'

Chapter Fourteen

A couple of hours later, Amy walked with Joss along the top terrace and down the steps to the Ashby Tallant gardens. There were four terraces in all, flanked by huge cedar trees, each with their own name and character. The top garden, nearest the house was the most formal; the bottom one, the wilderness garden, was an overgrown Eden with medieval fishponds and tumbling walls.

'I played here as a boy,' Joss said, tracing the lines on a stone-carved sundial as they stood in the central grassy court and looked at the tangled profusion all around. 'It was an exciting place for a child.' He gestured to a stone bench under the shade of a weeping willow. 'Shall we sit?'

Amy sat down. She was feeling strangely shy and it did not help that the only conversation between them since they had left the house had been of the most formal kind. She had wondered if Joss had just been waiting for a little privacy, waiting for the opportunity to rebuke her for coming to Ashby Tallant and having the audacity to set his circumstances before the Marquis. She wondered if he was angry and could not tell. The amber gaze, the living replica of the portraits on the wall, was as inscrutable as he had always been. She wished it was not so. She could not stand the uncertainly.

'Are you angry with me?' she burst out, when she could stand it no longer. Her fingers plucked nervously at the cambric of her dress. 'I am sorry, Joss, but I felt I had to come.'

Joss took her hand in his and her words dried on her lips. The look in his eyes was tender and rueful.

'Amy, I might wish that you did not rush so precipitately towards doing what you think is right, but I cannot be angry with you.' He smiled a little. 'Indeed, now that I am in a fair way to establishing a better understanding with my father, I suppose I should be grateful to you! It will take a little time for us to be on better terms, but we have made a beginning.'

Amy felt a rush of relief. 'I am glad that you were able to speak with him,' she said shyly. She moved a little closer to him. 'He was very kind to me, Joss. I like him very much.'

'He likes you,' Joss said drily. 'He told me that he would disown me for good this time if I let you slip through my fingers. But we will talk of that presently. I wanted to tell you first that Lady Spry's letters are safe and that I have returned them to her. I believe she has nothing further to fear in that quarter.'

Amy let go of his hand, but only so that she could throw her arms about him. 'Oh, how did you manage that?'

Joss released himself, laughing. 'It was not difficult.' The light went out of his face. 'It was Juliana who had the letters, not Massingham.'

'Juliana!' Amy frowned. She sat back. 'But Amanda was sure that Massingham had them.'

Joss shifted uncomfortably. 'You may have guessed that Juliana is Massingham's mistress. She had found the letters and used them for her own ends. As soon as you told me the tale, I suspected her. She has tried to pull such a trick before, you see.' He looked Amy in the eye. 'Juliana loves Massingham and she has been very unhappy. Do not judge her too harshly, Amy. For my sake, I beg you do not.' He took a deep breath. 'We could all have made things so very different for her.'

'Your father said as much to me,' Amy said softly. 'I cannot judge her, Joss. If all is well and Amanda is safe, those are the only things that truly matter to me.'

Joss's expression lightened. 'Lady Spry is very well. I left her discussing the remove to Nettlecombe with your mama. And Juliana is leaving for the continent for a space. I will tell you the whole in a little while, Amy, but I would rather speak of happier things.'

'There is one thing I have to ask first,' Amy said softly. 'Did you tell your father that the blackmailer was Juliana?'

Joss nodded. 'It is only fair that he knows the whole. Then, when the time comes for him to be reconciled with Juliana, there will be no secrets.'

'I hope that will be soon,' Amy said. There was a lump in her throat and she bit her lip to prevent the tears. 'Oh, I do hope so…'

'I hope so too.' Joss pulled her to her feet. 'Enough of this doom and gloom! May we speak on something I hope will be a happier subject?'

Amy nodded wordlessly. He was looking very serious. Her heart started to race.

'I have your brother's permission to pay my addresses to you, Amy,' Joss said formally. 'However, it is your good opinion that I value the most. If you consent to accept my proposal I shall be the happiest man alive, but I think that you should be very certain you are doing the right thing—'

Amy pressed her fingers against his lips, effectively silencing him. She tugged on his hand and he came to sit down beside her on the bench again.

'Joss, I must know why you are so persistent in trying to make me refuse you.'

She saw the laughter creep into his eyes, warm as sunshine, banishing the cold doubt there.

'Amy, you once told me that you detested gamblers and that your greatest happiness was when you won your money and achieved the security you craved.' Joss's fingers, long and strong, interlocked tightly with hers. 'You would be a fool to throw all that away to bind yourself to a man who embodies all that you despised—'

This time Amy silenced him with a kiss. 'Joss, it is not folly, it is love.' She freed herself and sat back a little so that she could see his face. 'I confess that at first I disliked you for your reputation—'

'No, you held me in contempt. That is far, far worse.'

'If you prefer.' Amy smiled slightly. 'Alas for me, my dislike was soon undermined by the pleasure that I took in your company. I was slow to realise it and when I tried to pull back it was too late.' Her voice sank to a whisper. 'I did not wish to avoid you. When I thought that I should not see you again it was the most dreadful torment.'

Joss pulled her close. He pressed his lips to her hair. 'Amy, you know I am a wastrel—'

'Stuff and nonsense! You do not gamble to excess and anyway, you always win! You told me so yourself!'

Joss gave a muffled groan. 'You know that makes no difference. Besides, I have been a rake.'

'Yes—' Amy raised her face to his '—but I shall be happy if you confine your attentions to me in future. Indeed, I have been hoping to see evidence of your rakish tendencies for I fear they have been overrated.'

Joss bent his head until his lips touched hers. 'I will let you be the judge of that. I do believe that you have disposed of all my objections, Amy.'

He made to kiss her properly, but Amy drew away from him. 'I have some concerns of my own, Joss. I mean that there are matters about which I feel *you* should be concerned...'

'Oh?' There was a light in his eyes now that made her heart skip a beat. 'What are they, my love? Can it be that your gambling is a far greater obsession than I had previously thought?'

'No...' Amy smiled despite herself, and then hesitated. 'It is simply that...I feel that I should be counselling you to think very carefully. You always said that you were wary of marriage, Joss, and I could not bear it if you were to find that it did not suit you after we were wed...'

Her hand was against his chest and she could feel the steady beat of his heart against her palm. It felt strong and reassuring.

'Amy!' Joss drew her to him again and this time she allowed herself to go. 'It is true that until recently I had absolutely no wish to marry. I could not imagine a time when I should ever feel differently. Worse, I dreaded sitting at one end of this cold mausoleum of a house whilst my wife inhabited a set of rooms as far away from me as possible. It seemed so bleak.' He smiled at her. 'Then I met you. At first I had no notion that I was falling in love with you. I knew that I enjoyed talking to you and found your company stimulating. I thought that there was no more to it than that, but…' he shook his head '…fool that I was, I did not realise that I was already in love.'

Amy made an inarticulate noise and pressed closer to him. She slid her arms about his waist and pressed her cheek against his jacket.

'Oh, Joss, that is by far the nicest thing that anyone has ever said to me! I have always been so plain and shy, and had no admirers—'

'That,' Joss said, tilting her chin up so that he could kiss her gently, 'is the most blatant fishing for a compliment that I have heard in a very long time! Let me oblige. For almost the whole time I knew you, I found myself looking at you and thinking how beautiful you were, Amy. You did not need the lottery money to buy pretty clothes.'

This time they kissed with rather more fervour and less gentleness.

'Besides,' Joss finished, 'if I discover that any other man has been professing himself in love with you, I fear I should have to call him out!'

'There is always poor Bertie Hallam,' Amy said thoughtfully. 'Proposing to me has become such a habit of his that I hope he may soon find another object for his gallantry!'

'He should confine his attentions to his cards,' Joss said callously, 'and then perhaps he might start winning!'

He drew Amy's arm through his and turned towards the steps. 'Come, let us go and tell my father the good news. I am happy that at last I have fulfilled one of his expectations!'

They were married two months later in the chapel at Ashby Tallant. Sir Richard Bainbridge gave the bride away and Amanda, Lady Spry, was matron-of-honour. The Duke of Fleet acted as groomsman and Lady Bainbridge graciously accepted the escort of the Marquis of Tallant to the wedding feast, where she was seen slipping several large slices of ham into her reticule to consume later. Mrs Benfleet travelled from Windsor in the Bainbridge carriage and Mrs Wendover and her children came from Whitechapel, travelling in the Tallant carriage, which miraculously kept all its wheels even whilst waiting in the street in Whitechapel.

Later, when the guests had departed, the bridal suite had been prepared for the happy couple and Lady Bainbridge had imparted some words of maternal wisdom to her daughter, Amy was finally left in peace to contemplate her wedding night.

Although she had spent a large part of the previous three months in Joss's company, she felt apprehensive and suddenly a little shy. As the wedding day had approached and the bustle of preparation had taken over it had been so difficult to hold on to the things that were really important. Even her charitable ventures had been curtailed through the necessary evils of dress fitting and consultations with Lady Bainbridge about the menu for the wedding breakfast. It felt to Amy as though there had been a buzz of activity about her for as long as she could remember and now all was suddenly silence.

Not quite silence. She could hear the sound of Joss's voice in the next room as he spoke quietly to his valet. Soon he would be joining her. Her head ached with the tension. The huge, opulent bedroom seemed unbearably stuffy.

She scrambled from the bed and flung up the window, leaning out and inhaling the fresh, summer air. It was not quite dark and a tiny crescent moon was rising above the lime avenue. The breeze caressed her face. Amy closed her eyes and felt a little of her tension evaporate.

'Amy?'

Amy jumped and almost hit her head on the window. She had not heard the connecting door open but now Joss was standing just behind her, the light burnishing his hair to dark bronze and shadowing his eyes. Amy felt her throat go dry. She swallowed hard.

'Oh. Joss. I…I did not hear you. I needed some fresh air. I have the headache.'

As soon as she said it she realised how lame it sounded, as though she were having second thoughts about her wedding night. Panic and shyness gripped her but, before she could blurt out that she did not mean to send him away, Joss had taken her hand, drawing her gently towards him.

'There is a balcony in the other bedroom. Let us go outside for a little. It has been an unconscionably long and tiring day.'

Grateful for his understanding, Amy went with him through the dressing room and into another, much smaller bedroom where one candle still burned. Joss drew back the heavy curtains and opened the long windows. A breath of wind stirred the wall hangings and set the candle flame dancing. They went out on to the balcony. Immediately the cool twilight wrapped about them.

The moon was riding high above the trees and the

first of the stars were coming out now. The cupola on the top of the great hall was outlined in black against a midnight blue sky. Amy stared entranced at the park-land, spread out before them in the fading light.

'Oh! It is so beautiful! It makes me feel quite wild! I want to run downstairs and out of the doors and across the grass in the moonlight—'

'Perhaps we may do that tomorrow night,' Joss said, a smile in his voice, 'and scandalise the servants.'

Amy sighed. 'Yes, I suppose… For tonight it would not be at all the thing. But I do thank you, Joss, for not going all stuffy and saying that that would be most un-seemly and that I must always act with a decorum that becomes a Countess.'

Joss pulled her into his arms with a swiftness that took her breath away. 'Amy, if you wish to run barefoot through the gardens clad only in your shift you shall not find me far behind!'

Amy turned her blushing face against his chest. 'Thank you. So…' she felt brave enough to address the subject on her mind '…how is this difficult matter of our wedding night to be managed? I feel a little self-conscious—'

'How is it to be *managed*?' Joss loosened his grip a little, holding her at arm's length so that his gaze could sweep over her comprehensively from her bare feet to her tumbling hair. 'Like this, I imagine…'

Before Amy was aware of what he was about, he had swept her up into his arms and carried her through the open windows, laying her on the tester bed. With one swift move he had drawn her silky dressing robe away from her. 'I suspect that you will soon forget your dif-ficulties…'

'Yes, but—' Amy struggled to sit up. 'The bridal bed is all prepared in the other room—'

'We shall go back in there presently. This will do perfectly well in the meantime.'

'Oh, but—' Amy lost the thread of her thoughts as Joss stripped off his own robe. In the candlelight his body was hard and lean and it was plain to see that he was aroused. Amy, whose experience of such matters was nil, felt her self-consciousness return even as something inside her responded to him.

'Joss, I am feeling even more apprehensive now,' she said in a tiny voice.

Joss smiled. He joined her on the bed, stretching out beside her and resting one hand gently on her stomach. Amy could feel the warmth of it through her gauzy nightdress and felt a delicious squirmy sensation inside.

'There is no need to be afraid, Amy,' Joss said softly. 'I swear I shall do nothing that you do not want.'

'It is not so much that I do not want it,' Amy said, eyes wide, 'simply that I am not sure how it will work.'

'Then it is best not to worry and just see what happens.' Joss's voice was as soothing as honey wine. Amy could feel herself letting go—at the same time as part of her was feeling very tense and excited indeed.

'Very well, I shall try…'

Joss bent and kissed her throat and she could not help the tremor that went through her. His hand slid to her hip, and she shivered again, eyes closing. When he started to unlace her nightdress she opened her eyes, but before she could speak he had silenced her with his lips on hers. The kiss was gentle but there was something hot beneath its sweetness. Amy wriggled, running her fingers into Joss's hair, holding him closer. She heard him groan against her mouth, then the kiss deepened and became hard and hungry, and she was swept with the most intoxicating sensual excitement she had ever felt.

'Oh, that is so very agreeable…'

Amy had not noticed when her nightdress had fallen open, freeing her breasts to Joss's touch. Now she arched against him as she felt his fingers brush one rosy nipple, circling, caressing. Then the nightdress came away altogether and she felt the warmth and hardness of Joss's naked body against her own, his hands pulling her closer still, and thought she might faint from sheer pleasure.

'Joss!'

Joss's eyes had darkened with desire and now he kissed her again with a concentrated passion. Amy knew instinctively that he was very close to losing control and the knowledge made her feel wicked and excited and powerful. Eagerly she returned kiss for searing kiss, sliding her hands over the strong muscles of his back, digging her fingers into his shoulders.

His hands and lips moved over her, provoking a blazing sensual awareness in her as they lingered on her breasts. Amy had long ago ceased to be afraid, ceased to think, wanting only the necessary consummation of all her desires. She shivered as she felt Joss's hand on her thigh, his fingers stroking the soft skin before he moved to touch her with an intimacy that was shocking but exquisitely exciting. Her mouth formed a silent 'oh' of pleasure and longing and he repeated the caress, moving on top of her, sliding one leg between hers. Amy squirmed, desperate to appease the delicious ache inside.

Joss took her face between both his hands. 'Sweetheart, I love you. I will try not to hurt you—'

As soon as the words were out his hands moved to her hips and he captured her mouth with his in an urgent kiss. He slid into her and smothered her instinctive gasp with his lips on hers.

The shock was enough to shake Amy out of the sensual trance that possessed her, but then Joss was kissing her again lingeringly, bending his head to her breasts with exquisite patience and skill, moving in long slow strokes that quickly built up the excitement to fever pitch again. Amy gasped and clung to him and felt his body go taut within her and watched his face as he took her, and the sheer excitement and the knowing pushed her over the edge, to shatter into a hundred shimmering pieces before she floated slowly down to earth. She lay entangled in Joss's arms, feeling his heart rate slow down and the sweat cool on their skin and she thought, *He is mine, now and for always.* Her heart swelled with love and she burrowed closer to his warmth and fell asleep.

'Amy, sweetheart, there is something that I must tell you.'

It was the following afternoon and Amy had taken Joss's arm for a stroll on the terrace after luncheon, for all the world, she had said laughingly, like an old married couple. Joss had stayed with her all night and most of the morning, first in the tester bed in the smaller room and then in the bridal bed, whose pristine perfection had been most satisfactorily disordered. He had finally dragged himself away only to dress and they had somehow managed to get themselves downstairs to eat.

The sun was warm and Amy felt drowsy. She leant against the terrace balustrade and smiled at him sleepily.

'You had better be quick then, for I fear I shall fall asleep soon! I think I need to take a nap this afternoon.'

'That will be delightful,' Joss said promptly. 'I will join you.'

Amy blinked at him. 'In the afternoon? But surely that would be most scandalous—'

Joss shrugged. 'I said that we should shake this old house up, did I not? I intend to start as I mean to go on. And tonight we may run barefoot through the gardens and—'

'Enough!' Amy held up a hand. 'I thought that you had something to tell me?'

'I did. You distracted me.' Joss came across and kissed her very gently, taking both her hands in his. 'Amy, when I tell you this I beg you not to be angry with me.'

Amy was starting to feel concerned. 'Joss, what is this?'

For once Joss seemed at a loss. 'I did think about never telling you—'

'Joss!' Amy broke in sharply. 'You are making me so nervous that I beg you will tell me at once!'

'Very well.' Joss gave her a lopsided smile. 'It is the lottery money, Amy. I have to tell you that it was my ticket that you found. It was my thirty thousand pounds.'

Amy stepped back, eyes narrowing. 'Yours? But you said that it was not! Are you making this up to tease me? What was the number?'

'Two thousand five hundred and eighty-eight,' Joss said obligingly. A smile was twitching the corner of his mouth. 'Oh dear, you look very angry.'

'I am not angry, precisely…' Amy was struggling with a variety of emotions. Indignation won. 'Well, upon my word! I have heard of people claiming prizes that do not belong to them, but why refuse a prize that does? It makes no sense! Why did you not tell me?'

Joss drove his hands into his pockets. 'I am not sure.'

Amy frowned. 'But I asked you! I asked you directly if it was your ticket and you said that it was not!'

Joss shook his head, turning slightly away. 'I would only have gambled the money away and I thought that you were more deserving…'

'You let me keep it out of pity?' There was a note of hurt in Amy's voice. 'Perhaps you thought that I might buy myself some pretty dresses and look halfway presentable—'

Joss caught her in his arms. 'To my mind you look most presentable without your clothes—'

'Joss!' Amy beat her fist against his chest in mock anger. She could feel her indignation melting like ice in the sun. 'Oh, this is too bad! To trick me like this! To marry me under false pretences! I suppose you thought that I needed the funds to pay for my charitable ventures?'

'The thought did cross my mind. I was so enjoying sharing them with you, sweetheart!'

Amy struggled. Joss held her fast and after a moment she relaxed against him.

'I suppose,' she said in a mollified tone, 'that the fact that you let me keep the money is really evidence of your noble nature, Joss. I have always said that you are an honourable man—'

'Minx!' Joss said. 'If you mention my noble nature one more time I shall kiss you until you reconsider your words.'

Amy smiled and tilted her face up to his. 'Is that a promise?'

She saw his eyes darken as they took in the captivating line of her lips. He lowered his head until his mouth was an inch from hers. 'It could be...'

They kissed again, breathless, happy.

'But, of course...' Amy pulled away and put her hand against his lips '...you have possession of my fortune now, Joss, so that you have regained your lottery win!'

'There is always the interest to pay on the sum,' Joss murmured. He moved her hand aside and bent closer, his lips an inch away from hers. 'You also owe me for the money you have already spent...'

Amy smiled as his mouth touched hers in a butterfly kiss. 'I fear you will never regain it. You will be forever out of pocket. You have gambled and lost, Joss Tallant.'

'No.' Joss was smiling at her with so much love it made her quite dizzy. 'I gambled and won, Amy Tallant, for I gained far more than the lottery prize.' He swung her up in his arms. 'That you cannot dispute. Winner takes all.'

* * * * *